One Week of July

Melissa Mastro

One Week of July

A Novel

Melissa Mastro

Cover design by Lucy Giller/Little Gem Studio
Line edited by Elyse Lyon
Copy edited by Anne-Marie Rutella
Typeset and proofread by Nicole Frail/Nicole Frail Edits, LLC

Paperback ISBN: 979-8-9914076-1-8
Ebook ISBN: 979-8-9914076-0-1

For my readers, especially those who are going through
a hard time.

This novel was written during one of the most difficult
years of my life, and it very much served as a therapeutic
outlet for me.

My hope is that you feel the same joy reading it that
I felt while writing it.

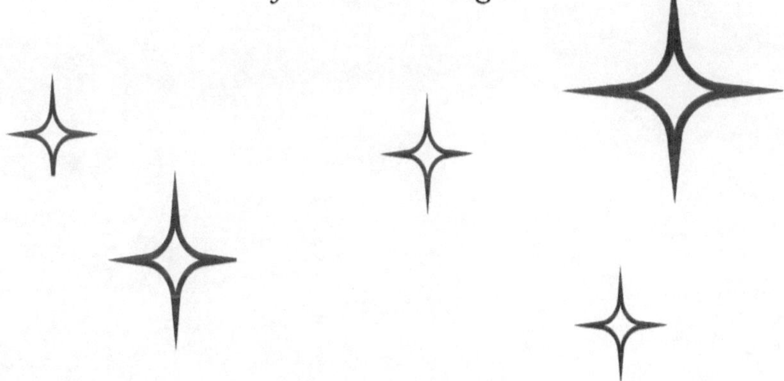

Prologue

IT WAS A QUIET SUMMER afternoon in Montclair, Georgia. The sun crept lazily through the dusty blinds of a used bookstore. Inside, a teenage boy was examining an old, beat-up paperback, knowing it had seen better days.

Twice Upon a Time was a quaint shop that hardly got any visitors, but the owner, Greta, was adored by everyone in that small Southern town, so the community came together to help keep her store open.

Not to mention, the shop had been a staple on Main Street since the 1970s, when Greta, and her late husband, Ivan, first opened it. Back then, Twice Upon a Time was always full of eager readers perusing the slim aisles, but as time marched on, the comers and goers steadily declined.

Still, Greta faithfully worked the store. After all, the memory of her beloved husband was present in every crack and crevice of that cozy shop. So, when time caught up to Greta, and she grew too old to maintain the store on her own, she gave a set of keys to the only other person who loved the shop as much as she and Ivan did.

Leighton Prescott had been visiting Twice Upon a Time since he was young. Growing up, his favorite days were always those when his mother would bring him and his sister, Kennedy, to the store to pick out a new hand-me-down book. He could never tire of the messy, overflowing shelves or the worn, velour sofa, so when Greta asked him to be the new caretaker, he happily accepted.

For the first few months, Leighton dedicated his evenings and his weekends to the bookstore, while his weekdays were spent completing his senior year of high school. But it was summer now, and he would be leaving for college in the fall. He had been spending even more time at the shop, knowing that he was going to miss it while he was away.

If it were up to Leighton, he would stay in Montclair and bring life back to the old bookstore that he loved so much, but boys like Leighton didn't get a choice. See, there was a plan for him, a predetermined path for him to follow. Leighton had expectations to fulfill, whether he liked it or not.

Day One

IT WAS RARE FOR A nonlocal to visit the bookstore. It was even rarer for said visitor to be a teenager. Lately, the only guests who came by Twice Upon a Time were the regulars, all of whom were older Montclair natives who hadn't yet switched to e-reading and probably never would. Yet there she was. A girl, an attractive girl, who looked to be right around Leighton's age, nestled into the old sofa in the corner of the shop; the same sofa Leighton had sat in so many times before.

Leighton had been in the back of the store, fumbling with a box of newly donated books, when he heard the soft jingle of the door.

Ding, ding.

Finally, he thought. He had been eagerly waiting for his sister to drop off some leftovers from her bakery, and it was right around the time when she usually came by.

"Hey, Ken, I'm in the back. I'll be up in just a minute!" Leighton shouted.

Ding, ding.

This time it was his cell phone.

Kennedy: Hey! Can't make it today, there was a rush at the bakery, and it doesn't look like it's letting up anytime soon. I'll make it up to you, I promise. xo Ken

Shit, Leighton thought as he quickly got up and dusted himself off. *I finally have a customer, and I'm screwing around in the back.*

"Be right there!" he called.

Leighton hurried to the front of the store to find a girl studying the titles in the first aisle.

"Hey, welcome to Twice Upon a Time!" He panted, catching his breath. "Sorry I wasn't around to greet you when you first came in. I was in the back sorting through a box of books. I'm Leighton, by the way. Is there anything that I can help you with?"

"Oh hey, no worries," the girl replied nonchalantly. "Um, I'm good right now. Just gonna look around, if that's okay?"

"Yeah, of course!" Leighton nodded. "If you need anything, just let me know."

"Will do, thanks!" She turned her attention back to the crowded shelves.

Leighton took a seat at the front desk while the girl slowly made her way down each aisle. He tried not to stare, but it was hard to fight his curiosity. Montclair was one of those small towns where everyone knew each other, so a nonlocal visitor naturally piqued his interest.

He watched as she made several trips around the store before she finally found what she was looking for. She smiled as she carefully wrestled the book off the crammed shelf. Once it was free, she hugged it close and proudly carried it over to the reading nook, which sat directly across from Leighton's desk. The girl fidgeted for a minute, then quietly settled into the antique green couch.

The girl stayed nestled on that sofa for the remainder of the afternoon and into the evening. She stayed there for so long, in fact, that the sun had started to set, and the moon was becoming visible in the Georgia sky. Leighton typically closed the bookstore around dusk, but she looked so peaceful sitting there, immersed in her story, that he decided it'd be best not to disturb her. He didn't really have any plans that night anyway. He was supposed to go to a party at his best friend, Carson's, house, but Carson's parents decided to stay home at the last minute, so the epic party that his buddy had planned had been called off.

Leighton and Carson had been best friends since the second grade. On the first day of school, Carson, who was new to town, had approached Leighton as he waited outside their classroom.

"Hi, I'm Carson, and you're going to be my best friend," he had declared.

A shy young Leighton looked at the assertive boy with wide eyes. "Um, okay," he'd stammered, grateful to have a buddy, but also a bit surprised by the new kid's candor.

Carson had been true to his word, though, and from that day on, he and Leighton were basically inseparable. Lately, Leighton and Carson hadn't been spending as much time together—they were both busy with work and college preparations—but the relationship that they had was one that could never be broken. They were more than friends; they were brothers.

Thump.

The noise was loud and abrupt, startling Leighton. He looked up to find that the girl had not only slammed her book shut but was now cradling her face in her hands. When he heard her hushed sobs, he realized she was crying.

He wasn't sure what to do. He didn't want to invade her privacy, but it also felt wrong to not console someone who was clearly upset. He contemplated his options for a moment then spoke up.

"Hey . . . are you okay?" he asked delicately.

She lifted her head, wiped her eyes, and looked at him. "Yeah, I'm . . . I'm fine. Sorry, I've just been having a hard time lately. I didn't mean to start randomly crying." She scrunched her face. "God, you must think I'm so weird."

Leighton gave her a sympathetic look. "You don't have

to apologize, and I don't think you're weird. Do you want to talk about whatever is bothering you?"

"To be honest, I'd rather talk about anything else."

"Okay, well then, why don't you tell me what you've been reading? And maybe your name, too? After all, I told you mine, but you never told me yours."

The girl let out a soft giggle, and Leighton was glad to see that she was starting to cheer up.

"I'm reading *The Outsiders*, and my name is July," she replied.

"July," Leighton repeated. "I like that name. It's unique. And *The Outsiders*, huh? Good choice—that's a classic."

"Thank you, my mom said that she wanted to name me something 'nontraditional,'" she said, making air quotes with her fingers. "And yeah, *The Outsiders* is one of those books that I always come back to. It was the first book that really made me feel something. I remember reading it in seventh grade and bawling my eyes out when Johnny died. I had always *enjoyed* reading before that, but my *love* for reading definitely began with this book." She gave the cover a pat.

"*The Outsiders* is a favorite of mine, too. And between you and me, I *might* have also cried during that scene. But only just a little." Leighton grinned sheepishly.

July smiled, and Leighton could tell that she appreciated his humility.

"So, what brings you to Montclair?" Leighton asked in an effort to keep the conversation alive.

"I'm just passing through, on my way down to Florida. It's a cute little town that you've got here. I've always loved the idea of a small, tight-knit community."

"Thanks. Yeah, Montclair is great. I'm lucky to call this place home. Where in Florida are you headed?"

"St. Cloud. It's about twenty-five miles south of Orlando."

"Is that where you're from?"

"No, I grew up in Brooklyn, with my mom. My dad lives in Florida. I'm going to visit him," July explained.

"Gotcha." Leighton nodded. "Have you been driving down? That's a long trip from New York."

"Yeah, well, kinda. *I'm* not technically driving. I'm taking the bus. I don't have a car or else I would've driven myself."

"Why not fly? It's so much quicker."

"I absolutely *hate* flying," she said, vehemently shaking her head. "So, the bus was really my only option. It hasn't been so bad, but I was beginning to get a little stir-crazy, so I figured I'd take a detour."

Leighton loved flying, but he kept that to himself. "Ah, that makes sense," he said instead. "The bus station is right around the corner."

"Yeah, I was surprised to see that the bus stopped in such a small town. Usually the terminals are in big cities. That was one of the reasons why I decided to get off here. I thought it'd be a nice change of pace."

"And how are you liking it so far?"

"Well, I've only been here for a few hours. This bookstore was my first stop, but so far, so good."

July returned to her book. Unsure what to do, Leighton took out his phone. He checked Instagram and then he opened Snapchat. He tried to preoccupy himself with the photos and videos of his friends, but the only thing he was really interested in was July. Every few seconds, he would look up from his phone to catch a glimpse of her reading. He struggled to think of a good conversation-starter. When his stomach growled, he got an idea.

"Hey," Leighton said, interrupting the quiet. "I've got a question for you."

"You've actually had quite a few questions for me," July said with a little smirk, "but what's one more?"

"You got me there," he said, tipping his head in acknowledgment. "So, um, what I wanted to ask you was . . . are you hungry, by any chance?"

July paused. "Yeah, actually, I am. To be honest, I'm starving."

"Me, too," Leighton happily agreed. "My sister was supposed to bring me something a few hours ago, but she got held up at work, so I haven't eaten anything since this morning. So, would you want to go and grab a bite with me?" He nervously scratched the back of his head. "I know that we just met, but there's this awesome burger joint right down the street . . ."

July hesitated again, and Leighton could tell that she was considering his invitation.

She tapped her pointer finger on her lips to pantomime her deliberation. "It depends," she finally said. "Does this awesome burger joint have a veggie burger?"

"They sure do. They make a killer black bean burger. I actually order it all the time, and I'm not even a vegetarian."

"Well, in that case, I can't say no."

"Really?" Leighton asked, a little too enthusiastic. He was trying to play it cool, but he wasn't doing a very good job. Despite his best efforts, he couldn't hide his excitement at the idea of spending more time with July.

"Sure, why not? I could use some company. Plus, if this burger is really as good as you say it is, then I wouldn't want to miss the opportunity to try it."

"You're going to love it, I promise."

"I hope you're a man of your word, Leighton."

"I am," he replied confidently.

Leighton could feel his face forming into a foolish grin, and it was taking everything in him to keep that from happening. But the truth was, the flirtatious banter between him and July was giving him butterflies, and he couldn't help but feel smitten. Hopefully, they would continue it at dinner.

Buster's Burger Bar had the best burgers in Georgia, maybe even in the entire United States. You wouldn't know it from the restaurant's modest appearance, but as soon as you walked in, you could smell that it was going to taste good. Buster's was always pretty busy on the weekends, but because it was later in the evening, the crowd had already come and gone. Leighton was glad to see there was no line.

"Well, if it isn't Mr. Leighton Prescott!" a large jovial man exclaimed from behind the counter.

"Hey, Buster!" Leighton replied.

"How have you been, son? And who is this lovely lady that you have with you?" Buster gave July a toothy grin when he said this.

"I'm good! This is July," Leighton said, motioning to introduce his guest.

"Hi." July waved. "It's nice to meet you."

"It's nice to meet you, too," Buster beamed. "So, what can I whip up for you two tonight?"

Leighton and July each placed their orders, and when they were finished, Leighton gave Buster a friendly handshake. Then he led July back toward the dining area where they chose a cozy booth in the corner.

It was in that booth, sitting face-to-face, when Leighton really got a good look at July.

Wow, he thought.

July was pretty in a way that he hadn't seen before. It wasn't her long, dark hair or her full, pouty lips, though those features were certainly beautiful, but it was her big brown eyes that really made her stand out. They were so warm and inviting, and he could see flecks of gold in her irises when the light hit them just right. What Leighton loved the most about her eyes, though, was how they mirrored her emotions. When she smiled, her eyes smiled, too.

Leighton imagined what it would be like to kiss July. He pictured his hands gently cupping her cheeks and his lips landing softly on hers. He fantasized about her taste, her smell, her touch . . .

"Can I help you?" July asked playfully, interrupting Leighton's daydream.

"S-Sorry," Leighton stammered, his cheeks getting hot. "I must've zoned out."

"Mm-hmm," July hummed with a mischievous grin.

Leighton winced. Could July somehow read his thoughts? He had never been so overwhelmed with feelings like this before. Fortunately, July started to talk about her favorite movies. They discovered that they were both huge Star Wars fans, though they couldn't seem to agree on which movie was best. July was in the middle of delivering a passionate and persuasive argument about why *Episode III* is the superior film when Buster came by to drop off their food.

"This looks amazing!" she exclaimed, wide-eyed.

"Wait 'til you try it," Buster replied.

July didn't keep him waiting. She quickly picked up the burger and took a huge bite. "Oh my gosh," she said, placing a hand in front of her mouth so she could finish chewing. "This might be the best veggie burger that I've ever had!"

Buster flashed her another toothy grin.

"See, I told you!" Leighton said matter-of-factly.

Buster let out a hearty chuckle. "Enjoy, kids! Holler if you need anything," he said before walking back to the kitchen.

The pair didn't speak much while they ate. Instead, they exchanged smiles here and there to let the other know that they were enjoying their food. Leighton appreciated the fact that he didn't feel uncomfortable due to the lack of conversation. He had been on dates before where he felt like he had to keep talking to avoid awkward silence. With July, though, everything felt so natural and relaxed. He didn't feel the need to force anything or act a certain way. He could just be himself. What exactly made him feel this way? Perhaps it was July's easygoing nature, or the fact that he felt like he'd known her for longer than just a few hours. Whatever it was, he liked it, and it made him like her even more.

"So, did it live up to the hype?" Leighton asked as he wiped his mouth with a napkin. They had each finished their burger and were picking at their fries.

"It totally exceeded my expectations! Eleven out of ten. I could eat that burger every day."

Leighton laughed. "I'm glad you liked it. So . . . what now?"

"I don't know, you tell me," July retorted. She gave Leighton another one of her little smirks.

"Well, I was thinking, if you aren't busy, maybe I could show you around downtown Montclair? It's not all that big, but it's a nice walk up and down Main Street."

He looked at July, hoping that she would accept his invitation. He wasn't ready for the night to end.

July smiled. "I would love that."

"Awesome! Okay, let me go pay our bill and then we'll head out." Leighton shuffled his way out of the booth.

"Wait!" July rummaged through her bag. "I have to give you money for my food."

"No, no, no. This was my treat. It's on me!" Leighton turned toward the counter, moving quickly so that July wouldn't have time to protest. By the time she looked up from her purse, he was already handing Buster his debit card.

There was a cool summer breeze in the air when Leighton and July stepped outside, and the sky was so clear that Leighton could see practically every star, planet, and constellation in the galaxy. The moon was full and just bright enough to create a warm glow that cascaded down the street. It was a perfect night.

The pair walked side by side as Leighton pointed out the

various local attractions. There was an eclectic record store, a trendy boutique, and a retro ice cream parlor, to name a few. They meandered down the cobblestone sidewalk while they looked at the buildings, all color-coordinated in alternating shades of pastel. It really was a picturesque little town.

At the end of the right side of Main Street was a Parisian-inspired bake shop, Mon Chéri Bakery, and it was the place that Leighton was most excited to show July. Why? Because it was his sister's bakery, and he had a key.

"How does dessert sound?" Leighton asked as he motioned toward the bakery.

"It sounds great, but it doesn't look like they're open."

"That's okay, I have a key." Leighton grinned. He pulled the key out of his pocket and gave it a little shake.

July raised an eyebrow. She looked confused.

"This is my sister's bake shop. She gave me a key, and sometimes I sneak in at night and steal some of her famous macarons. Would you like to be my partner in crime?"

"I don't know," July said, reluctant. "Won't she be mad?"

"No, she won't mind, as long as we don't make a mess. Plus, she owes me. Every Saturday, she comes by the bookstore with leftovers, but she bailed on me today."

July was quiet for a minute. "Okay, as long as she really won't mind."

"She won't. I promise."

Mon Chéri Bakery was one of Leighton's favorite spots in town, second only to the bookstore. Of course, he loved the shop for its delicious breads, pastries, cookies, and cakes, but he mostly loved it for what it meant to Kennedy. His sister had dreamed of opening her own bakery since she was a little girl, and she'd made that dream a reality, despite their parents' opposition. She was so tenacious when it came to what she wanted. If only Leighton could be more like his sister.

Leighton and Kennedy were four years apart, with Kennedy the older of the two. When she graduated high school, she decided to forgo college and open the bakery instead, much to the dismay of their mother and father. Their parents were so upset, in fact, that they threatened to cut her off and kick her out of the house if she didn't continue with her education. Kennedy didn't care, though; she took out a business loan and bought one of these pastel buildings. A few months later, Mon Chéri Bakery celebrated its grand opening, and today, it was one of the most popular shops in Montclair.

It was almost four years ago exactly when Kennedy made the decision to follow her dreams. She had been the same age that Leighton was now, in the same season of life: a recent high school graduate enjoying the final weeks of summer before heading off to college. Unlike Kennedy, though, Leighton would be following the path that had been carved out for him, rather than making his own. He wanted to be strong and unwavering like his sister, but he also didn't want to let his parents down. They expected him to carry out the family legacy. How could he disappoint them?

Leighton remembered the night his sister told their parents

that she wouldn't be going to college. It was during dinner, they were eating spinach and mozzarella ravioli, Kennedy's favorite.

"I'm not going to school," his sister blurted out between bites of pasta.

"Excuse me?" their mother said, dropping her fork.

"I'm not going to school. I'm opening a bakery instead," Kennedy clarified.

"Ha ha, very funny," Mom replied.

"I'm being serious, Mom," Kennedy said.

Their mother's face turned cross. "And I'm being serious when I say that I'm not entertaining this ridiculous fantasy. You're going to school—end of story."

What transpired after could only be described as explosive. Kennedy and Mom were at each other's throats for the better part of an hour, while Leighton and his father watched on in horror. Leighton wanted to speak up and defend his sister, but he was too scared to, and Dad probably knew better than to challenge his wife. The argument went on for over a week, with neither Mom nor Kennedy willing to surrender, and it ultimately ended with Mom kicking Kennedy out of the house.

The Prescotts hadn't all had a meal together, or spinach and mozzarella ravioli, since.

Leighton and July sat at a small, round table by the window of the bakery. Between them, they had a plate of macarons in a variety of colors and flavors.

"I've actually never had a macaron before," July admitted.

"I hadn't either, until Kennedy opened this bakery. Now I eat them all the time. My favorite is pistachio. Here, give it a try." Leighton handed her the light-green pastry.

July took a bite and nodded in delight. "Mmm, this is amazing!"

"I know, right?"

July nodded again, finished the macaron, and then asked, "Are you and your sister close?"

"Yeah, we are. She's honestly my best friend. Do you have any siblings?"

"Nope, I'm an only child. Growing up, it was just me and my mom. She was my best friend." July got quiet after saying this and shifted her gaze down toward her lap.

When she looked back up, Leighton could see a troubled expression in her eyes.

"Is everything okay?"

"Yeah," July answered, shaking it off. "I'm fine. So, what are your parents like?"

"They're pretty cool. They're just really involved in my life, I guess you could say."

"So, they're overbearing?" July asked bluntly.

"What?" Leighton said, caught off guard. "No, they just . . . want to see me succeed."

July gave him a skeptical look and Leighton paused for a moment, realizing that he was coming back to the hard truth that he had been avoiding for so long.

"But . . . ?" she asked, tilting her head. She must've sensed that there was more that he wasn't telling her.

Leighton laughed nervously. "It's nothing. Just typical parent crap. They . . . they have all these big plans for me, but sometimes, I'm not sure if what they want for me is actually what I want for me. You know?"

"I'm not sure that I do know, if I'm being honest," July said. "Is that typical parent crap? My mom never told me what I should do. She always encouraged me to follow my heart and live a life that makes me happy."

July's accusatory tone was making Leighton feel uneasy. What was she trying to imply? His parents certainly weren't perfect, but they only wanted what was best for him.

"I mean, I thought so," Leighton replied. "I don't know. I guess this is a sensitive subject for me."

July softened. "Parents are a sensitive subject for me, too," she admitted. "My dad walked out on my mom and me just a few weeks after I was born. I haven't seen him since then . . . if you even want to consider that seeing him. I was just a baby—I didn't know what was going on. Anyway, we just started talking again recently, and now I'm going to visit him in Florida. I don't know what to expect. He's more like a stranger to me than a father."

Leighton's mouth fell open. "Wow," he said, shocked at both her confession and the fact that she'd shared it with him. "I can't even imagine what that must be like. I wouldn't know what to do either. Were you mad at him for leaving? Are you still mad at him?"

July paused. "For the first few years of my life," she said, "I didn't even realize that having only one parent wasn't *normal*. It wasn't until I was older, like seven or eight, that I really started to question it. It was around that time when my mom finally told me what had happened, and I was furious. I hated him after that. Plus, growing up without a father really affected me. My mom did her best to fill both roles, and she did a damn good job, but it's not the same, you know?"

"Yeah," Leighton agreed, even though he didn't really know. He was lucky enough to have both of his parents in the picture, even if they were a little pushy at times.

"And to answer your question, yes, I am still mad at him, but I guess I have to give him a chance. I don't really have any other option . . ."

July trailed off. There was something that she wasn't sharing with Leighton, but he decided not to pry. After all, she'd already been pretty open about her circumstances.

"Well, I hope he treats you better now than he did back then. You deserve it." He picked up a macaron and raised it in the air, saying, "To family drama!"

July laughed, picked up a macaron of her own, and tapped it against Leighton's. "To family drama!"

They each took a big bite of their cookies before falling into a comfortable silence.

While they sat there, Leighton reflected on his day and on how unexpectedly delightful it had been.

What are the chances that this random girl would walk into the bookstore, and that we'd hit it off so well?

Leighton wasn't sure how the universe worked, but he was awfully thankful that it had brought him and July together. He hoped that she felt the same way.

After the bakery, Leighton and July made their way down the left side of Main Street. They traveled slowly, taking their time. Leighton was trying to keep July around for as long as he could, and it seemed like July was perfectly okay with that.

They passed by quite a few townspeople as they walked, which gave Leighton the opportunity to stop for small talk and prolong his evening with July even more. By the time they got to the end of the street, they had admired each and every pastel building and chatted with every person that they met along the way.

"Look at that!" July said as she ran up to the window of the final storefront, Petal Perfection, the local florist.

Leighton walked up beside her to see what she was pointing to. It was a beautiful arrangement of sunflowers.

"Sunflowers are my favorite," July continued. "Aren't they pretty?"

"Yes, they are," Leighton agreed. If only the shop were open so that he could buy them for her. What were July's plans? If she were to stick around, and he really hoped that she would, then he would stop in at some point to get her the bouquet.

"You know, I never asked you," Leighton said as they sat down on a bench. "Where are you staying while you're in town?"

"I'm staying at that little motel near the bus station. I think it's called the Montclair Motel. Speaking of, I should probably be getting back there. I haven't even unpacked yet. I just threw my suitcase on the bed and headed out to explore the area. And I'm starting to get really tired. It was a long day of traveling for me."

"Yeah, absolutely," Leighton said as he checked his watch. "Oh wow, it has gotten late. It's after eleven already."

July looked surprised. "Is it really? I guess time really does fly when you're having fun." She covered her mouth. "I can't believe I just said that. I'm such a dork." She laughed.

Leighton laughed, too. "You're not a dork. It has been a fun night, but it's time to get you back. I know the motel is just a few blocks over, but I don't want you walking alone at night. My truck is parked in front of the bookstore. How about we go get it, and then I'll give you a ride?"

"That sounds like a great idea. Thank you."

There wasn't much conversation on the walk back to Twice Upon a Time or on the drive to the motel. Leighton wondered if July wasn't feeling talkative for the same reason he wasn't—because she was upset that their time together was coming to an end.

Stop overthinking things, he thought. *She's probably just tired.*

When they pulled up to the motel, Leighton felt a knot in his stomach. He wanted her to go inside and get some rest, but he also didn't want her to leave. What if this was it? What if he never saw her again?

"Thank you for today," July said. "I really needed to take a break from everything that's been going on in my life, and you gave me that. For the first time in weeks, I didn't think about the past or the future, I just lived in the moment. It was really, really refreshing."

"You're welcome," he replied. "I want to thank you, too. Today was awesome. I really enjoyed your company."

It got quiet again before Leighton said, "Here, let me help you out."

Leighton got out of his truck and made his way around to the passenger side. He opened the door and July hopped down. When she landed on the ground, she was only a few inches away from him. It was the closest that they had been all night. They stood there like that for a few moments, face-to-face, with their gazes locked on each other. Leighton slowly inched closer until he was almost touching July. He knew what he wanted to do, but he wasn't sure if he should do it. He lifted his hand and tucked a piece of hair behind her ear. She smiled and he could see the flecks of gold dancing in her eyes.

He cleared his throat and started to ask, "Can I . . ."

But before he could finish, July's lips were pressed firmly against his, and the knot that was in his stomach just a few minutes earlier had turned into a flurry of butterflies.

"I want to see you again," he whispered as her mouth left his.

"I'll come by the bookstore tomorrow," she replied and walked off toward the motel.

Leighton was flooded with so much emotion in that moment that he had trouble finding the words that he wanted to say. He thought about asking July for her number, as a precautionary measure, just in case she changed her mind and left Montclair, but by the time he regained his composure, July was already in her room. He considered knocking on her door, but he chose to trust her word instead. If she was really the girl that he thought she was, then she wouldn't just disappear on him. Or at least that's what he hoped.

When Leighton got home, his parents were already asleep, which was okay with him. He didn't feel like explaining where he had been. He did want to tell Kennedy about his night, though, so he went out back to the guesthouse, where she was temporarily staying while her apartment underwent renovations. Although Kennedy still wasn't on the best of terms with their mother, she had reconciled with their father shortly after the bakery opened, and their dad had been able to convince Mom to let Kennedy stay in the guesthouse while her apartment was redone.

Leighton knocked on the guesthouse door a couple of times, but he got no answer. He tried once more, but it was clear that Kennedy wasn't there, which wasn't all that surprising. It was a Saturday night after all, and Kennedy loved to party. Leighton took his phone out of his pocket and sent her a quick text.

Leighton: Hey! Where are you?
Kennedy: I went out with the girls. I'll be home soon!
Leighton: Okay, cool. I want to tell you about my night!
Kennedy: Is everything alright?
Leighton: Yeah, everything is great! Come over to the main house whenever you get back. Mom and Dad are already asleep.
Kennedy: Okay, see you soon <3

Kennedy returned home around midnight. Leighton was waiting for her in the kitchen.

"Hey!" she said as she entered the room. She had that hazy look in her eyes that she always got when she had been drinking.

"Hey! How was your night?" Leighton asked.

"It was good! We went to some karaoke bar a few towns over. You should've heard me sing 'Bohemian Rhapsody.' It was fucking epic." She walked over to the fridge. "Do you want a beer?"

Leighton hesitated. His parents wouldn't be too happy to find him drinking, especially with his sister, who wasn't exactly welcome in their home, at least not when it came to their mother.

"Relax," Kennedy said before Leighton had the chance to respond. She had always been able to read him like a book. "What they don't know won't hurt them." She shot him a convincing grin and handed him one of the bottles.

"Okay, fine," Leighton said as he removed the cap.

Kennedy did the same and then took a big gulp. "So, tell me about your night! Something special must've happened, otherwise you wouldn't have waited up to talk to me."

Leighton took a sip of his beer and said, "I met a girl, and we really hit it off." He tried to say this as casually as possible, but he didn't do a very good job. He blushed and quickly took another sip, hoping Kennedy wouldn't notice just how smitten he was.

"A girl?!" Kennedy squealed. "Oh my God! What's her name? Where's she from? How'd you meet? Tell me everything!"

Leighton laughed. He'd known that Kennedy would be excited for him. She had always been his biggest supporter. So, he told her about his night, which wasn't exactly monumental, but she still sat there with shining eyes and an animated smile. When he told her about the kiss, she clapped enthusiastically, bouncing up and down.

It was nice to have Kennedy reacting in such a way. It made Leighton feel a little less crazy for crushing so hard on a girl that he just met.

Or maybe we're both crazy, he thought, but he brushed off that notion. After all, it had been a long time since he was interested in anyone. The only other girl that Leighton had ever seriously dated was their neighbor, Becca, during sophomore year. He'd been single, and pretty much keeping to himself, since they'd broken up two years ago.

Kennedy was always asking Leighton when he'd get a girlfriend, and it's not that he didn't want one, he just hadn't met anyone worth pursuing. That was until today, when July walked into his life.

"So, what now?" Kennedy said, interrupting Leighton's thoughts.

"She's coming by the bookstore again tomorrow."

"Nice!" Kennedy exclaimed, nudging Leighton's arm. "Do you have anything planned?"

"Not yet, but I'll think of something."

"How long is she staying in town?"

"She didn't mention. Hopefully a few more days, at least."

"You should invite her to Dad's reelection party, if she'll still be around."

"I don't know," Leighton replied apprehensively. "Don't you think it's too soon? We literally just met. I don't want to freak her out by moving too fast."

"Yeah, I see what you mean. Then again, it's not like it's a private party. The whole town is going to be there."

"True," Leighton agreed. "I don't know if I'm ready for

her to meet Mom and Dad just yet, though. I mean, they, well really Mom, can be so . . ." Leighton trailed off.

"Overbearing and opinionated?"

"Yeah. And I haven't even told July that Dad is the mayor yet."

"Why not?"

Leighton paused. "I don't know. I guess it felt good to be someone other than the mayor's son for a night."

Kennedy nodded. "Yeah, I know what you mean. That's why I go to random dive bars five towns over. Because no one knows me, and I can act however I want. It's liberating not to have to worry that someone is going to see me and tattle to Mom and Dad. If July is as cool as you say she is, though, then I don't think she is going to treat you differently based on who your father is."

"You're right. I'm probably just overthinking this."

"No offense, but—" Kennedy started to say before Leighton cut her off.

"Why do I have a feeling this is going to be offensive?" he asked with a smile.

Kennedy laughed. "You tend to overthink everything."

"You're not wrong."

"Why don't you see how tomorrow goes, and if things go well, then you can invite her to Dad's party?"

"That's a good idea," Leighton replied. "Yeah, I think I'll do that. If things go as well as they did today, then I'll tell her about the party."

"There ya go!" Kennedy gave him another nudge on the arm.

Leighton smiled and finished his beer.

"Well, I'm gonna hit the sack." He tossed the empty bottle into the recycling bin. "I'm exhausted and I've got to wake up early for work. Thanks for the talk, sis!"

"Anytime, broski!" Kennedy replied with a drunken grin.

Leighton gave Kennedy a hug. She smelled like cigarettes and beer, and it was actually comforting. Kennedy had always been the wilder of the two. She loved to go out while Leighton preferred to stay in. Kennedy always had some kind of boy toy, and Leighton was perpetually single. Most of all, Kennedy was bolder than Leighton. She didn't fit into what society wanted her to be. Leighton wished he could be more like that.

It was almost two in the morning when Leighton got up to his room. Despite the fact that he couldn't stop yawning, there was one more thing that he wanted to do before going to sleep. He walked over to his desk, flipped open his laptop, and pulled up Facebook to see if he could find July's profile. He didn't know her last name, but he figured that he could probably still find her, being that her first name was so unique.

He typed *July* into the search bar and then selected the People filter. He was surprised to see that there were a significant number of results. He scrolled through profile after profile, but none of them belonged to the girl that he had met that day. After fifteen minutes or so, he gave up.

Maybe she just doesn't have a Facebook account, he thought. It wouldn't really be all that strange, after all.

Leighton had plenty of friends who weren't on Facebook, opting instead for Instagram, Snapchat, and TikTok. Facebook was much more popular among the older crowd. Leighton reached for his cell phone so that he could do a quick search on one of the other platforms. The problem with those, however, was that it was much harder to find people. He tried Instagram with no luck and then Snapchat and TikTok, but they proved unsuccessful, too. Frustrated, he decided it was time for bed.

Leighton shut his laptop and stood up from his desk. Before he turned around, he caught a glimpse of his sister through his window. She was stumbling back to the guesthouse. He laughed and shook his head. *Typical Kennedy.* Leighton liked having his sister around. She was supposed to be moving back into her apartment in a couple of weeks, and he wished that wasn't the case. Then again, he was going away to college in a month, so it wouldn't really matter anyway.

Leighton changed into his pajamas and got into bed. As he fell asleep, he thought about July and the kiss that they had shared earlier that evening.

Day Two

LEIGHTON AWOKE THE NEXT MORNING to the smell of bacon. Normally, he would play around on his phone for several minutes before getting up, but he was eager to get to the bookstore. So, he hopped out of bed, took a quick shower, got dressed, and headed downstairs. When he walked into the kitchen, he saw his mom making breakfast while his dad drank coffee and read the paper. It was a typical Sunday morning at the Prescotts'.

"Good morning, hun!" his mother said cheerfully.

"Good morning," Leighton replied, hoping to pass through the kitchen and into the garage with as little conversation as possible. July hadn't said what time she'd be stopping by the bookshop, and he wanted to make sure that he was there when she arrived.

"Where were you last night?" Mom asked. "I noticed that you still weren't home when your father and I went to bed."

"I stayed late at the bookstore." Leighton had never been a good liar, but this time, the words rolled right off his tongue. His fibbing was for the greater good anyway. His parents didn't need to know about July, not yet at least. Leighton loved his mom and dad, but they had a habit of being judgmental, especially his mother. He could only imagine how they would respond to him staying out for hours with a girl that he had just met.

"What could you have possibly been doing at the bookstore all night? That place barely gets any customers these days," Mom scoffed. Despite bringing Leighton to Twice Upon a Time on a weekly basis when he was growing up, she didn't support his decision to work there, and she couldn't understand his deep affection for the shop.

"I was reading. We got a big box of donated books and there were some really great titles in there."

"Well, don't make it a habit," Mom tutted. "Remember, your father's reelection party is tomorrow night. You can't be late for that. You need to be there, supporting our family. We have an image to maintain."

Leighton hated when his mother lectured him, especially about things that she knew he already knew. He always did what his parents asked of him, even if it wasn't what he really wanted to do. He'd never let them down before. "Yes, Mom, I know," he replied, trying to hide the frustration in his voice.

Mom gave Leighton a pat on the back. "That's my boy."

Leighton forced a smile. "Well, I'm going to head out. I'll see you guys later."

"Wait," his mother called after him as he tried to leave the kitchen.

Leighton turned around.

"Don't you want to eat breakfast with us? We always eat breakfast together on Sunday mornings."

"Not today," Leighton replied. "Sorry, Mom. I want to get to the bookstore. Plus, I'm not even hungry."

Mom did not look happy with this response. She turned her attention to her husband. "Rod, is there anything that you'd like to say to your son before he leaves?"

His father looked up from the paper and shrugged. "Have a good day, son," he said, clearly oblivious to anything that had been going on the past few minutes.

Mom rolled her eyes as Leighton quickly exited the kitchen.

Dad had always been the passive parent, not because he didn't have rules, but because he preferred to avoid conflict with his wife. Mom liked to make the decisions, especially when it came to the kids, so Dad let her. Happy wife, happy life. Right?

Whenever Kennedy or Leighton wanted to do something that required parental permission, their father's response was always the same: "Go ask your mother."

One afternoon, when his mother was out, Leighton's father had told him that he could go to a friend's house. Leighton had been there for only around thirty minutes when his mom showed up.

"Leighton needs to come home now," she said politely, but Leighton could see the anger in her eyes.

When they got into the car, she had berated him. "Don't you ever go out without asking me first!" she barked.

"But Dad said that I could," Leighton cried.

"Your father doesn't make the decisions," she had said sternly. "I do."

Leighton never asked for permission from his father again.

On the drive into town, Leighton contemplated what he and July would do later that evening after he got off work. He wanted to do something special.

Maybe the roller rink in the next town over? It had a cool retro vibe, and it was a popular spot for dates. Leighton had gone with Becca a few times and they always had fun. Leighton wasn't exactly the best skater, but he was good enough not to make a total fool of himself.

Or they could drive down to the lake. There was a farmers' market on the way where they could pick up some snacks. It would be nice to have a little picnic by the water. He'd just have to close the shop early, or else there wouldn't be much daylight left by the time they got out there.

What about a movie? There were a few highly anticipated films that were just released that weekend. Plus, Montclair's local cinema had been recently renovated and Carson worked at the concession stand; it would be nice to introduce him to July. Other than a quick text saying that he'd met a girl, Leighton hadn't really told Carson anything about July.

There was always bowling, too, and on Sundays, the local bowling alley had half-off games. *Can't go wrong with bowling, right?*

Pleased with the options that he had come up with, Leighton decided to let July have the final say. He didn't care what they did, anyway, as long as he got to spend time with her.

When Leighton arrived at Twice Upon a Time, he was surprised to see that the lights were on, and the door was propped open. Inside, he found Greta and her caretaker, Monica, standing by the front desk. Leighton couldn't help but notice how tiny Greta looked, especially next to Monica's tall and muscular stature. Greta had always been petite, but now she looked even smaller and considerably frailer than when he had last seen her.

"Greta! Monica!" he said as he walked toward the women. "What a pleasant surprise!"

"Leighton!" they exclaimed in unison.

"It's so nice to see you, my dear!" Greta said with a big smile. She shuffled toward Leighton and then embraced him in a warm hug.

"How are you?" he asked. "You haven't been to the shop in so long. I've missed you!"

"I've missed you, too! I have been meaning to stop by for a while now, but my old age has been getting the better of me lately. I have my good days and my bad days. Today is a good day, so I thought why not pay my favorite young man a visit?" Greta gave Leighton a wink.

"I'm so glad you did," Leighton said, "and you, too, Monica," he continued, turning his attention to Greta's nurse. "It's been too long! How's the family?"

"They're great, Leighton. Thank you for asking. The kids have actually been wanting to come by the bookstore. I'll have to bring them in one of these days."

"Yeah, definitely! Drop them off whenever. I would love the company."

Monica took him up on his offer, promising to bring them in later that week. Then she excused herself and headed out to run a few errands.

"So, how are you, my dear?" Greta asked after Monica left.

"Pretty great," Leighton replied. "Life has been good to me lately." His mind flashed to July when he said this.

"Oh, I just love to hear that!" Greta beamed. "You deserve it. You've been taking such good care of this shop. I would have had to close this place down if it weren't for you. Thank you for all that you do. It means so much to me, and it would have meant so much to Ivan, too."

"Thank *me*? I should be thanking *you*, Greta! You've given me the opportunity of a lifetime. I love working at the shop. It's literally my dream job."

Greta's face lit up. "So, what else has been going on? Are you looking forward to school? You leave for college in a few weeks, right? Your parents must be so proud of you."

Leighton hesitated for a moment. Should he tell Greta the truth, or should he just tell her what he was expected to say? He opted for the latter; he didn't want to ruin the mood.

"I'm excited. Though, I hate that I have to leave the book-store."

"Oh, don't you worry about the shop. You have your studies to focus on. The bookstore will still be here when you get home, and you know that it's yours whenever you're in town."

Leighton knew that Greta was only saying this because she didn't want him to feel burdened by the bookshop, but what she didn't realize was that it wasn't a burden for him at all. In fact, staying at the bookstore was what he'd prefer to do. Going away to school was the real burden. He didn't say this to her, though. Instead, he smiled and said, "I know, I will," and "Thank you."

As the clock's hands inched closer to noon, Leighton found himself growing more and more anxious. He had faith in July, he really did, but he'd be lying if he said that a small part of him wasn't questioning if she was actually going to show.

He gazed out the shop's front window hoping to see her walking down the street, but although there were plenty of people passing by, none of them were July. He kept telling himself not to worry. After all, it's not like she was late. She couldn't be; she'd never told him when she planned to arrive. He just hoped that she'd get there soon, and not just because he was eager to see her, but also because he was eager to introduce her to Greta. Greta would adore July, and he had a feeling that July would feel the same way about the sweet old woman.

"Looking for something?" Greta asked, catching Leighton off guard. She had been in the back for the past several minutes, and Leighton hadn't heard her return to the front of the store.

"I'm actually waiting for someone."

"And who is this special guest that you're expecting?"

"Her name is July. We just met yesterday when she came into the bookstore, but we really hit it off so I invited her back here today."

"Well, isn't that sweet!" Greta exclaimed. "Did you know that Ivan and I met at a bookstore?"

Leighton cocked his head, surprised by Greta's revelation. "No, I didn't actually."

"It was back when I still lived in Sweden," she said. "I was eighteen years old at the time, and working at a quaint bookshop, much like this one. Ivan was a Russian soldier, stationed nearby, and he came into the store one afternoon. We eventually got to talking, and by the time we were done, it was dark out. Hours had passed without either one of us realizing just how much time had gone by."

Greta laughed.

"I remember it so vividly," she continued. "Ivan visited me every day until his platoon moved on to their next post. After he left, I was certain that I'd never see him again. After all, I was just another woman in one of the many towns that he passed through. So, I tried to forget about him, but he was always in the back of my mind. There are some people that just leave a mark on you, and Ivan left a mark on me, whether I wanted to admit it or not."

Greta paused. Her eyes were starting to get glassy.

She cleared her throat. "Weeks passed, then months, and then years, and although I had mostly moved on, there was still a glimmer of hope that I would see Ivan again. Well, to my surprise, five years after we had met, Ivan returned to that bookstore. I couldn't believe my eyes when I saw him."

Greta's face filled with joy. "That night, he asked me to be his wife, and of course I said yes. After we got married, we came to America to start a better life. We had a dream of opening a bookstore of our own, but we had to find the right place first. We tried living in a handful of states up north, but none of them felt like home. So, we traveled south until we landed right here in Montclair, Georgia. It only took one look around for us to know that this was where our shop was meant to be."

"Wow," Leighton said. "I can't believe that you've never told me this before. I had no idea that that's how you and Ivan met, or how you ended up here in Montclair with this bookshop." He paused. "I hope one day I'll find something like that," he admitted sheepishly, "like what you and Ivan had."

The old woman smiled with conflicting emotions in her eyes: loving and longing. Leighton couldn't imagine how hard it must be to lose your soulmate.

"You will, my dear, or perhaps you already have." Greta winked and gently squeezed Leighton's arm. "Come, come, I have a box of books in the back that needs to be carried up front. I tried to lift it myself, but it's much too heavy for my weak old arms."

The two made their way to the back of the store where Leighton retrieved the box of books. He carried it up front to the reading nook, where he and Greta sorted through the hodgepodge of novels: fantasies, historical fictions, biographies, romances, and mysteries, all in varying conditions. Some looked crisp and new while others looked worn and weathered.

Leighton and Greta made small talk while they worked. Greta asked Leighton about his parents and Kennedy, and Leighton gave his typical, politically correct responses. Leighton had been trained from a young age to paint the picture of a perfect family. The Prescotts had a squeaky clean image to maintain, and he knew better than to tarnish it.

The Prescott dynasty had begun with Leighton's great-grandfather, Lawrence, who was the first mayor of Montclair back when the town was founded in the 1950s. He served a handful of terms before his son, Leighton's grandfather, Warren, was elected in the 1980s. In 2005, Warren Prescott was succeeded by his son, Leighton's father, Rod. And in a few years, it would be Leighton's turn to fulfill the Prescott legacy. Hence why he was slated to attend college in a few weeks as a political science major. In Montclair, there were no term limitations for the mayor, so the Prescott lineage would continue until there wasn't an heir to fill the position, or until the townspeople voted someone else in, but the Prescotts were highly favored. So much so that there hadn't even been another candidate in the past several elections.

Leighton wondered if his father had actually wanted to be mayor, or if he, too, felt obligated to carry on the Prescott heritage, despite having dreams of his own. If his dad ever had felt this way, he certainly didn't talk about it. Maybe Leighton was just the odd man out. The black sheep. Maybe, instead of feeling resentful, he should be feeling grateful that he even had a path to follow. Leighton tried so hard to be the perfect son. He wanted to please his parents, but he couldn't help but wonder why that meant sacrificing his own happiness? Why couldn't he have both?

"Is everything okay, my dear?" Greta asked.

Leighton hadn't realized that he had zoned out. "Yes, everything is fine! I just got caught up in my own thoughts."

Greta laughed. "It happens to the best of us."

Leighton nodded and then continued to sort through the box of books. Near the bottom, he was excited to find a copy of *The Outsiders* Fiftieth Anniversary Edition. It was a beautiful hardcover and it was in pristine condition.

"Hey, Greta! Do you mind if I hold on to this one?" he asked.

"It's all yours."

"Thank you," Leighton said as he set the book aside.

It was quarter to two when Leighton and Greta finally cleared the box. The books were now organized in tidy piles based on genre, which would determine which aisle each one belonged in.

Leighton went to the back to retrieve the shop's ladder so that he could start putting the books away in their designated locations. When he got back to the front, Greta was sitting on the couch. She looked exhausted.

"Tired?" he asked.

Greta turned around to face him. "Yes, I am. I can't remember the last time I worked this hard. I think it might be time for me to head home. Would you mind calling Monica and asking her to pick me up?"

"Yeah, no problem. I'll do that now," Leighton said as he pulled his phone out of his pocket. Monica answered on the first ring and said that she'd be there in five minutes.

Leighton was disappointed, but he didn't show it. He really wanted Greta to meet July, but he understood why she needed to go. "I hope you didn't push yourself too hard," he said as he made his way over to the sofa to help her up. "And don't worry about the books. I'll make sure that they all get put away."

"Thank you, my dear," Greta replied as Leighton carefully lifted her off the couch. She gave him a hug. "It's always so nice to see you."

"You, too, Greta," Leighton said as he embraced the old woman.

After Greta left, and Leighton was alone, he found himself consumed with thoughts of July. It was nearly three now and she still wasn't at the bookstore. He wondered if she'd skipped town and continued on her trip down to Florida. *Surely she would have stopped by to let me know, right? Unless she felt like yesterday was a mistake and she left town hoping to forget it . . . to forget me.*

Leighton was notorious for overthinking, and this situation was no different. He knew that worrying about something that might not even be true wasn't doing him any good. So, he told himself to snap out of it and focused on the task at hand instead.

He was wheeling the ladder over to the first aisle when he heard the chime of the little bell on the shop's door.

"Hey," July said as she entered the bookstore.

"Hey!" Leighton exclaimed with a mix of excitement and relief.

July laughed. "What'd you think I wasn't going to come?"

Leighton blushed. "Maybe . . ."

July softened. "I wouldn't have bailed on you."

"Good thing, because I have something for you."

"What do you mean? You didn't have to get me anything!"

Leighton walked to the front desk and picked up *The Outsiders*. "It's just a little something," he said as he handed the book to July. "I found it in a box of donations, and I figured you might like it."

"Oh my gosh!" July exclaimed. "It's beautiful!" She ran her fingers over the cover. "Thank you so much. This was really thoughtful."

"You're welcome."

"The artwork on the cover is amazing."

"Yeah, they did a great job with it," Leighton agreed.

July pulled the book to her chest and hugged it. "I think this might be my favorite book that I own, and I own a lot of books."

"I'm so glad you like it."

"I love it!" July cradled the book, her eyes shining.

"So, what's on the agenda for today?" she continued, now flipping through the pages of her new hardcover.

"Well, I figure we'll hang out here for the rest of the day. I typically close around dusk, but we can head out early. I don't think all of these customers will mind," Leighton joked while motioning his arms around the empty room.

July laughed. "Wow, how courteous of them!"

"I know, right?" Leighton grinned. "As far as tonight goes, I came up with a few ideas. You can choose whichever one sounds best."

"Okay, let's hear 'em!"

"Alright. Option one: skating at an indoor roller rink. Option two: picnic by the lake. Option three: go to see a movie. Or option four: bowling."

July considered her choices. She tapped her pointer finger on her bottom lip while she deliberated.

"Tough call," she said after a few seconds. "They all sound like fun. Can we do whatever we don't do today on other days?"

"Does that mean that you're planning to stay in Montclair for a little longer?"

"I guess it depends on how you answer my question."

"Yes," Leighton responded. "We can definitely do all of those things. So now the next question is, which one would you like to start with?"

"I suppose it would make the most sense to start with option one and then move our way down the list, right?"

"Yeah, that makes sense to me."

"Roller rink it is, then!" July declared.

"Cool, we can leave here around five. The rink is in the next town over. It's a pretty quick drive. Like twenty minutes or so."

"Sounds like a plan!"

Over the next couple of hours, July helped Leighton with various tasks around the bookstore. First up was putting away the newly donated books. Leighton pushed

July on the shop's rolling ladder while she placed the novels on their designated shelves in their designated aisles. When they were done with that, they swept the floors and dusted the front desk. And after that, they cleaned the bathroom. Satisfied with their work for the day, the two headed over to the reading nook where they settled onto that worn, velour sofa and waited out the last hour.

They didn't talk much during this time; instead, they each curled up with a book of their choosing: Leighton had *The Alchemist* and July, of course, had *The Outsiders*. Occasionally, one would fidget and the other would look up, then they'd exchange smiles before returning to their novels and falling into another comfortable stillness.

At quarter past five, Leighton checked his watch and realized that it was time for them to go. He nudged July and the two got up from the sofa.

"For such a modest-looking couch, it sure is cozy," July said. "I was practically melting into it."

Leighton nodded. "This couch has been here since the shop opened. I remember reading on it back when I was just a kid, and even then, it was considered old. It's always been my favorite spot in the bookstore."

"I think it might be mine, too," July agreed.

As the two headed out, right before Leighton turned off the lights, he looked over at the old sofa. He saw himself as a young boy sitting on Greta's lap as she read him a children's book. Greta would point to a word and Leighton would sound it out.

"What does that say?" she'd ask gently.

"An-i-mal," Leighton said carefully, looking up at Greta for approval when he was done.

"Yes! Good job!" She beamed.

A few months later, Leighton was reading on his own.

The ride to the roller rink was Leighton's favorite kind. The weather was perfect so he and July drove with the windows down so that the summer breeze could caress their skin. Leighton put on a Led Zeppelin album and July sang along to "Stairway to Heaven." She was a terrible singer, but Leighton found that to be all the more endearing. When she belted out "and as we wind on down the road," Leighton couldn't contain his laughter any longer. She sounded awful. She was completely off-key and totally out of tune. It was adorable.

When the song ended, Leighton gave July a well-deserved round of applause and said, "You have the voice of an angel."

July pretended to take a bow and then erupted with laughter. It took her a minute to regain her composure, but once she did, she said, "When I was younger, I wanted to be a famous singer. I used to put on these shows for my mom, practically every night. And she always watched. It didn't matter how busy she was or if I was singing the same five songs that I had been singing for months. She never missed a show. Then, one night, after one of my performances, she pulled me into a hug and said, 'You know, I could listen to you sing forever. To me, your voice is perfect, but I think I might be a little biased because I'm your mom.' I asked her what she meant by that, and she said that she had something that she wanted me to hear. I didn't realize, but she had recorded me singing, and when she played it back for me, I was *mortified*. I sounded like a dying cat! I must've looked horrified, too, because when my mom saw my face, she started laughing hysterically." July smiled as she recalled the memory. "Seeing my mom laugh like that, well it made me laugh hysterically, too. We laughed until our stomachs ached and there were tears in our eyes, and even then, we couldn't stop. I'll never forget that night. It was the hardest that I had ever seen my mom laugh."

"Your mom sounds pretty awesome," Leighton said.

"Thank you. I got really lucky in the mom department."

He was about to ask July some more questions about her family and her upbringing, but they arrived at the roller rink before he had the opportunity to do so. After they pulled into the parking lot, Leighton quickly hopped out of his truck so that he could open July's door.

"You're such a gentleman," she said as she climbed out.

Leighton grinned and pretended to tip an imaginary cowboy hat. July giggled.

Walking into the roller rink was like stepping back in time: neon lights, disco balls, retro skates, and a 1970s soundtrack. The place was packed with couples holding hands as they moved round and round on the shiny wooden floor. Leighton could smell pizza and french fries from the snack shack in the front right corner of the building. To the left was a long count-er where visitors could rent skates.

As Leighton and July approached the front desk, they were greeted by a girl with blue hair and red lipstick. She told them that before they could rent their skates, they'd each have to complete a safety affidavit. The two agreed and began filling out their forms. While doing so, Leighton took a peek at July's paper and learned that her last name was Evans. He had been wanting to know what it was so that he could look her up on social media, but now he felt guilty for being sneaky and invading her privacy.

Leighton decided that it was better to be straightforward. "Do you have any social media accounts?" he asked casually.

"That's random," July said with a laugh, "but to answer your question, no, I don't. I did, but I deleted them all a few weeks ago. I needed a break."

Leighton wondered if there was a particular reason why July needed a break from social media. *Does it have to do with a guy? A recent breakup?* He was going to ask more questions but he let it go.

After they finished their paperwork, the pair went back up to the counter and got their rentals. It was clear that July was excited—she was practically skipping to the bench to change out of her sneakers and into her skates. The two laced up and put their belongings in a tiny locker.

Once on the slick surface of the rink, Leighton realized that he wasn't as good at skating as he used to be. While July glided effortlessly, he was shaking with instability. He could barely keep up with her. In fact, she made an entire revolution around the rink before he even moved a few feet.

"Are you okay?" she asked as she skated up behind Leighton. After she passed him, she turned around so that they were facing each other; casually showing off her ability to not only skate forward but backward, too.

"Yeah," Leighton lied. "I'm just easing into it. I'll be up to speed in no time."

July raised her eyebrow and gave him an I-don't-believe-a-word-you-just-said look. "No offense, but you look like you're teetering on the edge of disaster."

Leighton laughed and lost his balance, toppling to the ground as ungracefully as humanly possible.

July looked at him with wide eyes before bursting into laughter herself. Her knees began to wobble, and next thing Leighton knew, she was lying on the ground beside him.

"You made me fall!" She gave him a playful slap on the arm.

"Technically, you made yourself fall by making me laugh, which made me fall, which then made you laugh and ultimately fall down yourself," Leighton replied matter-of-factly.

July stuck her tongue out at him, then regained her balance and propped herself up. She looked down at Leighton. "You need my help, don't you?"

Leighton blushed. "Yeah, kinda."

July reached out her arms and Leighton grabbed her hands. They each tugged in an alternating fashion until Leighton was upright and somewhat stable, which was about as steady as he was going to get.

"Are you good?" July asked, still holding Leighton's hands.

"I think so," Leighton replied, with a bit of hesitation in his voice.

"How about we go around together?" She let go of Leighton's right hand but kept a tight grip on his left.

"I'd like that."

"Just promise that you won't take me down with you if you fall again."

Leighton laughed. "Deal."

The two made their way around the rink, fingers intertwined. They skated slowly at first, then picked up speed. Eventually, they fell into a comfortable rhythm. July softly sang along to "Dancing Queen," "September," and "Stayin' Alive." Periodically, Leighton would look down at her hand in his and revel at how perfectly it fit. Being with July was so easy for him, her company just felt natural.

Life is so crazy, Leighton thought. Twenty-four hours ago, July was just a strange girl who happened to wander into the bookstore, and now she was here, with her fingers laced in his, and she was quickly becoming someone he didn't want to be without.

After an hour or so, and many trips around the rink, the two traded their skates for their street shoes and headed over to the snack bar. While they ate, they talked about school and what was next for each of them. Leighton learned that July had also graduated that past June, but she wouldn't be attending college in the fall. Instead, she would be taking a year off to figure out what she wanted to do. She was interested in working with animals, but she wasn't sure if she wanted to pursue a degree in a field like veterinary studies or zoology, or if she wanted to skip school altogether and find a job at a place like a shelter or a sanctuary instead.

Leighton enjoyed getting to know July on a deeper level. It was nice to have her opening up to him, especially because sometimes, he felt like she was holding something back. Every now and then, he would catch a glimpse of sadness in her eyes, and he wanted to ask what was bothering her, but he also didn't want to pry. If she wanted him to know, she would tell him. Or maybe she wouldn't ever tell him what was troubling her, and that was okay, too. It was her secret to keep.

After learning about July's love for animals, Leighton suggested that they take a trip to the local wildlife preserve, knowing that it would be the perfect activity for her. When he told her about some of the exhibits that they had there, like giraffes, zebras, tigers, kangaroos, and other exotic animals, her eyes got big and she exclaimed, "I would love that!" The two decided that they would go the following day, after the bookstore, of course.

The conversation then turned to Leighton and what he would be doing now that he was done with high school. Leighton explained that he was leaving for college in just a few weeks. He would be attending Emory University, which was the alma mater of his father, grandfather, and great-grandfather. There, he would be studying political science.

July looked puzzled. "You don't seem like the political science type," she said.

"What do you mean by that?" Leighton asked.

"You come off as someone who would be into something more creative," she said with a shrug.

July wasn't wrong—Leighton loved to read and write, but he didn't tell her that. Instead he said that he had always been interested in politics. She wasn't buying it, though.

"Are these those 'big plans' that you mentioned last night?" she asked suspiciously.

"What do you mean?" Leighton replied, as if he didn't know exactly what she was talking about.

"Last night, at your sister's bakery, you said that your parents had all these big plans for you. Do these plans include you going to Emory University to study political science?" July looked Leighton directly in the eyes as she said this.

Leighton looked away, but he could still feel her stare piercing him. He looked back. "Yeah, maybe," he responded reluctantly before finally saying, "Okay, yes."

July's stern expression turned sympathetic. "You also said that you weren't sure if you wanted what your parents wanted for you . . ."

"Yeah, I did. The truth is, my dad is the mayor of Montclair, and my grandfather and great grandfather held the position before him. Since the town was founded, the Prescott family has been in office, and I'm next in line."

July opened her mouth as if she were going to say something but remained quiet, so Leighton continued, "My parents never really asked me what I wanted to do, I guess because they've always expected me to go down this path. I think they see it as an honor to maintain the family legacy. In their eyes, why wouldn't I want to do that? It's confusing, honestly, and I'm just trying to keep an open mind about it all. Maybe I'll actually end up enjoying it. And if not, at least I can take pride in knowing that I didn't let my family down, you know?"

"No, I really don't," July replied bluntly. "It sounds like you are being pressured to do something that you don't want to do, and that's not okay, regardless of who it is . . . even if it is your parents."

Leighton considered what July was saying to him. She had a point, but the situation also wasn't as black-and-white as she was making it seem. Leighton had never told his parents that he didn't want to pursue politics, so technically, they didn't know that they were pushing him to do something that he didn't want to do. Then again, they had been grooming him to carry out the family legacy since he was a young boy, so that could qualify as intentional pressure. *It's all so confusing*, Leighton thought.

"Maybe you should tell your parents how you're feeling," July suggested.

"But I don't even *know* how I'm feeling."

July scrunched her brows. "You know that you're having doubts. You know that you're not 100 percent positive that this is what you want to do, right?"

Leighton nodded and muttered, "Yeah."

"Just talk to them. It could end up being a really productive conversation that gives you the answers that you're looking for, but you'll never know unless you try," July said in an encouraging tone.

"You sound like my sister." Leighton laughed.

July smirked. "I hope that's a good thing!"

"It is. My sister has always been more headstrong than me. She's assertive and not afraid to speak her mind. After she graduated high school, she turned down a scholarship to Northeastern University. My parents were furious. They even kicked her out of the house, but she didn't care. She got a business loan and opened her bakery, and now it's one of the most popular shops in Montclair."

"That's what I'm talking about!" July exclaimed. "So, if she can do it, why can't you?"

"I guess because I'd feel guilty. My parents expect Kennedy to be unpredictable. She's the rebellious one, the wild child. Me, on the other hand . . . Well, I'm the one who always does what I'm supposed to do. I'm the *good* one, as my mom likes to say."

"It shouldn't be conditional. You can still be the *good* one without sacrificing your wants and your happiness."

Leighton sighed. "You make it sound so easy."

July reached out and put her hand on his. "It *should* be easy. Your parents are supposed to love you and accept you no matter what, and I'm sure yours will too regardless of if you pursue politics or whatever else your heart desires. But you haven't even given them the chance to."

"You're right. I'll talk to them."

July squeezed his hand. "Promise?"

"Promise," Leighton replied earnestly.

July shot him a triumphant grin. "Ready to go?"

Leighton nodded. "Yeah, let's get out of here."

The two got up from their little booth, cleared the table, and made their way toward the exit. Outside, the sun was hanging lower in the sky. It was half past seven now, and dusk was fast approaching. This was Leighton's favorite time of day, and he knew the perfect place to relish it, but they'd have to get there quickly or else they'd miss the sunset.

"Where to now, captain?" July asked playfully as they left the roller rink.

Leighton grinned. "It's a surprise."

Pine Meadows was a spacious park on the outskirts of Montclair. It had a sprawling green lawn that offered an unobstructed view of the big Georgia sky, making it an ideal location to watch day turn to night. It was a spot that Leighton and his buddies visited frequently. They spent many Friday and Saturday evenings on the lush, neatly trimmed grass, drinking beers while watching the sky turn pink, purple, and orange. Hopefully, July would enjoy it as much as they did.

The park was a fifteen-minute drive from the rink. Leighton turned on the radio, but instead of singing along, July stared out the window. Leighton could tell that she was curious about where they were going. When they arrived at their destination, she perked up and said, "Oh, this place looks nice!"

"You haven't even seen the half of it yet." Leighton beamed.

The park was encircled by a natural fence of pine trees. In the middle, there was a field where Leighton loved to lounge. You couldn't see that area from the parking lot, and Leighton was eager to show July. He hopped out of his truck, opened the passenger door, and grabbed July's hand.

"Follow me," he said as he led her past the pines.

As the two emerged from the trees, the picturesque meadow came into view. It was expansive with thick, plush grass sprinkled with a rainbow of wildflowers. The final rays of sunlight were shining down on the scenery like light leaks in an old photo.

"Wow, I was not expecting this. It looks like a scene from a painting!" July exclaimed.

Leighton was glad she appreciated the beauty of the park as much as he did. "It's one of my favorite spots. Not to mention, the absolute best place to watch the sunset. That's why I brought you here."

"What a great idea! I can't remember the last time I watched the sunset," July admitted.

"It's something that I try to do as much as possible, especially when I'm feeling stressed. Being out here always relaxes me," Leighton said.

"I can see why."

Leighton pointed to the center of the field and asked, "What do you think of that spot?"

"It looks perfect to me!"

Leighton remembered all the times that he and Carson sat in this very field, drinking beers and talking about girls.

"Dude, the next chick I date, I'm bringing her here to watch the sunset," Carson had mused one night. "I don't know why I hadn't thought of this before. No girl would be able to resist me after that," he continued, with his signature Carson smirk.

Leighton let out a laugh as he recalled the memory. Carson was always popular with the ladies. He was charismatic and a total flirt, with the kind of arrogance that was appealing instead of off-putting. Leighton, on the other hand, was much more reserved and far less experienced when it came to sex, relationships, and women. Who would've guessed that he'd be the one to bring a girl out here first.

Leighton and July situated themselves on the lawn and awaited the setting sun. They watched as the sky changed from blue to various shades of fruit sherbet: cherry, orange, grape. It was one of the most vibrant sunsets that Leighton had ever seen.

"What would you want to do if you don't go into politics?" July asked.

"I'd love to restore Twice Upon a Time to its former glory," Leighton replied. "I've honestly been so worried about what will happen to Greta and the bookshop while I'm away at school. I'd be devastated if she had to shut the doors for good because she couldn't find someone to fill in for me."

July nodded in understanding. "Have you always been close with Greta?"

"Yeah, I've known her my whole life. She's been like a grandmother to me for as long as I can remember, especially because both my Nana Jane, my mom's mom, and my Grandma Prescott, my dad's mom, passed away when I was young. Greta helped to fill that void."

"Well, she sounds amazing, and your idea to restore the bookshop does, too. I hope you get the chance to do it."

Leighton smiled. He hoped so, too.

After the multicolored sky had melted away like ice cream left outside on a hot summer day, and darkness had swept over the field, Leighton suggested that they return to town. July looked reluctant at first but then agreed. As they walked back to his truck, July grabbed Leighton's hand, and his heart nearly jumped out of his chest.

"I had a really great time today," she said once they were both inside the vehicle.

"I did, too," Leighton replied as he put his key into the ignition.

They sat there for a few minutes, quiet, with the only sound coming from the low hum of the idling engine. There was something in the air between them, a feeling that Leighton couldn't quite explain. It was like a charge of electricity mixed with the pressure of rushing water. Leighton wanted to touch July; he wanted to hold her and kiss her, but he also didn't want to come on too strong. If he moved too fast, would he ruin a good thing? It was so hard to keep his hands to himself, though, especially when it felt like July was a magnet pulling him closer. Did she feel it, too?

Leighton straightened in his seat and placed his hand on the gear shift. It was getting late, and his parents were going to question him if he didn't get home soon. He was about to put his truck into drive when something stopped him, a feeling in his gut telling him that he couldn't let this moment pass him by. Leighton brought his hand to July's cheek and pulled her to him. When their lips met, it felt like a fire igniting or waves crashing to shore. Leighton moved his hands to July's hair and ran his fingers through her soft curls. July squeezed his bicep and kissed him harder. They stayed like this for several minutes, breathing each other in and out, until Leighton finally pulled away. When he did, July looked flushed but satisfied. She took his hand and placed it in her lap, and as they drove back to the motel, she drew circles in his palm with her thumb.

"Today was pretty amazing," July said when they pulled into the parking lot.

"Yeah, it was," Leighton agreed, wishing he could freeze time so that he could stay with her for just a little bit longer. "Hey, I've been meaning to ask you . . . can I have your number? Or can I give you mine?"

July held out her hand with her palm facing up. "Phone."

Leighton pulled his phone out of his pocket, put in his passcode, and handed it to July.

She typed in her number and returned it. "Send me a text so I have yours."

"Done," Leighton said as July's phone chimed.

July smiled and unbuckled her seat belt. "Well, I guess I better get going."

"Yeah, I guess so." Leighton scratched the back of his head. It was a nervous habit of his.

July grabbed Leighton's hand and squeezed it gently. Then she pulled him in close and gave him a delicate kiss on the cheek.

"I'll see you tomorrow," she whispered as she moved her lips away from his face.

"Okay. You know where to find me."

July walked to her room, unlocked the door, and stepped inside. Leighton wondered how many more nights like this he had left. July was going to have to eventually continue her trip down to Florida. A knot grew in his stomach. He wanted more time with July, but each day spent together was another day closer to her inevitably leaving. It was conflicting to want time to simultaneously slow down and speed up. July had been gone for only a few minutes, and he already wanted it to be tomorrow so that he could see her again, but that also meant that he would be twelve hours closer to her departing for good.

Stop it, Leighton thought. *Today was awesome. Don't ruin it by overthinking. Stop worrying about the future. Live in the moment. Take it day by day.*

Leighton took a deep breath and drove away into the night. On the way, he repeated that mantra again and again until his mind was free of racing thoughts.

When Leighton got home, his mother was in the foyer, nursing a glass of chardonnay.

"Another late night at the bookstore?" she asked suspiciously as Leighton walked through the door.

"No, I went out with Carson after work."

Mom narrowed her eyes and gave Leighton an unconvinced look. "I really wish you'd tell me when you're not going to be home for dinner."

Leighton wasn't in the mood to talk, so he told his mother what she wanted to hear. "Sorry, Mom, I will next time, I promise."

She took a sip of wine. "Thank you," she said with a triumphant smirk.

Leighton nodded and then made a dash for the stairs. He wanted to get to his room before his mother asked him any more questions.

A few minutes later, Leighton sat in front of his laptop, a guilty feeling in the pit of his stomach. *This is wrong*, he thought. Leighton went to his bed and laid down. He stared aimlessly at the ceiling for several minutes before getting up again and returning to his desk. Google was still up, and before he could think twice, he was looking at search results for "July Evans New York." One of the first headlines caught his eye: One Dead After Small Plane Crash on Long Island. Leighton pulled up the news article.

One Dead After Small Plane Crash on Long Island

Riverhead, NY: Suffolk County Sheriff's Office said that one person died after a plane crash in Riverhead on Sunday night.

The plane, a twin-engine Piper PA-30, crashed at around 7:30 p.m. in a wooded area near Sound Avenue.

The pilot, later identified as Scarlett Evans, was pronounced dead at the scene, according to the Suffolk County coroner.

The Federal Aviation Administration and the National Transportation Safety Board are still investigating the cause of the crash.

Evans lived in Brooklyn, NY and is survived by 18-year-old daughter, July.

Leighton couldn't believe it. He read the article again and again, hoping the words on the screen would change, but they stayed the same.

The pilot . . . Scarlett Evans was pronounced dead at the scene . . .
Evans . . . is survived by 18-year-old daughter, July.

Leighton's stomach dropped. He checked the date to see when the article was written. Monday, June 28. The accident happened the day prior, Sunday, June 27. *July's mom passed away a month ago*, he thought. All of a sudden, it all made sense. This was why she started crying randomly, why she got quiet and distant when she talked about her mom, why she hated flying, and why she was going to Florida to reunite with her father. Leighton felt like he was going to puke, and he wasn't sure if it was because he felt bad for July or because he felt horrible for discovering this information. If she wanted him to know, she would've told him. This was an invasion of privacy, and he hated himself for it.

Leighton closed his laptop and started pacing around his room. If only he could go back in time. After a few minutes of self-loathing, he decided to take his mind off July's tragedy and his breach of privacy. He went downstairs for a late-night snack. Fortunately, his parents were already in bed. He looked out the kitchen window to see if Kennedy was home. Her lights were on, so he grabbed a gallon of ice cream and headed to the guesthouse.

Knock, knock, knock.

"One second!" Kennedy shouted.

Leighton could hear his sister running toward the door. When she opened it, he was greeted with a big smile and a bright green face. Leighton gave her a funny look.

"It's a face mask," she said. "Come in!"

Leighton followed Kennedy to the den. He lifted the cold tub that he was holding and said, "I brought ice cream."

"I can see that," she replied. "I'll go get us bowls and spoons."

When Kennedy came back, the two made their sundaes and then Kennedy put the remaining ice cream in the freezer. She returned to the den and sat down next to Leighton on the cappuccino-colored leather couch.

"So, what's up?" she asked with a mouth full of mint chocolate chip ice cream.

"I did something that I shouldn't have," Leighton confessed.

Kennedy looked at him, puzzled. "What'd you do?"

Leighton hesitated. "I did an internet search on July."

Kennedy gave him a nonchalant shrug. "Everyone does that when they first start talking to someone."

"No, this is different. She doesn't have any social media, but I found something else . . . a news article . . . about her mom. Apparently, she died in a plane crash. It just happened, only a month ago." Leighton looked down. He was so ashamed of himself.

"Oh my God," Kennedy said, shock and sympathy on her face. "That's terrible."

"I know. And it's even worse that I found out from the internet and not from July. I totally invaded her privacy."

"Don't be so hard on yourself," Kennedy said reassuringly. "It's normal to be curious about the person that you're interested in. And like I said before, literally everyone does it. I do it. All my friends do it. And ninety-nine percent of the time, it's totally innocent. You find the person's social media profiles. You confirm that they're not a sociopath or something. And you call it a day. You didn't do anything wrong—you just got unlucky."

Leighton moved his ice cream around the bowl with his

spoon. He still hadn't eaten any. "I appreciate you trying to justify my actions, Ken, but I still feel like shit for what I did."

Kennedy gave Leighton a compassionate look, set down her bowl, and wrapped her brother in a tight hug. "You're a good person. It was an honest mistake," she whispered in his ear.

Leighton shrugged. He didn't feel like a good person.

Kennedy turned on the television and finished her ice cream. When she was done, she asked Leighton if he was going to finish his, and when he said no, she finished his, too.

They sat there for a little while longer before Kennedy said that she needed to wash off her face mask. Leighton was ready to call it a night anyway.

"Do you think I should tell her that I know?" he asked as he was about to leave.

"I think you should relax. It's really not that big of a deal, I promise. But to answer your question, no, I don't. I think you should wait for her to open up to you."

Day Three

MORNING CAME QUICKLY, AND WHEN Leighton awoke, he felt as if he hadn't slept at all. He closed his eyes and accidentally dozed off for another hour. It would have been even longer if his mother hadn't knocked on his door. It was ten, and she wanted to know why he was still home. This was the time that he usually opened the shop.

On the drive to the bookstore, Leighton debated whether he should tell July that he found the article about her mom. He wanted to be honest with her, but he was also scared of how she would react. Withholding this information seemed wrong, though, plus Leighton was a terrible liar. He wasn't even sure if he'd be able to act normal around her, especially when he felt paralyzed by his guilty conscience.

When he pulled up to Twice Upon a Time, it was quarter to eleven and the door was propped open. Greta must've been there again. This made Leighton feel better. The old woman had a calming presence. Being around her would ease his stress and silence his mind. He carefully parallel parked in his usual spot out front, got out of his vehicle, and entered the bookshop.

Leighton expected to see Greta and Monica when he walked in, but to his surprise, it was July who was with the old woman instead. They were sitting close on the couch, engaged in an animated conversation.

"Leighton, my dear!" Greta beamed. "We've been waiting for you!"

"Hello, ladies," Leighton said. "I wasn't expecting any company this morning, but boy am I so glad to see the two of you!"

"It seems we've both decided to surprise you!" Greta smiled. "July and I were just getting to know each other. She's a lovely girl."

July blushed. "Thank you, Greta, you're lovely, too!"

Greta's face filled with joy when July said this. Greta waved to Leighton and said, "Come join us, dear!"

Leighton walked over to the sofa, and July scooted over so that he could sit between her and Greta. The three of them hung out there for quite some time, talking about this and that, sharing smiles and laughs, and just enjoying each other's company.

Leighton was so happy that Greta and July had the opportunity to meet, and that they were getting along so well. They really seemed to adore each other.

After an hour or so, Greta suggested that they order some lunch from the coffee shop next door, The Bean. Leighton offered to go pick up the food. When he returned, he found Greta comforting July while she wept on the couch. The old woman had July wrapped in a hug and was gently rubbing her back. Greta was saying, "Now, now, now, it's okay, let it all out, sweetheart."

Leighton hated to see July cry. What was upsetting her? She'd been in good spirits when he left for the coffee shop, and that was only fifteen minutes earlier. He assumed that it was related to her mom. After all, she'd just recently passed away, and July was obviously still grieving. Plus, this wouldn't be the first time that July was suddenly overcome with sadness. Just a couple of days ago, she'd started crying while reading *The Outsiders*. He couldn't imagine what she was going through. He felt so bad for her, but he also felt something else: a pang of jealousy. Had July told Greta about what happened to her mom? It certainly seemed so, and if that was the case, why did she feel comfortable talking to the old woman but not him?

Stop it, Leighton thought. *How selfish are you? This isn't a competition.*

Leighton felt guilty, once again, which seemed to be a recurring trend as of late. Was he really jealous of Greta? And how could he make July's situation about himself? The passing of her mother was July's tragedy, and she could talk to, or not talk to, whomever she wanted about it. Plus, Greta was the kindest and most compassionate woman that Leighton had ever met. It's no wonder that July felt comfortable talking to her. Not to mention, Greta understood the pain of grief. She had to battle it after Ivan's death. If anything, Leighton should be feeling happy for July because she'd found someone to vent to, and he should be feeling grateful for Greta for being July's outlet. July must have been bottling up her emotions for far too long, and that wasn't healthy.

Once Leighton's thoughts finally settled, he realized that he had been standing awkwardly in the doorway for at least a few minutes. Fortunately, Greta and July didn't notice. He took a few more steps into the building and cleared his throat. "Is everything okay?"

July pulled away from Greta and wiped her eyes. "Yeah, everything's fine." She forced a laugh. "I'm just being emotional."

"There's nothing wrong with that," Greta said with a tender smile.

Leighton nodded and then changed the subject, sensing that July didn't want to talk about it anymore. He lifted the to-go bag. "Ready to eat?"

"Yes!" both women exclaimed.

Leighton sat the bag of food on the front desk and took out Greta's and July's sandwiches. He carried them over to the girls on the sofa and then returned to the front desk. He figured he would eat there so that Greta and July had more room. The couch was small, and he didn't want to crowd them.

Leighton watched as Greta and July bit into their lunches. "Good?" he asked.

Greta nodded and July gave him a thumbs-up.

Leighton considered striking up a conversation while they

ate, but the girls seemed content being preoccupied with their food, so he let them be. Instead, he thought about the day when Greta gave him the keys to Twice Upon a Time, back when he was just a part-time volunteer. They were having lunch at The Bean, enjoying the same sandwiches that they were eating right now.

"I'm stepping away from the bookshop," Greta had said, wiping her mouth with a napkin.

"What do you mean?" Leighton asked, concerned. He loved the bookstore, it was his favorite place in Montclair, maybe even in the entire world.

"I'm getting old, my dear. It's just too much work for me."

Leighton's heart had sunk to his stomach. "But-but you can't just let it close."

Greta had chuckled. "Of course I can't, but I can find someone else to look after it."

Leighton hadn't been sure where she was going with this.

"Leighton," Greta said, "would you like to be the new caretaker of Twice Upon a Time?"

Leighton's face had lit up. He couldn't think of anything that he'd like more than that, and now, almost a year later, he still couldn't.

"So, what else do you kids have planned for today?" Greta asked as she wrapped up the remaining half of her sandwich.

"We're gonna go to the animal preserve later this afternoon, after I close up the bookshop," Leighton replied.

"What a great idea!" Greta said. "It's a perfect day for an outside activity. The weather is beautiful!"

"Yeah, it is," Leighton agreed. "I'm looking forward to it!"

"Me, too!" July chimed in.

"Have you been to the animal preserve recently, Leighton?" Greta asked. "They used to have a butterfly exhibit that I just loved to visit. I haven't gone in ages, though. I hope it's still there."

"It's still there. I went with my biology class a few months back, and that was one of the exhibits that we spent the most time in."

"Oh, I'm so glad to hear that!" Greta exclaimed.

"You should come with us, Greta," Leighton suggested.

"I appreciate the invitation, but I'm afraid it would be a bit too much for me. Plus, I don't want to intrude."

"You wouldn't be intruding!" July chirped. "We'd love to have you join us."

"You're both very sweet, but I'm going to sit this one out."

"Okay," Leighton surrendered.

"I have an idea," Greta continued. "Why don't you two head out when you finish eating? I can man the shop for the rest of the day."

Leighton looked at Greta apprehensively. She had grown quite frail, and he worried that her being alone at the store could be dangerous. God forbid something happened to her, he'd never forgive himself. "I don't know, Greta, don't you think it might be too much for you? I don't want you to over-work yourself, or worse, hurt yourself, especially if no one is around to help you."

"Oh, don't worry about me. I'll be fine! There isn't much to do around here anyway. I'll probably just stay cozied up on the couch with a book," Greta said. "Plus, Monica will be picking me up later. If I need help with anything before then, I can always call her and ask her to come by a little early."

Leighton considered what she said. She was right—there wasn't much to do. They hadn't received any new book donations to put away, and the shop was still in order from yesterday, when he and July cleaned and organized everything. Hanging out on the sofa and reading a book is probably what she'd be doing if she were home anyway. Plus, he didn't want Greta to think that he thought that she was unable to do things. He suspected that retaining her independence was important to her. She wasn't ready to surrender just yet.

Greta had always been a bit stubborn. Leighton really noticed it after Ivan's death when Greta was back at the store the day following his passing. Everyone in town told her to take some time off so that she could mourn, but she insisted on working. It wasn't until this time last year, after months of her doctor urging her to step down, that she finally conceded and asked Leighton to be the new caretaker of her beloved bookshop. Her body was weak by then, and it couldn't handle eight-hour workdays, seven days a week.

In the beginning, when Greta first gave Leighton the keys, she would still come by the store every few days, but her visits grew more and more infrequent. Now, she only popped in here and there, which was why Leighton was so surprised to see her the past two days. Of course he was thrilled to have her company, but it was unusual, with how much time had passed since her last visit. Maybe it meant that she was feeling better, but then again, Greta wasn't sick or unhealthy, she was just battling old age, and no one can reverse the hands of time.

"Okay," Leighton hesitantly agreed, "but if you need anything at all, and you can't get in touch with Monica, please give me a call. I'm happy to come back."

"Deal," Greta said.

Leighton and July headed out a few minutes later. The weather really was beautiful. Fortunately, it had been for the past few days. Leighton was looking forward to spending time outside, especially since he'd be with July. As much as he loved the bookstore, he spent the majority of his summer inside its walls. He was thankful to have a day that he could feel the sun on his skin. Leighton looked up at the sky and took in a deep breath of summer air before he and July got into his truck and drove off. He felt invigorated.

The animal preserve was only ten minutes away. It was a family-owned zoo, so it wasn't all that big, but they did have a good selection of animals: cats, primates, birds, reptiles, and a variety of other mammals. Leighton actually liked that it was smaller because it didn't take as long to tour. You could view every exhibit in one afternoon.

When they arrived, Leighton could tell that July was excited because she jumped out of his truck as soon as they pulled into a parking spot. By the time he exited the vehicle, she was already springing toward the entrance. Seeing July so happy made him feel good. At the gate, they got their admission bands from an older gentleman in a safari vest and matching hat. The man tried to talk with an Australian accent but his Southern drawl was too thick. Leighton appreciated the effort, and he suspected that July did, too, because she was grinning from ear to ear. Once inside, they followed a trail to the first enclosure and continued on a path around the grounds. It took Leighton and July three hours to see all the animals. The tour ended with the butterfly exhibit that Greta loved so much. Leighton made sure to take several pictures while they were in there. He would show them to Greta the next time he saw her.

After the exhibits, Leighton and July visited the petting zoo area where July fed baby goats. She was beaming the entire time and was so natural with the animals. When Leighton approached the goats, they seemed skittish and untrusting, but with July, they were curious and friendly. They walked right up to her and some even allowed her to hold them. It was obvious that she made them feel comfortable and safe. Leighton hoped that July would pursue her interest in animals. He had a feeling that she would excel in the field and that it would bring her a lot of fulfillment.

July spent almost an hour with the baby farm animals. After she fed them until their bellies were full, she came skipping out of the pen to Leighton.

"Today was the best day!" she proclaimed.

Leighton could see the joy in her eyes. She was like a kid on Christmas.

"You're so great with animals," he said as July sat down next to him. "I can see why you want to work with them. It's like they're naturally drawn to you."

"Thanks. I've been interested in animals for as long as I can remember."

"Well, it definitely seems like it's your calling. Did you spend a lot of time around animals when you were growing up?"

"No, actually, not at all," July admitted. "I've never had any pets or anything. But my mom, she grew up on a farm, and she always used to tell me stories about it."

"Oh really? Did you ever get to visit it?"

"No, unfortunately. My grandparents still live there, but I don't have a relationship with them. They pretty much disowned my mom after she ran off with my dad, and they never got around to reconciling things. I've always wanted to get to know them, but I felt uncomfortable reaching out. Plus, it goes both ways, you know? They never made an effort to get to know me either. I'm eighteen years old, and I've never even talked to them."

"Wow, I'm really sorry to hear that. I hope you know that it's their loss. You're incredible. They are totally missing out by not having you in their lives."

"Thanks," July replied with a tight-lipped smile.

Leighton considered changing the topic, but he was curious to hear more. He had been waiting for July to open up to him, and he wanted to learn as much about her as he could while she was willing to talk. "Why didn't they like your dad? If you don't mind me asking."

"He was a high school dropout who hung out with the wrong crowd. My grandparents wanted my mom to be with someone like them . . . an honest hardworking blue-collar family man. My dad was the opposite of that . . . a rebellious bad boy who swept my mom off her feet," July explained. "It's all so cliché."

"Yeah, I've definitely heard this trope before."

July giggled and Leighton was glad that the mood was light once again. He figured they would move on to something else, but to his surprise, July continued.

"So yeah, my dad had this grand idea to go to New York City where he and my mom could start their dream life," she explained. "My mom, being the hopeless romantic that she was, happily agreed, and the next night, she packed a tiny suitcase and left the farm, without even saying goodbye to my grandparents. They ended up getting a rinky-dink apartment that my mom had to work three jobs to afford, while my dad did God knows what. A couple of months later, my mom found out that she was pregnant with me. It definitely wasn't the dream life that my dad had promised, but she was happy. She thought he was, too, but a few weeks after I was born, he left without any explanation, and it was just my mom and me from then on."

Leighton shook his head in disapproval. "I can't believe your mom left everything for your dad, only for him to leave her. That really sucks. I'm so sorry that happened to her."

"Me, too," July agreed, "but I think everything happens for a reason, and my mom and I were better off without him. Life wasn't easy for us. We definitely struggled to get by, but my mom always made the best of it. We might not have had a lot of money, or a big house, or expensive clothes, but we had so much love for each other."

Leighton smiled and put his arm around July. "I know I've said this already, but your mom sounds really awesome."

July laid her head on his shoulder. "She was the best," she whispered so quietly that he could barely hear her.

Leighton wondered if July was finally going to tell him about the accident, but she turned her attention to the sky instead. It was clear that the conversation was over, and Leighton was okay with that. He was honestly surprised that she had shared as much as she did. From what he could tell, July was a guarded person, which was probably the result of the tragedy that she had suffered.

"Hey, I've been meaning to ask you something . . ." Leighton said after a few minutes.

July raised an eyebrow and looked at him curiously.

Leighton continued. "My dad is having a reelection party tomorrow night. He does it every year around this time. Would you like to be my plus-one?"

July was silent for a few moments, and Leighton could see the hesitation in her face.

"I don't know," she finally replied. "I think I'll feel out of place. And don't you think your parents will find it weird that you've invited a girl that you just met to a formal family event?"

"Not at all. My parents told me to invite someone to keep me company." That was a lie but Leighton was desperate to ease July's apprehension. He really wanted her to come. "It's really not that big of a deal."

July still looked reluctant. "It sounds like it is. And I don't even have anything to wear."

"It's not, I promise," Leighton said reassuringly. "And don't worry about clothes. I'm sure my sister has a million things that you could borrow. She'd be happy to lend you something." Leighton smiled at July. "Please," he begged.

"I want to hang out with you," July explained, "but I'm . . ." She looked down. "I don't know, I'm nervous to meet your family and to be in that kind of setting."

Leighton felt an ache of guilt in his stomach. Was he being selfish? Was he, once again, thinking only about his desires without considering July's feelings? He didn't want to pressure her into doing something that she didn't want to do, even if it meant sacrificing time together. "I understand," he said. "I don't want you to do something that makes you feel uncomfortable."

July's gaze stayed fixed on the ground and silence grew between them. Leighton wanted to say something to fill the void, but he bit his tongue.

"I'll go," July said suddenly, interrupting the quiet that was lingering between them like thick, humid air.

"No," Leighton replied softly. He put his arm around her again. "You don't have to."

"I know, but I want to. I was too quick to write it off. It could end up being a really great time."

Leighton squeezed her shoulder. "Are you sure?"

"Yeah." July nodded.

Leighton was thrilled to hear that she changed her mind about the party. He rubbed her back. "It will be a good time, I'm sure of it."

July looked up at Leighton and gave him a trusting smile. Leighton returned it and then the two got up and walked to his truck. His dad's party was less than twenty-four hours away, and July needed something to wear.

The ride to Leighton's didn't take long. When they arrived, July looked at his house incredulously.

"*This* is where your sister lives?" she asked with wide eyes.

"Kind of. This is my parents' house. My sister is staying in the guesthouse over there." Leighton pointed to a smaller building adjacent to the larger home. "It's temporary while her apartment gets renovated," he explained.

July continued to look, amazed. "So, this is where you live?"

"Yes. Why do you seem so surprised?" he asked playfully.

"I don't know, maybe because it's a *really* big house . . . with a gated entrance and perfect landscaping and a freakin' guesthouse. I just wasn't expecting this, I guess. You seem too, I don't know, humble and down-to-earth to live like this."

Leighton was quiet for a moment while he considered how to respond. His family was undoubtedly wealthy, and he was very much aware of his status and privilege. His parents had provided him with a comfortable lifestyle, and while he was thankful for that, it also made him feel self-conscious. He hated the thought of people assuming that he was just another spoiled rich kid. And he definitely didn't want July to think of him that way.

"Thank you," he finally said. "I know that I'm really fortunate to live like this, but I don't want it to define me. There are so many things in life that I value more than wealth and status."

"Sometimes I think you're too good to be true," July teased.

Leighton laughed. "I'll take that as a compliment."

The two sat there for another minute before Leighton unbuckled his seat belt. He was about to open his door when he realized that July wasn't doing the same.

"What's wrong?" he asked.

"I'm feeling anxious," she admitted.

"There's no reason to worry. You and Kennedy will get along great."

July let out a deep breath and exited the vehicle. As they walked toward the door, Leighton took July's hand in his and gave it a comforting squeeze. He could feel the tension leave her body.

Knock, knock, knock.

"Be right there!" Kennedy shouted from inside.

Leighton looked at July to make sure that she was still doing alright. She smiled and it seemed genuine. When he looked back toward the door, Kennedy was opening it.

"July!" Kennedy exclaimed with so much enthusiasm Leighton expected rainbows to shoot out of her mouth.

July looked surprised and confused.

"I might have told her about you . . ." Leighton whispered. He could feel his cheeks getting hot.

The door was wide open now and Kennedy was pulling July into a hug. Leighton was worried that this might be too much for July. When he heard her laughing, he let out a sigh of relief.

"Come in, come in," Kennedy said as she shuffled July into her temporary home. Once July's back was turned to them, Kennedy gave Leighton a thumbs-up, nodding in approval.

Leighton silently mouthed the words *stop embarrassing me* in return.

Once inside, the girls curled up together on the couch. Kennedy poured two glasses of rosé, and they spent the next hour getting to know each other. Leighton was thrilled to see them hitting it off so well, but he wasn't exactly interested in all their girl talk, so he slipped out to the kitchen and made dinner while July and Kennedy gossiped and got drunk on bubbly pink wine.

Leighton could hear them giggling while he stirred a pot of sauce and waited for the water to boil. He wasn't the most experienced cook, but he could make a mean plate of spaghetti. Plus, he wasn't too worried, anyway. He had a hunch that by the time the food was ready, the girls would be sufficiently buzzed and would likely find anything appetizing.

Once the pasta was cooked and the sauce had simmered, Leighton made two big plates and carried them into the den. When Kennedy and July saw him coming, their eyes grew big with excitement. He handed them their spaghetti and they each happily thanked him.

The girls ate quickly. When they were done, Kennedy took July into her room so that she could show her some outfit options. There was still half a bottle of wine left at that point, and Kennedy made sure to bring it with them. Leighton stayed in the living room and watched TV. From the other room, he listened as his sister enthusiastically played stylist.

Ten minutes later, July came out wearing a long, black satin dress and strappy heeled sandals. She looked incredible, despite being clearly intoxicated. She stumbled a little as she walked closer to him.

"What do you think?" she asked.

Leighton looked at her in awe.

"What?" July said, her cheeks turning red.

"I'm sorry," Leighton replied. "You just look really beautiful."

July hesitated. "Are you sure it's not too much? I don't usually dress like this . . ."

"It's perfect for the occasion," Leighton reassured her, "and it looks absolutely perfect on you."

July flashed him a shy smile. "Thank you."

The two looked at each other for a moment before July turned around and shuffled back to Kennedy's room. It was hard not to stare.

Kennedy and July returned to the den a few minutes later. July was back in her normal clothes and beginning to look tired. Kennedy opened another bottle of wine and offered July a glass, but she declined. It was clearly time to get July back to her motel. Kennedy was fun, but she had a way of wearing people out. Leighton knew this all too well; he was usually her guinea pig.

Leighton cleared his throat. "Hey, Ken, I think we're going to head out now. It's getting late and we've got a big day tomorrow."

"No!" Kennedy objected. "You guys just got here!"

"Are you being serious?" Leighton asked in disbelief. "We've been here for over two hours now!"

Kennedy gave him a big grin "Alright, fine," she said. Then she pouted. "I'll let you guys leave."

"I didn't realize we needed your permission," Leighton teased, "but thank you."

Kennedy stuck her tongue out at him.

Leighton got up and wrapped his sister in a warm hug. "Thank you for your help today, Ken. You're crazy, but you always have my back, and I really appreciate that."

Kennedy gave him a tight squeeze. "You don't have to

thank me. I'm always happy to help, especially when it comes to fashion. This was so fun!"

"I had fun, too!" July chimed in. "Thank you for everything, Kennedy."

Kennedy hugged July and said, "Anytime."

When Leighton and July stepped outside, the moon was full and the air was cool. Leighton loved nights like these—when the world was quiet and the only sound that he could hear was the steady hum of chirping crickets.

"It's so peaceful in the country," July said. "In New York, there's always noise. To be honest, I never realized just how loud it was until I came here."

"It *is* called the city that never sleeps," Leighton quipped, then flashed a playful grin.

July laughed. "You make a good point."

"Are you ready to head back to your motel?"

"Yeah, but not right this minute. I want to stay out here for a little longer. It's so calming."

"Okay. We can stay out here for as long as you'd like. Just let me know when you want to go."

"Okay." July returned her gaze to the night sky. Her body swayed gently as she looked at the stars. Leighton slowly laced his fingers through hers. Once they were interlocked, he could feel July drawing circles on his knuckle with her thumb. He loved it when she did that. A flare of heat traveled through his body. He tugged her arm and pulled her to him. When they were face-to-face, he put his hand on her cheek, then he placed small kisses on her forehead and her nose before landing on her lips.

July kissed him back, carefully at first before growing more urgent. When her tongue met his, Leighton felt a rush of electricity from his head to his toes. He pulled July closer, running his hands through her hair. July grabbed his arms, squeezing as she moved up his biceps. When she got to his shoulder blades, she scratched her nails back and forth, leaving goosebumps dotted along Leighton's skin.

Leighton moved his hands to July's neck. She melted into him. The desire was building between them. Leighton wanted more. He traveled his hands down her back, touching every curve along the way. When he got to her hips, he moved his hands to her front and slid his fingers underneath her shirt. He started traveling upward now, making sure to move slowly, but when he got to her bra, she stopped him.

"Not yet," she whispered before pulling away.

"I'm sorry," he winced, embarrassed.

"Don't be sorry," she replied, "I liked it."

So, why'd we stop? Leighton thought. He wanted to say it aloud, but he knew it was inappropriate.

"I guess we should get going, then."

July put her hand on his cheek. "Yeah, probably," she said before placing a tender kiss on his lips.

The drive to the motel was slightly uncomfortable. Leighton wasn't sure where he and July stood, and he couldn't stop his mind from racing. Was July mad at him? He was too nervous to ask. So, they rode in silence while Leighton battled his intrusive thoughts.

When they arrived at the motel, Leighton told July that

he'd pick her up at five the next day. July agreed, gave him a quick kiss on the cheek, and then hopped out of his truck before he had the chance to say anything else. Leighton thought about calling after her, but he let her go.

On the ride to his house, Leighton recalled the night when he and Becca broke up. It was the eve of his father's reelection party, exactly two years ago. They had been dating for several months, but Leighton had known for quite some time that he wanted to end things. Becca was a good girlfriend, but his feelings for her were not the same as her feelings for him. He knew that Becca was crazy about him, but the truth was, the only reason that he was with Becca was because her mother and his mother were friends, and Leighton's mom had pressured him to date her. He had hoped that with time, he'd grow more romantically interested in Becca, but that wasn't the case.

"Becca, there's something I want to talk to you about," Leighton had said as they stood under her front porch light.

"Sure, anything!" She giggled flirtatiously, clearly with no idea where the conversation was going.

Leighton had felt a twinge of guilt in his stomach. He considered backing out, like he had done the past few times he'd tried to break up with her. He didn't want to hurt her, but he couldn't lead her on any longer. He looked down at the ground and scratched the back of his head.

"I, um, I think we should break up," he said quietly.

Becca's mouth had fallen open. "What? Why?" Her eyes filled with tears.

"I-I'm sorry, Becca," he stammered. "It's not you, it's me."

Becca looked angry now. "Are you serious?" She seethed. "You're not really going to use that line on me, are you?"

Leighton felt terrible. "I never meant to hurt you. I just think we're better as friends," he pleaded.

"We will never be friends again!" Becca shouted. She walked into her house and slammed the door.

The next night, at the reelection party, Leighton's mother had asked him where Becca was, and when Leighton shared the news of their breakup, she was extremely upset. Mom had strong opinions not only when it came to Leighton's education and career but also about who he dated. To Mom, Becca was the ideal partner: a blond-haired, blue-eyed Southern belle from a prominent family in Montclair. Becca was polite, soft-spoken, and sweet-natured.

"How could you be so stupid? Becca's perfect!" Mom had shrieked.

Leighton swallowed hard. He already felt bad enough for ending things with Becca, and now his mother was just making him feel worse.

"She's not perfect for me, Mom," he'd said.

"Yes, she is. Trust me, I know a good girl when I see one. Please get back together with her."

Leighton shook his head. "I'm sorry, but I can't do that," he'd replied.

"You'll never find another girl like Becca," she threatened before storming off.

Back home, Leighton found his mother in the foyer once again. It was like a replica of the night before: same robe, same glass of wine, same unhappy expression on her face.

Leighton wasn't in the mood to be lectured, so he spoke up before she had the opportunity to say anything. "I know, I missed dinner again. I'm sorry. I didn't totally bail on family time, though. I was with Kennedy. I ate with her."

"I know," Mom replied bluntly, "I saw you. And I saw you with that girl."

Leighton froze as his mother's words danced menacingly around him. He could feel the blood rushing to his face. "What do you mean?" he asked nervously, as if he were guilty of a terrible crime.

"I saw my son being seduced by some girl in my own goddamn driveway," Mom snapped.

Leighton felt a flood of emotions: embarrassed that his mother had caught him in an intimate moment with July; violated that she had been watching him; angry that she couldn't respect his privacy; and defensive over July and the derogatory way that his mother was talking about her, calling her "that girl" and "some girl."

He clenched his hands into fists, digging his nails into his palms. *She's really crossed the line this time*, he thought. He couldn't let this go. Leighton hated confrontation more than anything else, but it looked like he had no choice.

"I can't believe you were spying on me!" he yelled. The aggression was so clear in his voice that it even took him by surprise. He didn't usually talk to his mother like this. "And she didn't seduce me. I'm the one who initiated it."

Mom rolled her eyes. "I don't care who initiated it. You

aren't usually like this, Leighton. You're not some playboy who takes strangers home, at least not to my knowledge. This girl is obviously a bad influence."

Her brazen tone made him angry. "First of all, her name is July, and she's not a bad influence. I've never acted like this before because I've never met a girl that I actually really liked. Until now."

Mom let out a laugh. "So, you're telling me that you really like this girl, huh?"

"Yes!" Leighton shouted.

"And how long has this been going on that you *really* like her?"

"Why does that matter?"

"Because I can't imagine that it's been very long, figuring this is the first time I'm hearing about her," his mother said sharply. "You do realize that you have an image to uphold, right, Leighton? You shouldn't be gallivanting around town with some girl that you hardly know. And don't forget, you're leaving for school in just a few short weeks. What's the point in pursuing a relationship, or whatever it is that you think you want with this girl, right now?"

"Yes, Mom, I am aware of all that, but I think you're making a problem out of nothing. Spending time with July isn't going to tarnish my image, and it's not going to get in the way of my future plans, so I'm going to continue to hang out with her and I'm going to see where things go, okay?"

Mom didn't respond, so Leighton continued, "Please just give her a chance because I plan to keep her in my life"—he paused—"and because I've invited her to Dad's party tomorrow night."

His mother's face filled with rage. "Are you out of your

damn mind? What in the world has gotten into you? I expect this shit from Kennedy, but not from you, Leighton. You've always been the good one. You've always been so obedient." Mom let out a sigh. She didn't look angry anymore, just upset and defeated.

Leighton felt bad. He hated to disappoint his mother. "I think you're making this a bigger deal than it actually is," he said in a kinder and more gentle tone.

"It *is* a big deal! The timing is all wrong. You're supposed to be focusing on school and on your future."

"I am focusing on those things."

Mom rolled her eyes.

"Would you be acting like this if it was Becca that I was with tonight?"

His mother let out a condescending laugh. "Actually, no. I wouldn't be acting like this because Becca is a sweet girl from a good family."

"And what makes you think that July isn't?" Leighton asked, frustration oozing through his words once again. "You're judging someone that you don't even know. Do you realize how problematic that is?"

"I know a good girl when I see one," Mom retorted. As if that was an acceptable explanation.

Leighton exhaled deeply. Fighting with his mother wasn't going to get him anywhere. He needed to try to reason with her. Calmly, evenly. "I know that you have this idea of the kind of girl that I should be with, and July might not perfectly fit that image, but she's special, and I really like her. I'm positive that you will, too. If you just got to know her."

Mom finished her wine and turned toward the stairs. "I'm going to bed," she said flatly.

"Mom, wait!" Leighton called after her.

His mother stopped but didn't turn around to face him.

"Can you please give July a chance tomorrow night? *Please.* For me?"

His mother remained silent. A few seconds passed before she continued up the stairs, all without saying another word.

Great, Leighton thought. He hung his head, dejected. He wanted to bring July around his family. He wanted her to be a part of his world. Was that such a good idea?

In the kitchen, Leighton grabbed a beer from the fridge. If his parents caught him, he'd be in trouble, but he needed to unwind. Leighton wasn't really a big drinker, he'd have a beer or two with his buddies on a Friday or Saturday night, but he didn't drink more than a few times a month and he rarely got drunk. There were times, though, especially those when he was feeling particularly stressed, when he just needed to relax. Tonight was one of those nights. Leighton brought the brown bottle to the island and sat on one of the bar stools, taking big swigs while he contemplated what to do.

He couldn't just uninvite July. What would he even say to her? *Sorry, July, but you can't come to my dad's party anymore because my mom thinks you're a seductress with a bad agenda.* Leighton shook his head. His mother was just going to have to get over herself. She was being dramatic anyway. But how was he going to get her to behave? His mother could be stubborn, especially when she had her mind made up. He moved the beer bottle back and forth along the counter before finishing it off. He went to the fridge and got himself another, opened it up, and took a long sip.

Leighton loved his mom, but sometimes she could be so difficult and controlling. He was eighteen years old now, though, and he would be leaving for college soon. She had to let him be independent and make his own decisions, even if she didn't agree with them. He took a few more swigs. *That's exactly what I'm going to say to her,* he thought as he finished his second beer. He tossed the bottle in the recycling bin and grabbed a third. This time, he drank it even quicker, in one long gulp. When he was done, his head felt hazy. He looked at the bottle and realized he had been drinking his dad's fancy IPAs, and they had a much higher alcohol content than the Busch Lights that he and his friends usually drank. Leighton was buzzed and all he wanted to do was see July.

He got up and moved toward the front door. He could feel his keys in the left pocket of his jeans. Leighton walked quietly so that he wouldn't disturb his parents. He wasn't sure if they were sleeping yet, but the house alarm was disarmed, which told him that they were probably still awake. Fortunately, they typically stayed in their bedroom once they turned in for the night. When he got to the door, he opened it slowly and slipped through the crevice as soon as there was just enough space for his body to fit. He wasn't safe yet, though. He still had to turn on his truck and get out of the driveway. That was going to be the hard part.

As Leighton approached his vehicle, he thanked his lucky stars that he hadn't parked in the garage that evening. If he had, he would have never been able to leave without the sound of the garage door alerting his parents. When Leighton got to his truck, he manually unlocked the door and got inside. He sat there for a moment, afraid that the sound of the engine would give him away. He put the key in the ignition and took a deep breath.

Bang! Bang! Bang!

Leighton jumped. He looked out the window to find Kennedy looking back at him.

"Where are *you* going?" she asked through the glass.

Leighton opened the door in an effort to control the volume of the conversation. "You scared the shit out of me!" he hissed.

"Sorry, I came outside to smoke a cigarette. I wasn't expecting to see anyone," she explained. "So . . . where are you going?"

"To see July."

"Are you sure that's a good idea?"

"Yeah . . . why?" He tried to act as sober as possible while saying this.

"Because you've been drinking, Leighton. Your eyes are foggy and your breath smells like beer. You can't drive right now. Give me your keys." Kennedy put her hand out, directing Leighton to drop them in her palm.

Leighton wasn't going to surrender. "I'm fine."

She gave him a stern look. "Don't make me get Mom and Dad."

Leighton let out a sigh. "Come on, Kennedy! Would you really do that?"

"To prevent you from drunk driving? Yes. You're being stupid. Now give me your keys and go to bed." She held out her hand again and this time Leighton relinquished the keys.

"Thank you," she said as she put the keys in her pocket.

Leighton was annoyed, but he knew that it was the right thing to do. God forbid he got pulled over, or worse, got in an accident and hurt himself or someone else. A sense of shame overcame him.

"Sorry," he said to Kennedy, "I don't know what's gotten into me."

"I don't know either. You're not usually like this. I'm just glad I was out here to stop you."

Leighton hung his head. "Me, too." Then he bid his sister good night. He was going to tell her about his conversation with their mother, but he was feeling too drained to revisit it. Plus, he wanted to go to bed before he made any more bad decisions.

Leighton went back into the house and headed upstairs to his room. He thought about texting July, but he wasn't sure what to say. After typing and deleting several messages, he gave up and went to sleep. As he drifted off, he thought about Greta and Ivan. The odds had been stacked against them, but they'd made it work. And if they could make it work, surely he and July could, too.

Day Four

THE NEXT MORNING, LEIGHTON AWOKE to a frenzy. When he left his bedroom, he found his normally quiet home packed with people preparing for the party that evening. The event planners were setting tables with perfectly folded napkins and shiny, ornate silverware. The caterers were chopping vegetables and marinating meats in fragrant herbs and spices. The landscapers were trimming the lawn and grooming the already-neat hedges. And then there was his mother, running around the house like a drill sergeant, micromanaging everyone's every move, even though it was obvious that they could all operate just fine without her interference.

Leighton was overwhelmed by it all, especially since his emotions were still high after the fight with his mother the night before. He retreated to his room to give his best friend a call. Carson knew how Leighton's mom could be, and he'd likely be able to offer some guidance on what Leighton should do next. Plus, Leighton wanted to tell his buddy more about July. They had been texting back and forth over the past few days, so Carson knew that Leighton had met a girl and that he was spending a lot of time with her, but he didn't know just how much Leighton actually liked July.

The boys talked for fifteen minutes while Carson got ready for the movie theater. He was working the matinee shift so he could attend Dad's party later that evening. Even though the phone call was quick, it was exactly what Leighton needed. With newfound confidence, courtesy of his best friend, Leighton headed downstairs to confront his mother. It was time for him to establish boundaries, per Carson's advice, and he needed to make sure that his mother not only understood them but respected them, too. Most importantly, he had to convince her to put her judgments aside and give July the fair chance that she deserved. It was essential that his mother treat July kindly, not just so July would feel comfortable, but also so she could get a good first impression of his mother. After all, he wanted July to like his mom just as much as he wanted his mom to like July. Despite his hard feelings toward his mother lately, it was still important to him that the people that he cared about all got along. This was especially true since the falling-out between his mother and sister. It upset Leighton that they had such a tumultuous relationship. If he could prevent any more conflict between the people in his life, then he was willing to do whatever it took to do that.

Leighton headed toward the kitchen, hoping to catch his mother's attention on the way. To his surprise, she noticed him right away, and she immediately addressed him.

"Hey, hun!" she said cheerfully. She was in the middle of preparing one of the many bouquets that would be displayed around the estate later that evening.

Leighton was caught off guard by her chipper attitude, especially with how they'd left things the night prior. Shouldn't his mom still be upset with him? Leighton decided not to question it, though, and to just be happy that there was no animosity. Plus, his mother's good disposition made him hopeful that the conversation that they were about to have might actually go well.

"Hey, Mom! How's it going?" Leighton asked.

"Great! Everything is moving along nicely. I think this is going to be the best party yet!"

Leighton laughed. His mother said this every year, and while she did always manage to outdo herself, it was still funny, and also endearing, to hear her declare it each summer.

"I'm sure it will be. You always throw the best parties."

Mom flashed him a proud grin.

"Hey," he continued. "Do you have a few minutes to talk?"

"Sure, what's going on?"

Leighton got serious as he contemplated what to say next. They needed to have this conversation, but how would his mother react? He was afraid to hurt her feelings. He decided to be as straightforward and transparent as possible. He took a deep breath and let the words spill out of him.

"It's hard for me to say this, but I want to be honest with you. I know how much you care about me, and I appreciate all that you have done to set me on the right path, but at this point in my life, I really need you to give me some independence."

Mom put down the flowers she was cutting and turned her focus to him. Her gaze was intense and unwavering, but her expression was hard to read.

Leighton shifted his weight. "I need you to let me make my own decisions, even if you don't agree with them. I know that you don't want to see me make mistakes, but that's part of growing up. I'm eighteen years old now, Mom, and I'm leaving for college in just a few weeks. I'm an adult, and I would like you to treat me like one."

Leighton paused, but his mother remained tight-lipped, so he kept going. "I'm always going to need you, and your opinion will always be important to me. I will always value your advice and take it into consideration when making choices, but at the end of the day, I'm going to do what I want to do. I really hope that you can respect that."

Another pause. Leighton tilted his head inquisitively in an effort to elicit a reply from his mother.

"Okay," Mom finally replied. She began tending to her flowers once again.

Leighton furrowed his brows and looked at her incredulously. "Okay? That's all you have to say?"

His mother laughed. "I guess you thought this was going to be a lot more difficult than it actually was. Come on, I'm not that bad, am I?" She set down the bouquet, nudged Leighton's arm, and then wrapped him in a tight hug. Leighton let out a sigh of relief.

"I didn't think you were going to take it this well at all," he admitted.

"Well, you've made a very convincing argument," his mother replied. "And you're right, you are an adult now and

I should be treating you like one. You don't need me to hold your hand anymore. You've got a good head on your shoulders, and I trust you to do the right thing." Mom pulled away and looked Leighton in the eyes. "I'm proud of you. I always have been and I always will be."

Leighton smiled and thanked her, relieved that their conversation had gone as smoothly as it did, and thrilled that his mother had agreed to his requests. Sometimes he questioned her integrity, but the moment that they just shared proved that she never had bad intentions. She wasn't controlling or dictatorial—she just simply wanted what was best for him.

Leighton spent the rest of the day running errands for his parents and helping them with party preparations. At half past four, he headed to the Montclair Motel to pick up July. On his way there, he stopped at Petal Perfection to pick up a bouquet of sunflowers. He wasn't able to get the exact arrangement that July had pointed out on their first night together, but he got one that was similar, and in his opinion, even more beautiful. The florist, Mrs. Garrison, even put the flowers in a pretty glass vase since July wouldn't have one of her own, being that she was traveling. Leighton couldn't wait to give it to her.

When he got to the motel a few minutes later, July was already outside. He watched as the sunlight danced across her face. She looked stunning. The dress that she borrowed from Kennedy hugged her body in all the right places, and her choice of hair and makeup—loose curls and dark red lips—really pulled the look together.

Wow, Leighton thought as he grabbed the flowers and hopped out of his truck.

When July saw the bouquet, her mouth fell open. "Oh my gosh! You remembered!"

"Of course I did." Leighton smiled as he handed her the vase.

"You didn't have to do this."

"I know, but I wanted to."

"Thank you so much." She beamed. "I love them!"

"You're welcome." Leighton grinned.

July brought the bouquet into her room so that it wouldn't be sitting in the truck during the party. When she returned, Leighton was waiting by the passenger door. As July approached, he could smell her perfume, a sweet, floral scent with a hint of musk. It fit her perfectly. Leighton opened the door. Before July got in, she turned toward him and placed a soft kiss on his cheek.

"You look incredible," Leighton whispered.

July giggled. "Thanks. You don't look too bad yourself."

On the way back to the Prescott estate, July sang along to every song that came on the radio. Leighton could tell that she was in a good mood, and he hoped it was because she was excited for the party. He had been worried that she was going to be nervous, but she seemed completely at ease.

When they reached his house, there were already dozens of cars in the driveway, indicating that most guests had already arrived. Fortunately, none of them were blocking the entrance to the garage. Leighton pulled in and looked over at July. "Ready?"

"Ready!"

It's going to be a great night, Leighton thought.

Inside was bustling with people holding champagne flutes and making small talk. Leighton said hello to a few familiar faces as he made his way toward the dining area. He was eager to find his parents so that he could introduce them to July. On the way there, he bumped into his sister, who looked a little too happy to be at the event. Typically, Kennedy hated these types of things.

"Leighton!" She squealed as she gave him a hug. When she noticed July standing behind him, she shoved Leighton out of the way and shrieked, "July! Look at you!" She grabbed July and squeezed her tightly.

July laughed. "Hey, Kennedy!"

"Are you drunk?" Leighton asked suspiciously. "You're never this chipper at family events."

Kennedy smirked and said, "Drunk? No. Stoned? Maybe."

"Are you kidding?" Leighton said with wide eyes. "If Mom and Dad find out, they're going to kill you, Ken!"

"Relax. They aren't going to know. I had to do something to put me in a good mood. Otherwise, I wouldn't have been able to play along with the perfect family facade."

"Oh, come on. We're not that bad."

Kennedy rolled her eyes. "Please, don't get me started."

Leighton laughed. "Oh, I won't. I know how that rant goes. Speaking of Mom and Dad, do you know where they are? I want to introduce them to July."

When Kennedy pointed straight ahead, Leighton took

July by the hand so he could lead her across the foyer and into the Prescotts' kitchen.

"Maybe I'll take a hit of whatever you were smoking later tonight," July whispered to Kennedy before Leighton whisked her away.

"Just tell me when!" Kennedy replied with a mischievous grin.

As Leighton and July made their way to the kitchen, Leighton couldn't help but reminisce on the reelection parties of days past. He found the different roles that he and his sister were expected to play interesting. Kennedy was supposed to be mild-mannered and to only speak if spoken to.

"Don't make a scene," his mother would tell her. "You are not to be the center of attention."

Mom wanted Kennedy to be a beautiful wallflower, an understated accessory to the perfect family. Leighton, on the other hand, was supposed to be confident and conversational.

"Make your rounds," his mother instructed.

"You know what to do, son," his father would say. "Firm handshakes, smart conversations, and strategic relationships."

What was funny about this dynamic was that between the two of them, Kennedy was far more outgoing and talkative, whereas Leighton was shy and preferred to keep to himself. Yet, year after year, at their father's reelection party, the extrovert had to play the introvert and vice versa.

It wasn't hard for Leighton to spot his mother when he entered the kitchen. She was wearing an emerald gown and talking animatedly to a group of women who were crowded around her. Near the back corner of the room was his father, wearing a suit and a patterned tie that matched his mother's dress. His father was engaged in conversation, too, but he spoke much less theatrically. His parents couldn't be more different. Mom was loud and ostentatious while Dad was soft-spoken and reserved. If the adage "opposites attract" was true, Leighton's parents were certainly a testament to it.

Leighton and July stood near the hors d'oeuvres table while they waited for Leighton's parents to notice them. Leighton asked July if she wanted anything to eat or to drink, but she declined. He noticed that she was picking at her fingernails.

"Don't be nervous," he said gently. "Everyone is going to love you, especially my parents." July gave him a half smile, the kind that screams "thanks but I don't believe you." Leighton put his hand on the small of her back and whispered, "I mean it."

Leighton looked around the room, attempting to make eye contact with his parents. His father was the first to notice him, unsurprisingly. Mom was still immersed in a spirited discussion with her posse. Leighton watched as Dad excused himself from his engagement and moved toward him and July.

"Hey, son!" Dad said as he approached them. Once he

was within arm's reach, he gave Leighton a pat on the back and then turned his attention to July. "Hi there! I don't believe we've met."

"Dad, this is July," Leighton said. "We've been spending a lot of time together lately. I'm excited to finally introduce you two."

"Hello, Mayor Prescott, it's so nice to meet you," July said shyly while extending her arm for a handshake.

Leighton's father returned the gesture. "Please, call me Rod," he said warmly.

July smiled and nodded.

Leighton's father continued, "So, how do you two know each other?"

"July came into the bookstore a few days ago," Leighton explained, "and we've been hanging out ever since."

"It seems you have similar interests, then," Dad deduced.

"Yeah," Leighton and July said simultaneously. This made July giggle.

"Are you from around here, July?" Dad asked.

"No, I'm from New York."

"Oh yeah? Where in New York?"

"Brooklyn," July replied.

"Very nice." Dad grabbed a mini crab cake from a waiter passing by. "So, what brings you to Montclair?"

"I'm traveling down to Florida to see my dad. I stopped here on the way, and it has seemingly turned into a four-day detour." She laughed. "Montclair is lovely. I honestly don't want to leave."

"It really is a great little town," Dad agreed and bit into the golden disc. When he finished chewing, he said, "Well, I hope you decide to stay a little longer, July. We love having visitors. And who knows? Maybe one day you'll decide to become a local."

Leighton could tell that his father was fond of July. He'd known that he would be. July was just so easy to be around. Her energy pulled you in. Leighton watched as she talked candidly with his father. He, too, hoped that she would stay in Montclair for a little bit longer.

A few minutes later, Leighton's mother joined the conversation, positioning herself between Leighton and Dad. "Hello, boys! Fabulous party, right?!"

Leighton and his father nodded.

"You always knock it out of the park, Daphne," Dad said.

Leighton nodded again, knowing his mother would appreciate the praise. Then he got ready to introduce her to July, but before he could say anything, Mom beat him to the punch.

"You must be July!" she said, turning her gaze to July. Mom had a tendency to be unpredictable when it came to her mood, so Leighton never knew what to expect. She seemed genuinely interested in meeting July, though. From what he could tell, her smile and her mannerisms were sincere.

"Hi, Mrs. Prescott," July replied politely. "It's so nice to meet you!"

Leighton's mom pulled July in for a hug. "It's nice to meet you, too! Leighton doesn't usually bring girls around. You must be awfully special!" Mom detached from the embrace and looked July up and down. "And I can see why! You're a cute little thing, aren't you?!"

July laughed and said "thank you," but Leighton could

tell that she was starting to feel uncomfortable. Her cheeks were turning red and she was beginning to fidget. He was happy that his mom was being nice to July, but she was almost being *too* nice. Her overzealous friendliness might be off-putting.

"Okay, Mom, that's enough!" Leighton said lightheartedly. He wanted to get July out of this situation without hurting his mom's feelings.

"Oh, you're no fun!" Mom teased while giving Leighton a playful slap on the arm. "I guess I won't hold you two up, though. I'm sure you probably want to go see your friends. There's a group of boys out back—I think Carson is with them."

"Cool," Leighton replied. "I was actually planning to find him next." He turned to July. "Carson's my best friend. I can't remember if I told you that or not already."

"You didn't, but I'm excited to meet him."

"Don't forget to say hello to our guests on your way out there," Mom interrupted, "especially the important ones."

Leighton sighed. "I know, Mom. You don't have to tell me."

Mom gave him a triumphant smile and then kissed him on the forehead. "That's my boy!"

"Alright, Daphne," Dad said to Mom as he gently pulled her away from Leighton. "Let's go make our rounds now."

Leighton was relieved that his father had stepped in. He was always good at reading the room and taking the necessary steps to keep everyone appeased.

"Okay, okay!" Mom replied as Dad put his arm around her lower back and gently tugged her away. "I'll see you two later!" She sauntered off.

Once Leighton's parents were out of earshot, July said, "It was nice to meet your parents."

"Are you just saying that because you feel like you have to?"

July laughed. "If I'm being honest, your mom is a little *much*, but that's okay! She was super nice. And I really enjoyed talking to your dad. He's pretty cool."

"Well, I appreciate your honesty. I know my mom can be a bit over-the-top, but she means well. My dad has always been the more laid-back of the two. They're like yin and yang, but the dynamic works."

For the next few hours, Leighton and July meandered around the party. They made small talk with nearly every guest there, picked at all the fancy appetizers, and even snuck a couple of glasses of champagne.

Leighton introduced July to Carson and two of his other closest friends, Reilly and Hunter; they all loved her. He'd known that they would.

"I can see why you've fallen for this girl so quickly," Carson whispered in Leighton's ear. "She's awesome." He gave Leighton a pat on the back. "I'm so happy for you, man."

"Thanks," Leighton said, blushing. He was excited to hear that he had his best friend's approval. Carson had been a fixture in Leighton's life for nearly a decade, so his support was important to him.

After spending time with the boys, Leighton and July caught up with Monica, who was enjoying a rare night out alone. She usually had her kids with her, but she'd hired a babysitter for once.

"I'm so glad you came," Leighton said to Monica, "but I was expecting to see Greta with you."

"Greta was feeling more tired than usual today," Monica explained, "so she decided to turn in early. She wanted me to tell you that she was sorry she couldn't make it, though. You know she would have been here if she was feeling up to it."

Leighton wished that Greta had been able to attend the party, but he understood why she stayed home. All in all, the night was going even better than he could've hoped for.

At half past nine, Dad was scheduled to give a speech, and he insisted that Leighton join him to say a few words. He said it was part of the "grooming process." Leighton didn't want to leave July alone, but his father wasn't going to take no for an answer.

"Will you be okay by yourself for a little while?" he asked July.

"I'll be just fine," she assured him. "I can always hang out with Kennedy if I feel like I need a buddy."

Leighton was relieved. He didn't want to have to choose between his father and July, and now he didn't have to. He pulled July to him and gave her a kiss on the forehead.

"We'll meet back here as soon as the speech is over, okay?"

"Okay," July replied. "Good luck!"

"Thank you." Leighton headed toward the small stage that had been set up in the front right corner of the living room. He turned to look back at July on his way up, but she had already walked away. He tried to find her in the crowd, but he couldn't seem to spot her.

Why did she run off so quickly? Will she be back to hear me speak? His mind was beginning to race, like it was so accustomed to do. He needed to ground himself, otherwise he wouldn't be able to focus on the task at hand. His father was expecting him to perform, and Leighton couldn't let him down. He took a deep breath. *She's probably just in the bathroom*, he thought. He took another deep breath. And then he climbed onto the stage.

The speech took twenty-five minutes, with Dad talking for the first fifteen and Leighton talking for the final ten. When they were done and the crowd's applause finally dwindled, Dad gave Leighton a firm pat on the back. "Good job, son," he said. "You spoke eloquently and confidently. I think the people were more impressed with you than they were with me. I'm really proud of you."

Leighton smiled and thanked his father. Dad wasn't one to hand out compliments. He gave praise only when it was warranted. Leighton must've actually done a good job, which was surprising because the whole time he was up on that stage, all he could think about was July. He'd scoured the room again and again, scanning every face in the dense crowd, but none of them belonged to her. Even while delivering his speech, Leighton had to fight himself to stay on pace. All he wanted to do was get his words out as quickly as possible so that he could go and look for July sooner.

Stepping down from the stage, Leighton noticed that the room was still packed with people. He couldn't see his and July's meeting spot from where he stood, which gave him hope that she was waiting for him there, but when he arrived, she was nowhere to be found. *She has to be here somewhere,* he thought. Leighton trudged through the crowd, trying his best to stay on task, but with each step, there was someone wanting to talk to him. He tried to keep the engagements short, but it wasn't easy when he was also trying to be polite. Thirty minutes and a dozen conversations later, he'd successfully traversed the room, only to find that July was still missing.

Leighton made his way toward the kitchen and spotted Kennedy on his way there.

"Have you seen July?" he asked her abruptly.

"Easy, tiger," Kennedy teased. "I saw her going to the bathroom before your speech, but I haven't seen her since then. I figured she was with you."

"I haven't seen her since then either. We were supposed to meet in the corner of the living room after I was done, but she wasn't there."

"Take a deep breath. I'm sure she's around here somewhere. You were great up there, by the way."

"Thanks, but I really don't care about that right now. I just want to find July."

"Have you tried calling her?"

"No."

"Well, why don't you start there," she suggested.

Leighton took out his cell and called July, but it went straight to voicemail.

"It didn't even ring. I guess I'll send her a text," he said as he typed a quick message.

When he finished, Kennedy gave Leighton's arm a comforting squeeze and said, "Come on, I'll help you look for her."

Over the next twenty minutes, Leighton and Kennedy searched every inch of the Prescott estate to no avail. July wasn't there.

Leighton tried calling her a few more times, but he kept getting her voicemail.

"I don't understand," Leighton said to Kennedy with dejection in his voice. "She obviously left, but why and how? She has no car. Did she leave with someone? Did she call for a ride? And why did she decide to leave all of a sudden? Everything was fine before I went up to the stage. It just doesn't make sense."

Kennedy gave him a sympathetic look. "I wish I had the answers."

They were quiet for a moment.

"So, what are you going to do now?" Kennedy asked.

"I'm gonna go to her motel," Leighton replied with a sense of newfound confidence.

Kennedy hesitated for a second before wrapping Leighton in a tight hug. "I hope you find her."

"Thanks, me, too." He headed out the door.

Once Leighton was in his truck, his emotions started to run wild. He wasn't going to let them get the better of him, though. *Stay strong*, he thought. *There's an explanation for all of this. It's going to be okay.*

He gripped the steering wheel and started to drive. He moved slowly through his neighborhood. When he neared the exit of his street, right before the turn toward Main, he saw her, walking briskly in the night. He blinked to make sure that he wasn't imagining it, but there she was, in his sister's silk dress, marching in and out of the pools of light cast by the streetlamps.

Leighton rolled down the window and pulled up next to her. "July!" he shouted. She looked at him. "What the hell are you doing?"

She didn't answer. Instead, she turned her face forward and began to walk faster.

Leighton inched his truck up so he was next to her again. "July, please. Tell me what's going on," he begged. He didn't care that he sounded pathetic and desperate. He just wanted answers.

July didn't look at him this time, but she did slow down her pace.

Leighton inched his truck up once again. "At least let me give you a ride to the motel. You still have a ways to go and I can't imagine it's all that comfortable in heels."

July stopped. "Okay," she said quietly.

When she got into his truck, Leighton could see that she'd been crying. Her eyes were red and her makeup was running.

"Do you want to talk about it?"

July shrugged. "What's there to say?"

"Well, you can start with why you suddenly left the party."

July hesitated. "It seemed like the only option," she finally replied.

Leighton's eyebrows scrunched together as he looked at July with a confused expression. "What does that mean?"

July didn't answer.

"Please, July. Talk to me."

Still no response.

"Does it have to do with your mom?"

July quickly rotated her body so that she was facing Leighton. He could feel her glare burning on his cheek. He turned his head to meet her stare, and was frightened to see a look of fury in her eyes.

"Why would you say that?" she seethed.

Leighton realized that he'd messed up, but there was no going back now. He swallowed hard.

"I . . . um . . ." He scratched the back of his head nervously. "I know about your mom," he admitted.

July's eyes widened, but she didn't say anything. Leighton could see her posture stiffen. It looked like she was clenching her jaw.

He continued. "I looked you up online. I just wanted to see if you had any social media accounts. I know you said that you didn't, but, I don't know, I thought maybe I could find something . . . and, well, a news article came up. It was about your mom and the accident."

July wasn't looking at Leighton anymore. She was just staring out the windshield. He was hoping she'd say something, but she just sat there.

"I'm so sorry, July. I'm sorry for your loss. And I'm sorry for not minding my own business. And I'm sorry for not being honest with you." Leighton looked at her with pleading eyes, but she wouldn't meet his gaze.

"Please just bring me back to the motel."

"Okay." He thought about saying more but didn't. July was upset, understandably so, and she probably needed time to cool down. Leighton was going to let her decide when *she* wanted to talk to *him*; like how he should've let her decide when, or even if, she wanted to tell him about her mom.

The remainder of the ride was tense and uncomfortable. Thankfully, it took only another five minutes or so to arrive at the motel, but it felt like an eternity.

When they pulled into the parking lot, July quickly gathered her belongings and exited the vehicle.

"By the way," she snapped, "it was never about my mom. . . . It was about yours." She slammed the door shut before Leighton could even process what he had just heard.

What? he thought. He needed clarification, but July was already in her room. *What the hell did my mom do this time?*

Leighton sped back home, growing angrier the closer he got to his house. He was mad and confused, and quite frankly, sick to his stomach. *How did it come to this?* Everything had been going so well and now he felt like his life was spiraling out of control. His mom obviously said or did something hurtful to July, and then he went and made it even worse by not only assuming that July was upset about *her* mom but then admitting to totally invading her privacy and learning something about her that she wasn't ready to share.

What a fucking mess.

Leighton couldn't help but remember the last time he felt this afflicted. It was the night when his mother kicked his sister out of the house. They had been arguing for well over a week, ever since Kennedy shared her bakery news over their infamous ravioli dinner. For the next several days, Mom insisted that

Kennedy reconsider, but she refused. Both women had a tendency to be stubborn, but Leighton was sure that any outsider would agree that Mom was wrong in this situation.

"You are going to college and continuing your education," Mom screamed on that fateful night.

"No, Mom, I'm not!" Kennedy fired back. "You can't tell me what I can and cannot do with *my* life!"

Mom let out an exasperated sigh. "You're right, but you know what I can do?" she asked, utter disdain in her eyes.

"What?"

"I can choose who lives under my roof, and you, my dear," she said with a bite, "are no longer welcome here."

Kennedy didn't even bother to fight back. She packed up her things and got picked up by a friend less than thirty minutes later. Leighton watched as she went, tears in his eyes. He'd known that his sister was going to be out of the house eventually, but he hadn't been ready for her to leave just yet.

Leighton had stayed at the front door, looking through the glass, for the better part of an hour, but his sister didn't return. He'd known that she wouldn't. When he finally turned around to go up to his room, he found his mother standing behind him in the foyer. She was in her robe, nursing a glass of chardonnay with a sneer on her face. He had never been so mad at her.

When Leighton got home, he ripped through the driveway and into the garage, then slammed on the brakes. He got out of his vehicle and marched into the house, still heaving with partygoers. He wove through the crowd with his head down, not caring who was in his way. When he got into the kitchen, he saw Mom, standing with her posse. They were in the middle of conversation, but he didn't care. He approached the group and looked directly at her.

"We need to talk," he said sharply.

"Now, that's no way to greet your mother!" Mom exclaimed before breaking out into laughter. She winked at the ladies around her, and they started laughing, too.

Leighton dug his nails into the palms of his hands. *Here we go with another one of her performances*, he thought. His mother was trying to make a joke of it all, but he wasn't having it.

"This is serious, Mom. I need to talk to you . . . alone . . . now."

"Okay, okay. Hold your horses!" She looked at the group of women around her. "If you would please excuse me, ladies, it seems my son has a pressing issue that requires my immediate attention."

They all smiled and nodded and pushed her along, just like they had been groomed to do.

Leighton led his mother out of the kitchen and up the stairs, toward the master bedroom. Mom tried to make small talk on the way, but Leighton wouldn't respond. He wasn't going to make this easy on her. When they got into the bedroom, he closed the door and Mom sat on a chaise lounge in the corner.

"What's this all about, hun?" she asked innocently.

"Don't play nice with me, Mom," Leighton retorted. "I know that you said or did something to July. And whatever it was, it must've been bad, because she left the party over it.

I found her walking back to her motel because she was too uncomfortable to stay here! What the hell did you do?"

"Oh please!" Mom rolled her eyes. "Let's not be dramatic. I merely told July that you were going away to school in a few weeks, and that it would be silly for her to expect any type of relationship to work out between the two of you."

"I love how you're acting like this isn't a big deal, meanwhile you, once again, overstepped your fucking boundaries," Leighton shouted.

"Don't you dare cuss at me. I don't care how mad you are, I'm still your mother, and you will speak to me respectfully."

"Why did you have to say something to July? Why couldn't you just keep your mouth shut? We just talked about boundaries this morning. It hasn't even been twenty-four hours and you've already gone back on your word. You said that you were going to respect me. You said that you were going to treat me like an adult."

"Leighton. I did it to *help* you. Your future is already laid out and I just don't see July fitting into it. She'll get in the way of everything that you've worked so hard for. I'm sorry, I know you don't want to hear that, but it's the truth."

"You don't know that!" Leighton shouted, his face hot with fury. "And this *future* of mine that you keep talking about isn't actually mine at all. It's the future that you've created for me. I have never had a say in any of it. You've never even asked me what I want to do or who I want to be. You've always just decided for me. I'm so sick and tired of you controlling me!"

"I knew this girl was bad news!"

Leighton looked at his mother in disbelief. "That's your

response to everything that I just said? Are you being serious right now?"

"You've never spoken to me like this before!" Mom was visibly upset, but Leighton didn't care. He wasn't going to tiptoe around her feelings anymore. He couldn't allow her to keep doing this.

"You've never questioned my motives," Mom continued. "But now that you've been hanging out with this girl, you're rebelling against me. She's a bad influence, Leighton. I need you to realize that."

Leighton scoffed. "You're out of control, you know that, right? You're blaming July for something that she has nothing to do with. The problem is *you* controlling me and making decisions for me and thinking that you can dictate my damn life. I've never said anything before because I've always just wanted to be a good son. I've always been afraid of disappointing you and Dad. But it's come to the point where I'm sacrificing my own happiness to make you happy, and that's not fair. I'm done, Mom."

She looked at him. For once, his mother seemed to be at a loss for words. Leighton didn't care to hear anything else that she had to say anyway. He was ready to give her his ultimatum and leave. Enough was enough.

"If you want to continue to be a part of my life, then you will back off. You will respect my boundaries and let me make my own decisions. You will no longer determine what is best for me. You will simply support me in the things that I want to do. This will be our new dynamic moving forward, otherwise, I can't have a relationship with you anymore."

Mom's eyes began to fill with tears. Leighton wasn't going

to let her guilt-trip him, though. He turned toward the door. "I hope you understand," he said on his way out.

Leighton didn't look back. He didn't care that he could hear his mother crying. Normally he would turn around and try to console her. He would apologize for upsetting her and beg for her forgiveness. She'd act hurt for a little while but then she'd forgive him, and they would fall back into the same old cycle. Leighton finally saw it for what it was now, though—manipulation. And he wasn't going to succumb to it anymore.

Leighton had always been mild-mannered and sweet-tempered. He was a textbook people pleaser. As a result, he rarely got into fights with his parents. There were only two exceptions, both of which were arguments with his mother, though not nearly as explosive as the one that they just had. The first was on the night when Mom kicked Kennedy out of the house, when Leighton found her standing behind him in the foyer while he looked out the front door, wishing that his sister would come back home. Leighton remembered the smirk that was on his mother's face. It'd made him so angry, and he couldn't bite his tongue any longer. He told his mom that she was spiteful and heartless. The second was a few months later, on the bakery's opening day. Mom had pretended to be happy for her daughter while in front of the townspeople, but as soon as everyone was gone, she went back to being cruel and critical. The facade made Leighton sick, and he'd called his mother out for her duplicity. Both of those arguments ended the same way: with Mom crying and Leighton apologizing, even though he didn't feel like he had done anything wrong. Speaking up was the right thing to do, but his mother was so good at playing the victim that she was able to convince him otherwise. He wasn't going to let that happen this time, though.

Once downstairs, Leighton found Kennedy hanging out in the corner of the living room. When she made eye contact with him, he mouthed the words *let's go*, and Kennedy nodded. They met at the back door and slipped out of the party undetected.

"I need to smoke," Leighton said as they walked into the guesthouse.

Kennedy raised an eyebrow, but she didn't say anything. Instead, she grabbed some bud from a glass jar in the kitchen cabinet and started rolling a joint. While she rolled it, Leighton recounted the night's events. Kennedy listened intently, throwing in a "wow" or an "unbelievable" every now and then. When Leighton finished the story, she asked if he wanted to keep talking about it. He shook his head and said he just wanted to relax.

"This should help," she replied with a smile.

Leighton didn't really smoke much anymore, but he was glad to have made an exception that night. He actually felt calm and his mind was totally at ease. *Man, I miss getting stoned*, he thought. He had grown so used to racing thoughts that he'd forgotten what it was like to have a clear head. He was feeling so good, in fact, that he couldn't even think about what had happened with July or his mom earlier that evening even if he wanted to.

At around midnight, Leighton saw himself out. Kennedy had already fallen asleep by that point, her quiet snores like a children's lullaby. Leighton was tired, too. He had been fighting his eyelids for the better part of an hour, but he was too lazy to get up. He'd get a better night's sleep in his bed, though, so he pulled himself out of the couch that he had been slowly melting into and left for the main house. When he got to his room, he didn't even bother to change. He sprawled out on top of the covers and quickly fell into a deep slumber.

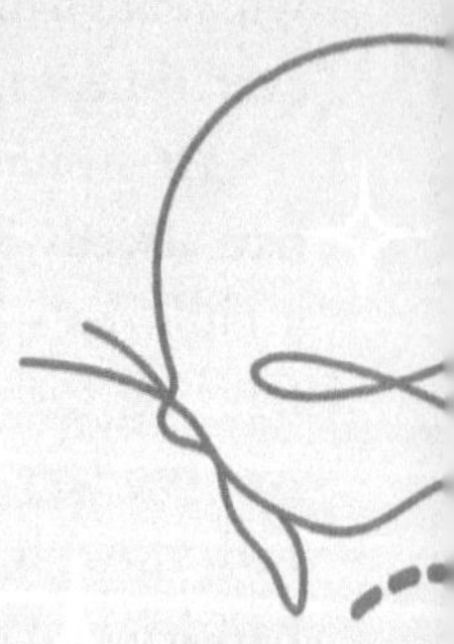

Day Five

KNOCK, KNOCK, KNOCK.

Knock, knock, knock.

Knock, knock, knock.

"Leighton! Are you up? Unlock the door. I need to talk to you!"

Leighton was still half asleep when his mother started pounding on his door. Her voice seemed distant in his groggy haze even though she was right outside his room.

Knock, knock, knock.

Knock, knock, knock.

"Open the damn door, Leighton!"

Leighton rolled out of bed, trying to wake himself up. When he unlocked the door, his mother pushed her way in before he had the chance to open the door himself.

Once inside, Mom furrowed her brows and gave Leighton

a confused look. "Why are you in your dress pants and sports coat?"

Leighton shrugged. He was still feeling pretty out of it and didn't feel like answering questions. "So," he said, "what's so important that you had to wake me up?"

His mother looked down at the ground for a moment. When she looked back up at him, she had a somber expression on her face. "I have some bad news."

The words hit him like a wave of ice-cold water, and all the exhaustion that he had just been feeling was replaced with a rush of panic and unease. "What is it?"

"Greta. She passed away."

Mom continued to speak, but Leighton couldn't hear a word she was saying. Her mouth was moving but there was no sound. *This isn't real*, he thought. *This can't be real.*

When the room started spinning and the air got heavy, he took it as confirmation that this was all just a nightmare. *Wake up*, he pleaded to himself. *Wake up.*

He closed his eyes for what felt like an eternity, praying that when he opened them, he'd be back in his bed, waking up for the day.

On the count of three, he thought, making a deal with himself that when he got to that magic number, he'd open his eyes. His stomach twisted and turned into tight knots while beads of sweat dripped down his forehead. He took a deep breath.

One . . .

Two . . .

Three—

"Leighton!" His mother's cry pierced the silence. He

opened his eyes in a frenzy and found his mother's face just a few inches away from his own. She was grabbing his arms. "Are you okay?"

No, Leighton thought, *I am anything but okay*. He could feel the defeat and despair sweeping over him, forcing him to surrender to reality.

Greta is gone.

"Leighton," his mother begged, this time with even more urgency in her voice. "Talk to me, please. You're worrying me. I know this must be so hard for you. I know how close you two were."

Leighton tried to speak, but he couldn't find the words. He felt detached from his body, like a lost soul, hovering in limbo, trying to reconnect with its physical form but unable to do so.

Mom tightened her grip on Leighton's arms and suddenly he was back in his body, which had felt like an empty shell just moments ago. He winced as his mother's nails dug into his skin, but at least he could feel something, even if it was pain.

"When did this happen?" Leighton asked, his voice shaking.

"Last night. Monica found her this morning. She said that Greta died peacefully. In her sleep."

"I don't . . . I don't understand. I was just with her less than forty-eight hours ago. She seemed fine."

Mom gave him a sympathetic look. "Greta was old, sweetheart. I guess it was just her time to go. God called her up to heaven."

It was that last part that broke Leighton; he couldn't fight the tears that were coming. He sobbed like a child for the next half hour. Mom held him while he wept, and everything that had happened between them the night before suddenly didn't matter anymore. He'd never needed his mother more than he did right then. She rubbed his back and whispered "It'll be okay" over and over again, until his eyes dried out and he couldn't cry anymore.

"I have to get to the bookstore," Leighton mumbled as he pulled away from his mother's embrace.

"Maybe you should take the day off, hun," Mom gently suggested.

"No, I want to be at the shop. I think it would be good for me. I think it's what Greta would have wanted."

"Okay, if you insist." Mom chewed on her bottom lip. Leighton could tell that she was worried about him.

"I'll be okay, Mom, I promise."

His mother nodded passively, and Leighton was grateful that she not only acknowledged his wishes but respected them, too. Normally, she would pressure Leighton into doing what she thought was best for him. *This is progress*, he thought.

Downstairs, Leighton's father was in his usual spot at the end of the kitchen table, reading the paper and sipping his coffee. He looked up as Leighton entered the room. "I'm so sorry, son," he said sympathetically.

Leighton gave him a half-hearted smile. "Thanks, Dad."

"I know how important Greta was to you," his father continued. "She loved you so much."

"I know. I loved her, too." Leighton could feel himself getting emotional, but he didn't want to cry again. He took a deep breath and examined the room. The house was still decorated from the night before. He couldn't believe that his dad's party was just twelve hours ago. Leighton felt a lump forming in his throat as another thought came to mind. Twelve hours ago, Greta was going to bed for the very last time, unaware that she wouldn't be waking up the next morning. Leighton closed his eyes and tightened his jaw. He wasn't going to let himself get upset again.

"What are your plans for the day?" his father asked, interrupting Leighton's melancholic thoughts.

"I'm going to the bookstore."

Dad's eyebrows scrunched together. "Are you sure you're feeling up to it?"

"Yeah. It's what Greta would have wanted me to do."

"Alright," his father replied apprehensively, "just don't push yourself too hard. It's okay to take time to mourn."

"I know, Dad. I won't."

Dad gave Leighton a tight-lipped smile. "I guess I'll see you later, then." He returned to his paper.

"See you later." Leighton grabbed an apple from a basket on the kitchen island. He wasn't hungry, but he always took a piece of fruit before heading out for the day. It was second nature, and right now, he was just trying to go about the motions as usual. If he treated today like any other day then maybe he'd be able to forget about the hole growing in his chest.

Leighton drove into town with the windows down and his

favorite playlist on. Feeling the sun on his skin and the breeze through his hair helped to ground him. Ever since his mother shared the news of Greta's passing, he'd been experiencing waves of disconnect between himself and his body. It was a strange sensation of detachment, and he didn't like it. He assumed that this was a side effect of grief, though he had never felt this way before. Then again, he had never experienced such a substantial loss, at least not at an age when he really understood it. Both of his grandmothers had passed away when he was a child, and Ivan passed away not too long after; although Leighton was a little bit older at the time, he had still been too young to fully comprehend what was going on. Plus, as much as he loved his grandmothers and Ivan, he hadn't been as close with them as he had been with Greta.

Leighton reminisced on all the special moments he and Greta had shared over the years. They played in his mind like a movie montage. He pictured himself running into Twice Upon a Time as a young boy and Greta scooping him up into a big bear hug. He saw her smiling proudly from the other side of the sofa as he read their favorite children's book for the first time on his own. He thought about her cheering him on at T-ball games and spelling bees, school concerts and moving up ceremonies. He imagined her laughing from his passenger seat on the day that he got his license, when he took her on his in-augural ride. Greta was always there for him, through the good and the bad, the big and the small. Leighton knew that he had been incredibly lucky to have these experiences with her, but he couldn't help but wish that he could have just a few more.

At the shop, there were already several people waiting outside with flowers. Leighton wasn't surprised to see them. Montclair was small and word traveled quickly, plus Greta was beloved by so many, it made sense that the locals would come by to share their condolences. He parked his truck and met them on the sidewalk.

Monica was the first to greet him. "Leighton," she whispered as she pulled him into a tight embrace. He could feel her pain. Could she feel his, too?

When Monica released Leighton, Mr. O'Hara, the town's handyman said, "I'm so sorry to hear about Greta."

"She will be so missed," chimed Mrs. Kinzer, Leighton's high school math teacher.

"This town isn't going to be the same without her!" Leighton's ex-girlfriend, Becca, lamented.

"You okay, man?" a comforting voice asked. Leighton saw Carson making his way through the crowd. He placed a hand on Leighton's shoulder.

Leighton nodded and put on a brave face. He wished that he could be alone at the bookstore, but that wouldn't be fair. After all, this wasn't just his loss to mourn. So, he unlocked the door and led the visitors inside. They set up their flowers throughout the shop and shared their favorite stories of Greta. By noon, the store was filled with at least two dozen people. It was the most visitors that Twice Upon a Time had seen in years.

At half past twelve, Kennedy came by with an assortment of baked goods. Leighton still wasn't hungry, but the other guests munched away while they made small talk with each other. Leighton was thankful for the distraction. While it was nice to have so many people at the shop, he also felt a responsibility to entertain them while they were there, and playing host for the past few hours was beginning to get exhausting. Fortunately, the visitors were so preoccupied with Kennedy's treats that he was able to slip away for a few minutes and get some time to himself. He snuck out the back door to hang out behind the building for a little bit.

Leighton leaned against the pastel wall of the bookstore and closed his eyes. He directed his face toward the sun so he could feel the heat radiate his skin. There was a comforting quiet around him, despite the background noise that he could hear from afar: a bird singing a cheerful melody, the steady hum of cars moving up and down Main Street, a child crying for his mother. But where Leighton stood, there was a bubble of solace, keeping him wrapped up and protected from the cacophony. It felt like a warm hug and he was certain it was Greta.

Thump.

The sound of the door startled Leighton. His body tensed and his eyes quickly opened. He looked to his left to find his sister standing beside him.

"Hey," Kennedy said as she inched closer.

"Hey."

"How are you doing?"

"I'm okay. Better than I thought I'd be."

"That's good." She sounded relieved. "I've been worried about you. I couldn't wait to close the bakery so I could come over here and check on you."

"I'll be alright, Ken."

Kennedy nodded in acknowledgment. She looked up at the sky, then down to the ground. She took a pebble beneath her shoe and started moving it back and forth along the pavement. "I just can't believe she's gone . . ."

"Me neither."

"I wish that I had made more of an effort to visit her. The last time that we really hung out was at the grand opening of my bakery. . . . That was four years ago." Leighton could hear the shame in his sister's voice.

"Aw, Ken. Don't feel guilty. You were spread so thin those first few years, and when you finally got into your rhythm, Greta had already stopped working at the bookstore and was barely spending any time outside her home." Leighton tried to sound persuasive, but he knew he'd probably feel the same way if he were in Kennedy's position.

"Yeah, I guess you're right," she agreed. Kennedy spoke the words, but Leighton could tell that she didn't believe them. He decided not to push, though. After all, he'd done the same thing when he told her that he was okay. It wasn't a total lie, but he'd definitely used the term loosely.

The two stood in silence for a few minutes before Kennedy interrupted the quiet.

"I could have gone to her house," she said with defeat still present in her voice.

"And I could have hung out with her for longer when she was at the bookstore the other day, but I left early to spend time with July."

"Speaking of July, have you talked to her? Or seen her?"

"Nope. For all I know, she could be on a bus on her way to Florida right now."

Kennedy gave Leighton a sympathetic pout. "You know I'm here if you need me, right?"

"I know." Leighton forced a smile. He didn't want his sister to worry about him. Hopefully his performance was convincing enough.

Kennedy hesitated before reluctantly saying, "Alright, well I guess I'm going to head back inside."

"Okay."

Kennedy turned toward the door. Leighton knew that he should probably go back, too, but he needed just a few more minutes to himself.

He waited while his sister let herself back into the store. When he heard the familiar thump of the door, he leaned his head back toward the sun and closed his eyes again. As he enjoyed the warmth on his skin, he thought about Greta and the story she had told him the other day, the one about her and Ivan. If there was anything that provided him with comfort through all of this, it was the thought that she was finally reunited with her husband. Greta and Ivan's love story made Leighton believe in the possibility of soulmates, which was something that he had never really considered before. It also made him realize that there were different degrees of relationships, and while more than one *could* work, a successful partnership didn't necessarily mean that you found the person that you were fated to be with. For example, his parents had a good marriage, and they definitely loved each other, but Leighton wasn't sure that he would call them soulmates. Had his mother or father ever had the opportunity to meet the person who could've been better for them? Or had that never happened because they'd found someone who was good enough? Was finding your soulmate something that happened to only a select few? And of those people, were they just the lucky ones who happened to meet their destined lover early in life? Or did they wait knowing that the best was yet to come?

Leighton didn't want to settle, and maybe he was jumping to conclusions assuming that people like his parents had settled. Maybe they really believed that they had found their soulmate, or maybe they just didn't believe in the notion of soulmates at all. Either way, Leighton knew that he wanted a love like Greta and Ivan's, and he was sure that he would know it when he found it, and he was beginning to believe that maybe he already had.

He thought about the night prior and the events that had transpired before this awful tragedy. He hadn't thought it could get any worse, but somehow it had. Surely this was rock bottom, though. Things had to get better from here. Leighton would visit July later that evening, if she was still around. He had to try to make things better with her. Greta would have wanted that.

Content with his decision, Leighton finally headed back inside. As he placed his hand on the door's handle, a monarch butterfly landed on his wrist. He looked at it incredulously as it fluttered its orange-and-black wings before gracefully flying away. Monarchs were Greta's favorite, and Leighton was certain that this was a sign from her. If he knew Greta as well as he thought he did, then this was her way of telling him that she was okay and that he shouldn't give up on July.

When Leighton returned to the bookshop, he was surprised

to see that his mother and father were there; it wasn't like them to break from their schedules, especially when the election was only a few months away. He was certain that his father had campaign work to do, and the thought of his mother going out before she had the chance to get the house back in order after last night's party seemed absurd. Leighton hoped that they were there for the right reasons and not just to make an appearance. He knew that they were mourning the loss of Greta. After all, they were close with her, too, but his parents were also calculated, and reputation and political gain impacted much of what they did on a day-to-day basis. These were special circumstances, though, so he let go of his skepticism and gave his parents the benefit of the doubt.

"Mom, Dad! I wasn't expecting to see you guys here," Leighton said as he approached his parents.

"Of course we were going to come by," Mom said while pulling Leighton into a hug. "Greta was so dear to us." She leaned back and cupped Leighton's face. "Plus, we've been worrying about you."

Dad placed his hand on Leighton's shoulders. "How are you holding up, son?"

"I'm good," Leighton responded, and he actually meant it. Seeing the butterfly gave him hope that Greta was in a better place. He truly believed that she was finally reunited with Ivan, which is what she had been yearning for since her husband's passing.

"Well, if you need to talk, your mother and I are here for you. We don't want you to feel like you're in this alone," his father said comfortingly.

"I know, Dad. Thank you."

It took an hour and a half for the bookstore to completely clear out. No new visitors arrived during that time, and the people who were already there slowly began to trail out until it was just Leighton and Kennedy left in the shop.

"Are you going to head home soon?" Kennedy asked while flipping through a novel that she'd found on the coffee table beside the old green sofa.

"I don't think so," Leighton replied. "I want to hang out here for a little while longer."

Kennedy gave her brother an apprehensive look. "Are you sure?"

"Yeah, aside from like fifteen minutes, I haven't gotten any time to myself since Mom told me about Greta earlier this morning. I'm looking forward to being alone for a bit," Leighton explained.

His sister narrowed her eyes and shot him another look, the one she gave when she didn't believe him.

"I'm fine, Ken. I promise."

Kennedy surrendered. "Okay, okay. But if anything changes, you call me. Deal?"

"Deal."

Kennedy returned the worn book to the coffee table and gathered her belongings. When she reached the door, she turned to Leighton once again with furrowed brows and an are-you-sure-about-this look in her eyes.

Leighton gave his sister a reassuring smile and a nod. Kennedy let out a dramatic sigh and then exited the building. Leighton followed her to the door and turned the wooden sign from Open to Closed.

Finally, he thought, *peace and quiet.* He took a deep

breath and walked around the shop. Now that he was by himself, he wasn't sure what to do. He searched the room for a worthy task, but the store looked neat, despite the number of visitors that had been there that day. After scanning the shop for several minutes, he found a few books that needed to be put away. He picked them up and slowly returned them to their designated shelves. Despite taking his time, he still finished sooner than he would have liked. He dusted the counters next, and then he swept the floors. When he finished that, he could shine the windows. Surely that would kill some time. Anything to keep himself busy.

While Leighton cleaned, he recalled when Ivan passed away around eight years earlier. Leighton remembered visiting Twice Upon a Time the day after it happened. When he walked in, he saw Greta sitting on the sofa. She was holding a bouquet of roses as tears streamed down her face. Leighton learned that the flowers were from her late husband. Ivan had planned the surprise posthumous delivery to console his grieving wife.

"Greta," Leighton said quietly as he sat down on the couch next to her, "are you sure you want to be at the bookstore right now?"

Greta had wiped her eyes and chuckled. "There's nowhere else I'd rather be," she said, clutching the floral arrangement close to her heart. "As long as this shop is open, then a piece of Ivan will always be alive."

Leighton ran his fingers along the walls of the bookstore

as he returned to the present day. Now the same was true for Greta, too.

An hour later, Leighton had completed everything that he had set out to do, but he still wasn't ready to leave. Something was willing him to stay. He turned on the radio and paced around the room. It was nearing five now, and he knew that he should be going home for dinner. He had bailed on his parents the past few days, and his mother made it clear that she wasn't happy about it. He pulled his car keys from the left front pocket of his jeans only to quickly drop them back in. If ever there was a night when he could get away with skipping a family meal, it was tonight. His parents wouldn't give him a hard time under the circumstances. He might as well take advantage of it.

Leighton continued to pace around the quaint shop. "Simple Man" was playing on the radio now; it was one of his favorite songs. Dad was a huge Lynyrd Skynyrd fan and he'd passed his love for the Southern rock band down to Leighton. Leighton hummed along as he walked in tiny circles, weaving in and out, creating figure eights on the floor. When the song ended, he turned off the radio and made his way down the aisle of fiction books by authors whose last names began with the letters *A-L*. He finally knew what he needed to do.

Leighton ran his left pointer finger across the leather bindings until he found the one that he was looking for: *Little Women*, by Louisa May Alcott, the Vintage Children's Classics edition. It was Greta's favorite novel, and while the shop had several copies in stock, it was this particular cover that the old woman always reached for. Leighton remembered watching her admire the illustrations on the front. He could still hear her saying how much she loved the hand-drawn sketches, and how perfectly the artist captured each of the March girls.

Leighton pulled the pale blue book from the crammed shelf and opened to the first page. Inside, he found a letter penned on old floral stationery. He didn't need to see the ornate cursive handwriting to know who it was from.

Dearest Leighton,

I'm not sure when you will find this letter, but I predict it won't take you long. You have always known where to look for me.

By now, my reason for writing is probably clear. My time here is coming to an end. You needn't be sad, though. I'm ready to be with my beloved Ivan again.

The bookstore is yours to do what you please. You could open it only when you are home from college, or you could find someone to work it while you are away. You could even close the doors for good and keep it as your own private collection. Whatever you choose will be the right decision.

Continue to be your most authentic self and always, always follow your heart.

With love,
Greta

Leighton finished reading the letter and then he read it again and again. After the third time, he brought the paper close to his chest and held it there as tears filled his eyes. He didn't fight them this time, though. Instead, he let them fall freely, cupping the note to shield it. He cradled Greta's letter as he cried, and it felt so good, because these were happy tears. This was a cry of relief. Greta was where she wanted to be, and Leighton took solace in her peaceful passing.

Ding, ding.

"We're closed for the day!" Leighton called from the aisle, tucking Greta's letter into his pants pocket. He could have sworn that he'd locked the door.

"I know, I saw the sign, but I was hoping you could make an exception."

"July?" Leighton quickly made his way to the front of the building, drying his eyes as he walked so that there weren't any lingering tears.

"Hi," she said quietly once Leighton was in view. She was shifting her weight from one leg to the other, and Leighton could tell that she was nervous.

"Hey," he said with a small smile. July was the last person that Leighton had expected to show up at the bookstore today. He was so glad to see her.

"Can we talk?" she asked apprehensively, tucking a loose hair behind her ear.

"Yeah, of course. Do you want to go sit on the couch?"

"Sure. I actually came by earlier," she explained as they made their way to the sofa, "but when I saw all the people here, I figured it was a bad time. The store was busy today, huh?"

"Yeah, it was, but not with customers."

July looked confused.

"They were here for Greta," Leighton explained as he and July each sat down on the couch. "She . . . she passed away last night."

Pain, sadness, and empathy filled July's eyes. "Leighton, I am so sorry," she lamented. "I know how hard it is to lose someone that you love. Are you okay?" She wrapped her arms around him. "This must be so hard for you."

"Yeah . . . I'm okay. I wasn't at first," he admitted. "When I found out this morning, I was a fucking wreck. I don't think I've ever cried so hard in my life. But as the day went on, it got better."

July squeezed Leighton's arm, but before she could say anything, he continued.

"This is probably going to sound crazy, but I kept feeling like Greta was trying to send me a message . . . like she wanted me to know that she was in a better place." He took the folded note out of his pocket. "And then I found this. It's a letter that she left for me before she passed away. I found it in her favorite book."

July's mouth fell open, and she placed her right hand over her heart. "Can I read it?" she asked timidly.

"Of course." Leighton handed her the small piece of stationery.

July took the note and opened it. Leighton watched as her gaze moved along the page. When she finished reading it, she whispered, "This is so beautiful." Leighton could see a few tears falling down her cheek. "It was so thoughtful of her to leave you this," she said as she wiped them away.

"I know." Leighton choked. He could feel his eyes welling

up again, too. "She must've left it the other day, when we were at the animal preserve."

July gave Leighton a tight-lipped smile and then pulled him to her again, holding him for even longer this time. When she let go, she handed him back the letter. Leighton looked it over one more time before folding it up and placing it in his pocket once more.

"I'm gonna miss her so much," he said, "but it makes me feel better knowing that she was at peace before she passed."

"That would make me feel better, too," July agreed, her voice quiet.

Leighton felt a pang of guilt. Even though she wasn't showing it, he imagined that this couldn't be easy for her to talk about, especially given the circumstances of her mother's death. Unlike Leighton, she didn't get any closure.

"I'm sorry," he said with shame in his voice.

"For what?"

Leighton was pretty sure that she knew why he was sorry, but he continued anyway. He figured that this would be a good time to apologize for his behavior the past few days. "For everything," he said. "For invading your privacy, and then for not being honest with you about it. For making assumptions about how you're feeling or why you're feeling a certain way. For being insensitive to your situation."

He paused and then let out a deep breath. "I handled everything like a total jackass."

"You don't have to apologize," she said. "I actually came here to apologize to *you*."

Leighton, confused, raised an eyebrow. "But you didn't do anything wrong."

"Yes, I did. I completely overreacted last night. It's normal to look people up on the internet. And in most cases, you find their social media accounts, you look through their pictures, no big deal. It's not your fault that you found something darker. And as for not telling me, I understand why you didn't. It must've been uncomfortable for you. What would you have even said? If the tables were turned, I would have done the same thing. The reason I got so angry was because it took me by surprise, and instead of taking a step back and evaluating the situation, I freaked out."

"I think you reacted how most people would have reacted," Leighton replied. "Plus, you were already upset about what my mom said to you. I'm sorry about that, too, by the way. She totally overstepped her boundaries, but you don't have to worry about her doing that again. I talked to her last night and made it clear that I won't tolerate that shit anymore."

"You did?" July asked, tilting her head to the side. Leighton could see that she was a bit shocked by his revelation.

"Of course I did," Leighton replied. "I was furious when I found out what she did to you. I never want you to be put in a situation like that ever again."

July's face softened. "Thank you," she said as she met Leighton's gaze. "For everything."

Leighton was getting ready to tell her that she didn't need to thank him, but before he could, July placed her palm on his cheek and pulled him to her. It felt like he was moving in slow motion as he waited for his lips to meet July's, but once they touched, he couldn't move fast enough. He cupped the back of July's head in his hand and ran his fingers through her soft wavy hair. Every time she moved, he caught the scent of coconut and vanilla. He wasn't sure if it was her shampoo or perfume, but he wanted more of the sweet, sensual aroma. He wanted more of her. July pressed her lips against his harder, with an intensity that he wasn't expecting. He grabbed her hips and moved her so that she was positioned on top of him. Her legs wrapped around his body and Leighton could feel her warmth radiating on his thighs.

Leighton and July stayed like this until they were both flushed in the face and nearly out of breath. When they couldn't kiss any longer, July pulled away and put her hands on Leighton's cheeks.

"I like you," she said with a wide-eyed, schoolgirl grin.

"I like you, too," Leighton replied, feverish. He kissed July's forehead and then her nose before helping her off his lap and back beside him on the sofa.

They sat on the couch for several minutes without saying a word. It wasn't awkward, though, at least not for Leighton. He needed the time to regain his composure.

"Do you want to know more about my mom's accident?" July asked, interrupting the silence.

Leighton looked at her apprehensively. "Only if you want to tell me about it. I don't want you to feel like you owe me an explanation or anything."

"I know. I want to talk about it."

"Okay. I'm all ears."

July smiled. "Thank you." She shifted her body so that she was facing him, and then she began her story.

"A few years ago, my mom decided that she wanted to start a new hobby. I was expecting her to try knitting or join a dance class or something, but she said that she wanted to get into aviation. She had never mentioned an interest in flying before, so I thought it was a weird midlife crisis–type deal and it would pass, but she started taking lessons and totally fell in love with it. I wished that she would have chosen something, I don't know, less extreme, I guess, but my mom worked her ass off to give me a good life, so how could I not support her in something that she really wanted to do?

"She eventually got her pilot's license, and she started doing solo flights a few times a month, like the one that she was on when she"—July closed her eyes for a second—"died. She had done that same trip several times before. I was actually supposed to go on it with her that day, but I decided to go out with my friends instead."

July looked down at her lap, and when she looked back up, Leighton could see the pain and regret in her face. "They still don't know what happened, and all I can think about is 'what if?' What if I had gone with her that day? Would we have been in a different plane that didn't crash? Would she still be here? Maybe the crash would've happened either way, and if I were there, I would've gone down with her. Would that have been so bad, though? Losing my mom was the worst thing to ever happen to me, and sometimes I think it would've been better if I was in the crash, too."

July's eyes filled with tears. "I just feel so guilty, and mad. So, so mad. Why did this have to happen to me? Why did I have to lose my mom?"

She was bawling now, and Leighton's heart was breaking as he watched her fall apart. He wanted to pick up the pieces.

He needed to make her feel better. So, he pulled her to his chest and cradled her in his arms.

"Shh," he whispered. "It's okay, let it out. I know it hurts, and you have every right to be angry. I would be, too. No one should have to go through what you went through, but please don't blame yourself. Your mom wouldn't want that. And don't you dare say that things would've been better off if you were on that plane, too. You're meant to be here, July. The world needs you. I need you."

July's crying slowed and quieted until all Leighton could hear were faint hiccups. He rocked her while her eyes dried and her grief subsided.

"I'm sorry," she finally said. "I didn't mean to break down like that." She pulled away from Leighton and chewed on her bottom lip. "Thank you for listening to me and for consoling me, too. I think I've been needing to get that out for a while now. It's like I had been fighting back my emotions for months." She took a deep breath. "It actually felt good to cry," she admitted with a small smile.

Leighton was relieved to see July in better spirits, and he felt good knowing that he was the one who helped get her there. "Thank you for opening up to me. I know you didn't have to, and it would have been perfectly okay if you didn't, but I was really hoping you would. I want to be the person you can talk to about anything. I want to be your shoulder to cry on. Most of all, I want to be the person who can put a smile back on your face whenever you're feeling down."

July reached for Leighton again, and he wrapped his arms around her.

"Today you proved that you can be that person," she whispered.

The words hit Leighton straight in his heart.

She moved back to her side of the couch. "We should do something tonight, something to celebrate my mom and Greta."

"What did you have in mind?"

July gave the ceiling a pensive stare. "I don't know. What if we had a celebration of life? We could light some candles, play their favorite music, have a few drinks. It doesn't have to be anything fancy, just a little something to honor them."

"I like that idea. A lot. Do you want to do it here at the bookstore or somewhere else?"

"We can do it here. It's obviously the perfect location for Greta, and it's fitting for my mom, too, because she loved to read."

"Okay, cool. We'll need to get supplies," Leighton said. "I have a Bluetooth speaker that we can use to play the music, but we'll have to go to the store to get candles and a lighter. And what did you want to drink?"

July smirked, and Leighton could see a playful twinkle in her eye.

"I was thinking of tequila," she said, "in which case, we'll need to get salt and limes. Oh, and a couple of shot glasses, too!"

"Okay, we should be able to find shot glasses at the store, and I can ask Kennedy to pick us up a bottle of tequila. I'm sure she won't mind," Leighton said.

"I can get us the bottle. I have a fake ID," July replied with a mischievous grin.

"Oh, *really*?"

"Yes, sir. See?" She pulled the card out of her wallet.

Leighton leaned in to get a good look at it. "Wow, that's pretty legit."

"That's kind of the idea."

Leighton laughed. "True."

The two were quiet for a minute before Leighton continued. "Should we head out to the store now? The sooner we get everything, the sooner we can get this party started."

July placed her hand over her mouth before erupting with laughter.

"What's so funny?" Leighton asked.

"Did you really just say 'get this party started?' That's such a, I don't know, middle-aged man thing to say," she teased.

Leighton could feel his face growing hot, but he laughed it off, hoping that July wouldn't notice that his cheeks were turning red from embarrassment.

When Leighton was growing up, one of the things the adults in his life always used to say was "you're such an old soul." Leighton never thought much of it when he was young, but as he started to get older, he couldn't help but notice that they never made that comment to any of the other boys his age.

"Do you think I'm an old soul?" Leighton had asked his sister one night while they were watching a movie.

"Is that a serious question?" Kennedy laughed. "Yes, you are definitely an old soul."

Leighton looked down in disappointment.

"What's wrong?"

"I don't know. No one says that about the other guys."

Kennedy nudged his arm. "So what? It's cool to be different. Why would you want to be like everyone else anyway?"

Leighton shrugged and Kennedy pulled him into a hug. "Life's too short to pretend to be someone you're not."

The local Walmart wasn't in Montclair but it was still no more than a fifteen minute drive away. It was right off Interstate 85. Leighton always thought it was strange how his small, sleepy town was just a stone's throw from the busiest highway in Georgia. Montclair's Main Street was like a time capsule. It looked like a picture from the 1950s, dotted with mom-and-pop shops on both sides of the road, yet it took only one left turn to find a busy freeway and a large commercial area with every big box store you could imagine.

Leighton and July took their time shopping, perusing every aisle of the department store. They tried on hats and sunglasses, browsed the five-dollar movie bin, and smelled every candle that they could get their hands on. When they were done fooling around, they rounded up their supplies and checked out. Fortunately, they were able to find everything that they were looking for, including a pair of light-up shot glasses that July was particularly excited about.

After Walmart, they visited the liquor store. Leighton, nervous that someone he knew might see him, stayed in the truck while July went inside. He watched through the windshield as July found the bottle and walked it up to the cashier. It looked like everything was going smoothly. His observations were confirmed when July exited the building and she held up the brown paper bag, giving it a little shake to show him that she got it. He didn't need to see the bottle, though, to know that it was a success—July's triumphant smile easily gave that away.

"I have a confession," July said as she got back into the vehicle.

Leighton looked at her curiously. "Oh yeah? And what would that be?"

"That was my first time using my fake ID," she admitted. "I was actually really nervous."

"You didn't look nervous, at least not from what I could see."

"I'm glad I got the opportunity to use it. I paid over two hundred dollars for this thing!"

"Jeez, that's a lot of money to spend on a fake ID."

"Too much," July agreed. "But I thought it would be worth the investment. I had all these crazy plans to have a wild summer of clubbing, parties, and music festivals . . . but then the accident happened, and, well . . . I quickly realized that none of that shit matters."

Leighton looked at July sympathetically. "I think tragedy has a way of making us reevaluate *everything*."

"Yeah." July turned her gaze toward her lap. Leighton could see that she was starting to get upset.

"What are we doing?" he asked playfully. "We're supposed to be celebrating! There's no time to be sad. We have shots to take and candles to light and songs to sing!"

July looked up at Leighton and gave him a small smile.

"Cheer up." He nudged her arm. "We're going to have a great night!"

July brightened. "Hell yeah, we are!"

Leighton gave July a nod of approval. "Let's get out of here," he said as he pulled out of the parking spot. He gripped the steering wheel with his left hand and the shifter with his right. Just as he was about to return his right hand to the wheel, July grabbed it and wrapped her fingers around his. When she touched him, the hairs on the back of his neck stood up. She was electric. Leighton closed his eyes and took a deep breath. He was trying to keep his cool, but it was hard when July ignited every nerve in his body. He opened his eyes and focused on the road ahead of him. Then, he began to drive. Fortunately, he preferred to do so one-handed.

Back at the bookstore, Leighton and July quickly started decorating. They were both eager to begin the celebration. The pair set up snacks and drinks on the main counter and then strategically placed candles around the shop. They filled the ceiling with a plethora of balloons and set Leighton's speaker on the side table next to the sofa. When they were done, they put on party hats and got ready to take their first shot. Leighton cut the lime while July rimmed their glasses with salt.

"Ready?" July asked as she poured each of them a hefty serving of tequila.

The shot glasses were doubles, and July took full advantage of the extra room, filling each one right up to the brim.

Leighton eyed his glass, trying not to feel intimidated by the task at hand. If he was being honest, he wasn't much of a tequila person, or any type of liquor really. He much preferred beer, but today was a special celebration, and he wasn't going to wimp out. Leighton took the tequila in one hand and a lime wedge in the other, careful not to spill.

"To your mom and to Greta!" He clinked his glass against July's.

"To my mom and Greta!" July repeated before biting her lime and throwing back her shot.

Leighton followed, wincing as the strong liquor hit the back of his throat. He forced it down until it burned in his stomach. He let out a deep breath, water filling his eyes.

"You okay, bud?" July asked playfully.

Leighton blushed and gave July a sheepish grin. "Yeah, I'm good. Apparently, I need more practice if I want to be on your level, though. You took that like a champ."

July winked and said, "One more?"

Leighton hesitated. He wasn't ready to take another shot, but he couldn't let July know that. He didn't want her to think he was lame. So, Leighton faked his best smile and replied, "Let's do it!" with as much optimism as he could muster. *Hopefully this one goes down easier than the first*, he thought.

It didn't, but the next one did, and the two after that were basically a cakewalk. One hour and several shots later, Leighton was feeling more than a bit buzzed. Alright, he was drunk, and based on July's crooked smile and glazed eyes, he figured it was safe to say that she was, too.

The two danced around the cozy shop and sang along to

"The Chain" by Fleetwood Mac, July's mom's favorite song. Outside, the sun had almost set, which was good, because that meant that the café next door was closed, and with how loud Leighton and July were, they would almost certainly be disturbing the people inside had they still been open.

As the night transitioned from dusk to dark, the light in the bookstore grew faint. The only illumination came from the piña colada–scented candles placed haphazardly around the room. Leighton watched the flames dance along with him and July, casting shadows on the walls that seemed to mirror their own movements. He couldn't remember the last time he felt so weightless. Every now and then, he leaned his head back and took in the sweet aroma of coconut and pineapple. He liked the rush that he felt as his head got dizzy with the tropical fragrance.

"Do you believe in fate?" Leighton asked when their playlist came to an end.

July raised an eyebrow. "Are you about to get soft on me?" she teased.

Leighton laughed. "No, no. I'm just wondering."

July hesitated as if she were considering his question. "No, I don't," she finally replied. "Maybe I did at one time, but I can't anymore. If I did, then that would mean that I believe that my mom was fated to die in a horrific plane crash, and I refuse to believe that God or the universe or whatever else you want to call the divine, supernatural force that controls our lives would ever want that for me, or for her."

July's answer made Leighton uncomfortable. He looked down at his hands and fidgeted, hoping she wouldn't turn the question around on him, because the truth was, Leighton hadn't believed in fate . . . until July walked into his life. After spending these past few days with her, though, he felt a strong sense that they'd been destined to meet. He would even go as far as to say that they were destined to be together. He couldn't tell her that, though, not after what she just said about her mom.

"What about you?" July asked, much to Leighton's dismay.

He hesitated. "I haven't given it much thought. I honestly don't even know why I brought it up." Leighton scratched the back of his head. "I guess the tequila really got to me."

July narrowed her eyes and Leighton could tell she wasn't buying it.

He fidgeted awkwardly again. *I need to change the subject*, he thought. He looked around the room and saw the snacks on the main counter. The sight of the pretzels and popcorn made his stomach growl. It had been hours since he last ate.

"I don't know about you, but I'm starving," he said, hoping July would take the bait.

July paused for what felt like an eternity. "I'm pretty hungry, too," she replied at last.

Leighton let out a sigh of relief. He walked over to the main counter and grabbed the snack bowls. "Want to bring these over to the couch?"

"Sure." July made her way toward the sofa. Leighton watched as she curled up on it, shifting a few times before settling into a comfortable position.

"Pretzels or popcorn?" Leighton asked as he presented each option.

"Popcorn, please!"

"You got it," he said, handing her the bowl.

July pulled the bowl to her chest and scooped up a large handful. "Thank you!" After a few bites, she began tossing the pieces in the air, trying to catch them in her mouth, but she missed, in dramatic fashion, each time. Leighton smiled as he watched popcorn land everywhere but where she intended it to go: on her forehead, in her hair, down her shirt. He laughed quietly as a wave of warmth passed through his chest. He was such a sucker for July's little quirks.

"Are you going to join me or what?" July asked.

He hadn't realized that he was standing there staring at her.

"Yeah, sorry. I was zoning out, I guess." He took a seat next to her on the couch.

"Catch," July said as she threw a piece of popcorn his way.

Leighton leaned forward just in time for it to land perfectly in his mouth.

"Show-off," July said with a playful smirk.

Over the next few hours, the two bounced around from snacking to chatting to making out, though not necessarily in that order. They even took a few more tequila shots. It wasn't until Leighton got a text from his mother that he realized just how late it had gotten.

Mom: Are you still at the bookstore?? It's almost 11. Your father and I are worried sick. It's time to come home.

Shit, Leighton thought as he stared at his phone.

"Is everything okay?" July asked. She looked concerned.

"Yeah, sorry. It's my mom," he explained while quickly typing a reply to his mother.

Leighton: Sorry, I lost track of time. Be home soon!

"She wants me to come home," he continued. "It's a quarter to eleven."

July looked surprised. "Is it really? Damn, it got late fast. I should be getting back, too," she said as she unsteadily lifted herself up from the couch. She was clearly still feeling the effects of all that tequila. Leighton was, too.

"Okay, I'll help you clean up and then I can walk back to my motel," July continued. "Can you have your sister pick you up? You obviously can't drive."

Leighton stood up from the sofa, feeling a bit wobbly himself. "Yeah, I'm sure that won't be a problem," he replied, "but I'm not letting you walk to the motel alone. I'll go with you and then I'll have Kennedy pick me up here when I get back."

July paused. "Are you sure? It's only a five-minute walk. I think I can manage on my own."

"One hundred percent positive," Leighton insisted. "Montclair is safe, but you still shouldn't be walking alone in the middle of the night. Plus, it'll make me feel better knowing that you got back to your room okay."

"Fair enough," she conceded.

"Thank you."

"Thank *you* for being a gentleman."

Leighton wrapped her in a quick hug. "My pleasure," he said into her soft hair. "Alright, are you ready to clean this place up?"

"Let's do it."

Despite their drunkenness, it didn't take Leighton and July all that long to tidy up the bookshop, probably because they were too tipsy to be fussy. They gathered the candles and put them in a spare box, moved the leftover snacks to the back closet, and dumped the remaining tequila down the bathroom sink.

"I think I've had enough tequila for the next year," Leighton said as he poured the potent golden liquor down the drain.

July held her nose so she couldn't smell it. "Me, too."

At that point, the only thing left to do was take care of the balloons. July insisted that they deflate each one so that they could properly dispose of them. While they did this, she gave a heartfelt speech about the danger of releasing balloons outside and the threat that it could pose to wildlife.

Leighton smiled, not because he didn't take what July was saying seriously but because of the passion in her voice when she said it. He loved that she had something that she cared so deeply about; knowing that this was important to her made him like her even more than he already did.

"You know," he said, "you're going to be really great at whichever one of those jobs you decide to pursue."

July blushed. "Thank you, that was a really nice compliment."

Leighton pulled her to him and gave her a small kiss on the forehead. "Ready to go?"

"Yeah," she said as she grazed her nails along his lower back.

The walk to the motel was idyllic. The moon hung, picturesque, in the night sky, casting light on the pair as they strolled hand in hand down the cobblestone sidewalk. They chatted and laughed and shared flirty grins every step of the way. When they arrived, July wrapped herself in Leighton's arms, resting her head on his chest. Leighton held her and rocked her back and forth for a few minutes.

"I had a great time tonight," she whispered.

"Me, too."

They shared a sweet kiss before July turned around to head for her room.

"Don't forget to call Kennedy for a ride!" she called over her shoulder.

"I won't!"

Leighton watched as July let herself in. Before closing the door, she gave him a small wave. He returned the gesture. He hated this part—the part when they said goodbye. Each time, he'd felt a lump forming in his throat, and tonight was no different. He tried to fight the feeling, but it was no use. It had happened every night since he met July five days ago. It was doubt and uncertainty manifesting itself. He never knew if this was going to be the last time he would see her, and while he was slowly growing more confident— after all, she hadn't left yet—he still questioned if tomorrow might be the day when it would all fall apart.

Leighton tried and failed to swallow past the thing that seemed to be stuck in his throat. *Here we go again*, he thought. He wished he wasn't so inclined to worry, but unfortunately, anxiety had been a growing problem for him as of late, even before he met July. It had really started to get bad this past year, as his plans for college, and the future, became more of a reality. The pressure, the expectations, the image; at times it was just too much to bear. Leighton swallowed again, harder this time, but it was to no avail, the lump wasn't going anywhere, at least not yet.

On his way back to the bookstore, Leighton thought about Greta and Ivan, and all the memories that he had of the two of them together. In every one, they seemed so happy and so in love. He remembered when he caught them slow dancing at the bookshop one night. It was a Friday evening and he had gone to Twice Upon a Time to pick out a book to read that weekend. As he approached the pastel building, he saw a candle flicker in the front window while two silhouettes moved in perfect unison. He watched for a few minutes before turning around and heading home. He didn't want to disturb the special moment.

A vibration in Leighton's pocket brought him back to the present day. He pulled out his phone to find a text from July: *Goodnight Leighton :)* it said.

Leighton felt a foolish grin spread across his face. *Goodnight July :)* he quickly texted back.

Greta's story of how she and Ivan met came rushing over him. He couldn't help but notice the similarities between their meeting and his and July's. Was July just a passerby in his life, someone he would only know temporarily, or was there a possibility of her becoming a permanent fixture? He hoped for the latter, but he wasn't sure how realistic that was. After all, he would be leaving for college in just a few short weeks and July eventually had to continue her journey to Florida. *If Greta and Ivan could make it work then why can't we?* he thought.

When Leighton returned to the shop, he gave his sister a call, but she didn't answer. He tried again and then again once more, but it went to voicemail each time. *Where are you, Kennedy?* He didn't feel like waiting around but calling his parents was out of the question. *Maybe Carson can pick me up*, he thought, but Carson didn't answer his phone either. He thought about trying Monica, but she was probably in bed already, plus she couldn't leave her kids home alone. Leighton contemplated what to do. He was definitely still feeling the effects of the alcohol, but he wouldn't say that he was drunk anymore. He waited a few minutes in hopes that his sister or his best friend would call him back. If they didn't, then he'd just have to drive home himself. *It's only a short trip*, he reasoned. *I'll be fine.*

Fifteen minutes later, Leighton still hadn't heard from Kennedy or Carson. It was nearing midnight now, and he desperately wanted to go home. Drinking and driving was wrong, he knew, but enough time had gone by since his last shot and he was feeling only a little buzzed. Plus, this would be a one-time thing. He would absolutely not be making a habit of it, which made him feel a little bit better about doing it just this once. Content with his justification, Leighton reached into his pocket and grabbed his keys. Then he locked up the shop and unlocked his truck. Once in the driver's seat, he felt a twinge of guilt. He wasn't usually this reckless. If anything, he was quite the opposite—overcautious and always overthinking his next move. He rarely took risks; he much preferred to play it safe. But tonight, he had to get home, and he was out of options, other than walking, but that would take upward of thirty minutes and it was far too late for that. He took a deep breath, put his truck in drive, and pulled onto Main Street. *It'll be fine; it's just a five-minute ride.*

Leighton crawled down the quiet street, trying his best to go unnoticed, despite being the only vehicle on the road. Now that he was driving, he couldn't help but feel like he wasn't in as much control as he should be. He wouldn't say that he was drunk by any means, but he was definitely under the influence, and he was hyperaware of it now that he was behind the wheel. Fortunately, the trip to his house was pretty straightforward. Travel south on Main Street, turn right at the only intersection/stoplight, and then make the first left onto Dixie Circle; it was a cul-de-sac and his was the house at the end.

Despite being able to see the intersection from the bookstore, it seemed to take an eternity to actually get there. Leighton wanted to speed up so that he could get home sooner, but every time he tried to push down harder on the pedal, something stopped him. When he finally got to the traffic light, he let out a sigh of relief. He was off the main road and in the homestretch now.

Weewoo.

The sound, a stark contrast to the sleepy silence of the little town, startled Leighton so much that he could practically feel his heart leaping out of his chest. Panic descended on him as he saw the flashing red lights dance around his vehicle.

This can't be happening, he thought.

Leighton looked in his rearview mirror, desperate to see anything other than the grim reality he was so afraid to accept. He grimaced as his eyes focused on the object in the reflection—a police car trailing closely behind him. He was being pulled over.

The next few minutes were a blur. Leighton pulled to the side of the road and waited for the officer to approach. When she did, Leighton was met with a flashlight to his face. He winced as his eyes adjusted to the intense beam.

"Leighton Prescott," she said as she shifted her flashlight so that it was no longer blinding him, "you're out awfully late on a weeknight."

"Hi, Sheriff Montgomery," Leighton replied. "Yes, I suppose it is pretty late. I was just heading home."

"I see," she said, "and do you know why I pulled you over?"

"No, ma'am."

"You were driving barely fifteen miles per hour when the speed limit is thirty miles per hour." She tightened her gaze. "Is everything okay?"

"Oh," Leighton replied with genuine surprise. "Yes, everything is fine. I didn't even realize I was driving so slow. I guess I was just trying to be cautious."

The sheriff leaned her head in closer to the window, so that she was face-to-face with Leighton. "I've known you for a long time, Leighton. I can tell when you're not being honest. Are you sure there's nothing that you want to tell me?"

Leighton felt a bead of sweat drip down his forehead. He swallowed hard. "No, ma'am," he said with as much self-assurance and composure as he could muster.

Sheriff Montgomery let out a sigh. "I can smell the alcohol on your breath, son. It's obvious that you've been drinking," she pointed out flatly.

Leighton's chest was pounding now. He felt himself spiraling out of control. "I took a few shots earlier this evening," he confessed, "but I swear, I'm fine now. I'm not even a little bit drunk."

"It doesn't matter." The sheriff shook her head. "Montclair has a zero-tolerance policy for drinking and driving. I'm sorry, Leighton, but I'm going to have to take you back to the station."

"Please don't do this," Leighton pleaded. "I'm only two minutes away from my house. I'll walk the rest of the way." He looked at Sheriff Montgomery desperately. "And I promise to never, ever do this again. Just please, please let me go home."

"I'm sorry," she replied, "but I can't do that."

The sheriff's expression was stern and unwavering, and Leighton knew that he wasn't going to change her mind.

"Okay, I understand." Leighton looked down at his lap in defeat. *My parents are going to kill me*, he thought.

The ride to the station was short, but that didn't make it any less shameful. Sheriff Montgomery was kind enough to forgo the handcuffs but sitting in the back of a police cruiser, cuffed or not, was still a humbling experience. When they arrived, the sheriff swiftly ushered Leighton out of the car and into a holding cell. *As if this couldn't get any worse*, he thought, *I'm literally behind bars.*

Leighton slumped on the cold metal bench. Fortunately—if you could call any of this fortunate—he was the only detainee.

"You get one phone call," Sheriff Montgomery said from the cell door.

Leighton looked up but didn't say anything. It wasn't that he didn't know who to call; it was that he wasn't ready to call them. He knew exactly who it had to be. There was only one person who would be able to get him out of this mess, but that didn't make it any easier. So, he hesitated, as if procrastinating was going to weaken the blow.

"Would you like to take advantage of that now, or do you need more time to figure out who you'd like to contact?" the sheriff asked.

Leighton let out a deep sigh. "I'll do it now. I'm going to call my father."

"Okay, follow me."

The police station was quite small. There was a front desk immediately upon entry, two cubicles in the center of the room, the holding cell toward the back, a makeshift kitchen to the left of it, and then a private office to the right, which he assumed belonged to Sheriff Montgomery. Leighton followed her to a telephone on the wall.

"There you go," the sheriff said.

"Thank you, ma'am."

She gave him a nod and sat down at one of the cubicle desks.

Leighton slowly picked up the receiver and dialed his dad's cell phone number.

Ring.

Ring.

"This is Rod," his father answered sleepily.

Leighton felt guilty for waking him up, especially with the news that he was about to deliver. "Hi, Dad," he said apprehensively.

"Leighton?" his father asked with both surprise and concern. "I thought you were home by now. Is everything alright?"

"Yeah, well, kind of . . . I was on my way home when there was an, um . . . incident."

"What's going on, son?" Dad asked in a noticeably more alert and awake tone. "You're worrying me."

Leighton was terrified to speak the words, but he couldn't drag this out any longer. He had to rip the bandage off quickly. "I'm at the police station. I was arrested for drinking and driving."

His father was quiet for a few moments. In the background, Leighton could hear his mother pestering him with a brigade of questions.

Rod, what's going on?

Rod, is that our son?

Rod, where is he?

Rod, why won't you answer me?

"I'll be there in ten minutes," his father finally said before abruptly hanging up the phone.

Leighton let out a long sigh. Ten minutes wasn't enough time to prepare himself for the wrath of his father. See, Rod

Prescott was calm and collected ninety-nine percent of the time, but when he got mad, he got *really* mad, and Leighton was sure that tonight's incident was going to unleash that side of him. *This is going to suck*, he thought as he returned to the holding cell.

Dad came barging into the station not long after Leighton's phone call. Leighton was surprised to see him looking so disheveled: unbrushed hair, wrinkled T-shirt, baggy sweatpants, weathered tennis shoes. His father never left the house like this. Whenever he was out in public, he looked like he had just stepped out of a *GQ* magazine spread.

"What the hell is going on in here?" he asked as he entered the building.

Sheriff Montgomery stood up from the cubicle where she had been sitting. "Good evening, Mayor Prescott," she said. "I've brought your son in for driving under the influence. I found him going fifteen miles per hour under the speed limit. When I pulled him over, I could smell alcohol on his breath, and it became apparent that he had been drinking. As you know, Montclair has a zero-tolerance policy for this behavior."

"Yes, I am very much aware of the policy, Sheriff." Dad turned his attention to Leighton. "Son," he asked, "are these accusations true?"

"Yes," Leighton said, his gaze fixed on the ground. The shame he felt was overwhelming. He couldn't bear to look his father in the eyes.

"Well," his father replied, disappointment heavy in his tone, "we're going to have a serious discussion about this when we get home."

"Okay," Leighton mumbled.

"Sheriff, do you mind if we have a word alone? Perhaps in your office?" He gestured toward the small room.

Sheriff Montgomery hesitated. "Sure," she replied, a hint of apprehension in her voice. She walked over to the office. "After you."

"Thank you," Dad replied.

The sheriff followed him. When Leighton heard the door shut, he finally found the courage to look up.

Sheriff Montgomery's office wasn't very private; in fact, it wasn't private at all. It had a big window, like the ones that you'd see in an interrogation room, exhibiting everything that was going on inside. Leighton watched as his father and the sheriff engaged in what looked like a semi-heated discussion, and although he couldn't hear a single word that they were speaking, he knew exactly what was being said. It's why he'd called his father here instead of Kennedy. See, being a Prescott came with privilege. Leighton couldn't pretend that he wasn't aware of that or that it hadn't benefited him in the past. On an average day, he disliked the special treatment that he received for being the son of the mayor, but there were times when he needed to exploit it, and this was one of them.

His father would be able to strike up a deal with Sheriff Montgomery, and Leighton would get a slap on the wrist instead of a mark on his record. It didn't make him feel superior or proud, quite the opposite actually, but it had to be done. The stakes were too high.

As the minutes marched on, Leighton noticed that his father's efforts were being met with opposition. The sheriff was putting up a fight. Dad was clearly trying to negotiate some sort of deal, but Sheriff Montgomery didn't seem to be having it. She kept shaking her head, a stern look on her face. Leighton tried not to worry—after all, his father was incredibly persistent. But the sheriff appeared to be unwavering. Dad was beginning to look desperate. Finally, Sheriff Montgomery threw up the white flag, metaphorically of course. Dad let out a visible sigh of relief and the two shook hands. *Thank God*, Leighton thought.

"Let's go, son," his father said as he exited the office.

Leighton got up quickly and walked over to the holding cell gate, waiting for the sheriff to unlock it.

When she did, he politely said, "Thank you, ma'am," but Sheriff Montgomery didn't reply. Instead, she met his gaze with bitter, scornful eyes. She wasn't trying to hide her displeasure in Mayor Prescott coercing her into disobeying the law. Leighton could understand her contempt, but it didn't make it any easier to be regarded in such a way. Leighton had always been well-behaved and agreeable. He was easy to get along with and he rarely ever got into trouble. He didn't want the sheriff to dislike him, but he was afraid it might be too late. He exited the police station swiftly, head down, vowing to never make this walk of shame again.

"What the hell were you thinking?" Dad roared when he and Leighton got into his sedan.

"I-I wasn't thinking," he stammered. "It was a stupid mistake. I'm sorry. I'm so, so sorry."

"Sorry isn't good enough, Leighton. You almost ruined everything that we've worked so hard for. Do you understand that? Not to mention, the fact that you could have hurt your-self or someone else!"

Leighton was about to reply, but Dad continued before he could mutter anything. "You can't be doing shit like this. You have a reputation to uphold. You're a goddamn Prescott, for Christ's sake! Our family has an image to maintain. How dare you jeopardize that!"

Leighton knew he had to choose his next words wise-ly. He couldn't remember the last time that his father was this angry, and he needed him to calm down before they got home, otherwise he'd have to face the wrath of both his parents at the same time. If he could just rein in his father then he'd only have to worry about his mother, who would almost certainly be waiting to berate him as soon as he entered the house.

"I know, Dad, and all I can say is that I am so sorry," Leighton said. "I had a lapse of judgment, but I swear, it'll never happen again. I feel like an idiot. I hate myself. I wish I could go back in time and do it all differently, but I can't, so I'm going to use this as a learning experience, and I'm going to grow from it."

Dad didn't respond right away. Had Leighton's attempt to appease his father been unsuccessful?

"Good," his father replied at last, and that was all that was said for the rest of the car ride. Leighton was thankful for the silence, even if it was only for the five minutes it took to get to his house. It gave him time to relax, which he suspected was true for his father, too, who looked considerably more temperate now.

When they pulled into the garage, Dad spoke up again. "I

would imagine that your mother is not too happy with you. She's probably not happy with me either. She must've called at least a dozen times while we were at the station. But I'm thinking that she'll be so distracted with you that I should be able to get off the hook for not answering her calls." He flashed Leighton a mischievous smirk when he said this, and Leighton felt a flood of relief and appreciation that he and his father were already on better terms.

"Yeah, I figured as much. I can't say that I'm looking forward to it, but I know it's what I deserve. I'm glad that I can at least be your scapegoat," Leighton said with a laugh.

Dad laughed, too. "Why don't you head inside? I'll be in shortly."

"Okay."

As Leighton exited the vehicle and walked toward the door, he thought about the last time, and the only other time, that he had ever screwed up so royally. It was homecoming night, freshman year. His buddies had convinced him to steal alcohol from his parents' liquor cabinet so they could get drunk before the dance. Leighton didn't want to do it, but he also didn't want his friends to think he was lame. So he swiped a bottle of Jack Daniel's and the boys passed it around until they were slurring and tripping over their own feet. When they got to the school gymnasium, it didn't take long for the chaperones to discover they were all intoxicated.

Fifteen minutes later, Dad and Mom were there, and Leighton was in the most trouble he had ever been in. Whiskey was supposed to cloud your memory, but no amount of alcohol could have made Leighton forget just how angry his parents were at him that night. They berated him for the better part of an hour. When they finally finished, his mother looked at him and solemnly said, "You're supposed to be the good one."

Leighton remembered how conflicted that had made him feel. On the one hand, he wanted to be the well-behaved and dutiful son. On the other hand, he hated the pressure that came along with being "the good one." He already had enough expectations to fulfill; he didn't need any more.

When Leighton entered the house, his mother was sitting at the kitchen island. He expected to see her there, but what he didn't expect to see was his sister perched beside her. Despite acting amicable at his father's reelection party, his mother and sister weren't exactly getting along. In public settings, they pretended to be civil, but it was all a facade. Behind closed doors, they rarely spoke or even interacted. Yet here they were, together. Kennedy was even rubbing Mom's back as if to console her.

"Leighton!" Mom shrieked when she caught sight of him. "Oh, I have just been sick with worry! I swear I must've called your father over a hundred times." She got up and rushed over to Leighton. "It was all a misunderstanding, right? What am I saying? Of course it was," she continued before Leighton could respond. "That sheriff was probably just bored and looking for something to do. How dare she falsely accuse my son of such misconduct! I should have your father dismiss her of her duties. I was never fond of her anyway, if I'm being honest. Surely, there is someone more qualified for the position—"

"Mom, stop!" Leighton finally exclaimed. He took her hands, which were cupping his cheeks as if he were a child, and pushed them toward her chest. She looked at him with startled eyes. "Sheriff Montgomery didn't make anything up. I had a few drinks tonight and then I tried to drive home."

Mom's mouth fell open.

"It was a mistake. I'm sorry. I'll never do it again."

His mother paused for a moment and Leighton could see her bewilderment turning into something else—rage.

"A *mistake*?!" she cried, throwing her arms in the air. "That's what you think this was? A *mistake*?"

"Yes, Mom. An incredibly stupid mistake, and one that I will never, ever make again," Leighton promised in a calm, reassuring tone despite his oncoming frustration with his mother's theatrics. He knew that she had every right to be angry with him, and he had suspected that she was going to act like this, but it didn't make it any less aggravating. He deserved this, though, so he would continue to stand there until her inevitable lecture was complete.

"Leighton," she said, "leaving the milk out to spoil is a mistake. Forgetting your wallet at home is a mistake. Making a wrong turn and getting lost is a mistake. Drinking and driving is much more than a fucking *mistake*, especially when you are the mayor's son who is being groomed to hold office next. How could you be so stupid? How could you be so selfish?"

Mom began to cry, and Leighton felt that familiar pang of guilt.

"I'm sorry, Mom. Really, I am. Please don't cry," he pleaded.

"Did you ruin everything? Everything that we worked so hard for?"

"No, Dad made a deal with Sheriff Montgomery. She dropped the charges. There's no record that it ever even happened."

"You're lucky your father is the mayor," Mom replied haughtily.

"Yes, I am."

Before Mom could say anything else, Dad came in and disrupted the conversation. "I hope I'm not interrupting anything," he said, as if he wasn't fully aware that his wife and son were in the middle of a heated exchange. "We have to go pick up Leighton's truck." He scanned the room and Leighton could see that he, too, was surprised to see Kennedy there. "Ken, would you mind driving Leighton's truck back home? It's right around the corner. I'll give you a ride."

"Yeah, no problem." Kennedy got up from her seat and hurried out of the kitchen.

Leighton's sister was probably relieved to have an excuse to get out of there. She had been on the receiving end of Mom's condemnations many times, and he wouldn't be surprised if this episode, even if it wasn't directed toward her, brought back bad memories.

"I'm incredibly disappointed in you," Mom said to Leighton once they were alone.

"I'm incredibly disappointed in myself," Leighton replied. He looked at the ground.

"You should be," Mom said. "What you did was totally unacceptable. Absolutely asinine. You know better than this,

Leighton. I'm just hoping this major lapse in judgment was the result of grief and not something else."

Leighton knew what she was insinuating, of course, but he chose not to let it get to him, at least not visibly.

"It was. I haven't been thinking clearly all day."

"Well, maybe you should go talk to someone. After all, we really can't afford for you to be making any more life-altering *mistakes*. You got away with it this time, but next time you won't be so lucky, and then you can kiss your future goodbye. Everything that we worked so hard for will be thrown out the window!"

"I don't need to talk to someone. This was a one-time thing. I've learned my lesson, I promise."

Mom narrowed her eyes in suspicion. She waited a few moments before letting out a sigh. "Fine," she said, "but if I notice any more unusual behavior, I'm scheduling a therapy appointment. Grief can make you act in ways that you otherwise wouldn't, so if you are struggling with the passing of Greta, then we need to do something about it."

"Okay." Leighton extended his arms and invited his mother in for a hug. It was his way of offering her an olive branch. If she accepted, then he would know that their spat was over.

Mom hesitated at first, trying to play coy, but after a few seconds, she gave in. She always had a soft spot for Leighton, and he'd be lying if he said that he didn't exploit it sometimes.

That could've been a lot worse, Leighton thought as he embraced his mother. He smiled as he held her, thankful that she hadn't made their exchange any more difficult.

When he released her, he could see that she was smiling, too, despite her attempt to quickly change her expression.

"I'm gonna go to bed now, if that's okay?" he asked.

"Yes, of course. You must be exhausted."

"I am. It was a long day." He started to walk away, but he only made it a few steps when his mother called after him.

"Hey!"

"Yeah?" He turned around to look at her.

"Give me your phone," she demanded with an out-stretched hand.

"What? Why?"

"Because you're grounded. No phone, no truck, no leaving the house for the next twenty-four hours."

Leighton's mouth fell open. "Are you being serious? This isn't fair! I'll give you my phone, but can you at least let me go to the bookstore tomorrow?"

"No," Mom replied firmly. "This isn't up for discussion. I've made up my mind. You should just be grateful that I'm punishing you for only twenty-four hours. If it weren't for the fact that we just lost Greta, and I'm chalking up your horrible decision to emotional distress, you'd be grounded for a hell of a lot longer. Do you realize how monumentally you screwed up?"

She has a point. "Okay, fine," Leighton said as he surrendered his cell phone.

"Thank you," Mom said as she took the mobile device and put it in the pocket of her silk robe.

"I'm going to bed now," Leighton said, despite having no intention of actually doing so. A few minutes ago, before he was informed of his punishment, he had planned to go right to sleep, but now he had to figure out a way to contact July and let her know that he wouldn't be at the bookstore tomorrow. After all, the two had an unspoken agreement to meet there each day. What would July think if she showed up and Leighton was nowhere to be found? Leighton had to relay a message to her, but how? Calling or texting her was out of the question, and she didn't have social media, so he couldn't reach out to her through there either.

I'll write her a letter, he thought, *and then I'll have Kennedy deliver it to her.* Sure, it seemed a bit archaic. He couldn't remember the last time he'd penned a handwritten letter. How many guys his age were actually penning notes to the person they were crushing on? But he couldn't think of any better option. Plus, maybe July would find it endearing, like something out of a Hallmark movie. He needed to suck up to her anyway, because once she read the letter and learned about what he had done, she would more than likely be upset with him. Hopefully this gesture would help to make her a little less angry, or maybe even not angry at all, though the latter was probably wishful thinking.

Once in his room, Leighton changed into sweats and sat down at his desk. Before he began writing, he looked out the window and noticed Kennedy walking back to the guesthouse. He tried to get her attention by tapping on the glass, but his attempts were unsuccessful, so he messaged her on Facebook instead. Fortunately, his mother hadn't thought to confiscate his computer.

Leighton: Hey, Ken
Kennedy: Hey

What's up?

Why are you messaging me on FB??

Leighton: Not much. Mom took my phone away so I couldn't call/text.

I wanted to ask if you could do me a favor?

Kennedy: Ah, gotcha.

That sucks : /

Sure, what do you need?

Leighton: Can you bring a letter to July tomorrow morning?

Kennedy: A letter?

Leighton: Yeah, I need to tell her that I won't be at the bookstore tomorrow. I'm on house arrest for the next twenty-four hours :/ and I have no other way of contacting her.

Kennedy: Okay, I can drop it off before I head to the bakery.

Does that work?

Leighton: Yeah, that's perfect.

You can just slip it under her door.

She's room 13.

Kennedy: Sounds good.

Are you gonna come by to give it to me?

Leighton: Yeah, I just have to write it.

I'll be over ASAP.

Thanks, Ken.

Kennedy: No problem <3

Leighton closed his laptop and pulled a notebook out from his desk drawer.

July,

I hope you don't think it's weird that I'm writing you this letter, but it's my only way of getting in touch with you (more on that later).

I wanted to let you know that I won't be at the bookstore today because I'm on house arrest until later this evening (see next paragraph).

I screwed up last night. When I got back to the bookstore, I called Kennedy (as promised) as well as Carson, but when neither of them answered, I decided to drive myself home. Big mistake. I got pulled over and arrested for DUI. Fortunately, the charges were dropped and I was released, but my parents have justifiably grounded me (though only for twenty-four hours, which will be more like twelve by the time you read this).

I know you are probably upset with me, but I need to see you tonight. I'll come by the motel after my parents go to sleep. It will probably be around 10:00 or 11:00 p.m. I hope you'll be there.

Leighton

Leighton read over the letter a couple of times. It wasn't perfect, but it would have to do. After all, it was nearing the early hours of the morning now, and Kennedy, who was already doing him a favor by delivering the note to July, was waiting up for him to drop it off. So Leighton folded it up and put it in an envelope with **JULY** written in big block letters across the front. Then he took the quick trip out back to give the letter to his sister.

When Leighton approached the guesthouse, he lifted his hand up to knock, but before he could do so, Kennedy was already opening the door.

"What are you psychic or something?"

"My Spidey senses were tingling," Kennedy replied with a grin.

Leighton laughed and handed her the envelope. "Thank you for doing this for me," he said.

"It's the least I can do," she responded, her face somber. "I saw that you called me a bunch of times tonight, which I assume was for a ride home. If I had only answered, then none of this would have happened. I'm really sorry. I was watching a movie and my phone was on silent."

Leighton could see the guilt in his sister's eyes, and it made him feel terrible. "Aw, Ken. Don't blame yourself for what happened tonight. I could've called Mom or Dad or even an Uber, when you didn't answer, but I chose to be stupid and drive myself home instead. The only person at fault here is me."

Kennedy gave him a sympathetic look.

"And honestly," he continued, "it could've been a lot worse. The charges were dropped, I'm only grounded for a day, and most importantly, I've learned a valuable lesson."

"That's true."

"Plus, it looks like my screw-up might've had one positive

thing come out of it . . . you and Mom . . . ? It seemed like you two were actually getting along."

"Yeah," Kennedy said with a laugh, "believe it or not, we were. She came by here shortly after Dad left to go to the police station. She said that she was going crazy with worry and she needed company. So we went back to the house and had a glass of wine, and we had a pretty good conversation, too. It was actually really . . . nice." She smiled, and Leighton could tell that she wanted to fight it, but she couldn't.

Leighton pulled Kennedy into a hug. "I'm so happy for you, Ken. I've been wanting you and Mom to patch things up for so long now."

Kennedy paused. "Me, too," she quietly confessed.

Leighton gave her a tight squeeze before releasing her from their embrace. "You should probably be getting to bed now," he pointed out. "You've got a bakery to run in the morning."

"And a letter to deliver," Kennedy replied, waving the envelope.

"Thank you again for doing this for me."

"No problem."

"Room 13!" Leighton called as he turned toward the main house.

"Room 13!" Kennedy repeated before closing her door.

Leighton felt a grin spread across his face. He loved having Kennedy home again, even if it was just temporarily, and it wasn't because she was willing to help him with things, like delivering his letter to July, but because she was genuinely his best friend.

When they were younger, they would do everything together: ride bikes, climb trees, play hide-and-seek. Even when Kennedy got older and it was obvious that she'd rather hang out with her friends, she still always made time for her little brother. In fact, up until she got kicked out, they had a weekly tradition where they'd watch a scary movie together every Sunday night. They called it Spooky Sunday. Leighton was sure that he and his sister had seen every horror flick ever made, from big-ticket blockbusters to low-budget indie films.

Leighton recalled the last Spooky Sunday that they shared.

"I have something to tell you," Kennedy had said as the *Halloween* theme song played in the background.

Leighton perked up. "What is it?"

"I got a business loan. I'm opening a bakery!" His sister beamed.

She'd been so happy, and he was so happy for her, too. "But what about school?" he asked, knowing that his parents would be wondering the same thing.

"I'm not going," she stated matter-of-factly. "I'm doing what I want to do."

Leighton had pulled her into a hug. "I'm so proud of you, Ken." And he was so proud, but he couldn't help but feel a little worried as well. He knew how his parents could be, especially his mother, and he'd feared that they wouldn't approve of Kennedy's change of plans, but he could have never predicted just how bad the falling-out would be. The contempt, the resentment, the years of little to no contact.

Could they have finally moved past it? Leighton thought as he walked back to the main house. Maybe it was wishful thinking, but after seeing them together, he was hopeful that his mother and sister might finally reconcile.

Day Six

LEIGHTON SLEPT IN THE NEXT morning, which wasn't something he often did, being that he usually had to wake up for school or for work. But without any obligations or any responsibilities for the day, he figured that he might as well take advantage of the opportunity for some extra shuteye. It was nearly noon when he finally got up, and he realized that July had probably already received and read his letter. He wondered what she was thinking and feeling. Was she mad at him for what he did? Did she feel betrayed that he'd broken his promise? Was she disappointed that they wouldn't be spending the day together? Would she be waiting for him at her motel later that night? Did she even want to see him?

Stop it, Leighton thought. He needed to calm his racing mind, so he splashed some water on his face and headed downstairs to see his parents. He could always count on them to provide distraction.

Once on the main floor, Leighton found his mother exactly where he'd expected to—in the kitchen. She was preparing a colorful salad for lunch.

"Hey, hun!" she said cheerfully as he entered the room.

"Hey, mom," he replied, "you're in an awfully good mood."

"I am! We've got a busy day ahead of us!"

"We do?" he asked, confused. "I thought I was grounded?"

"You are," she said as she poured dressing over the bowl of vegetables, "but I thought it'd be nice if we went to the store and picked up some things for your dorm room. You know, to get you excited for school! It's only a few weeks away now and you hardly ever talk about it. You spend all your time at that bookstore"—she turned to face him—"but this is what kids your age *should* be doing." She pointed a pair of tongs in his direction. "So far, I've done all of the shopping myself. Don't you want to choose your own bedding and desk supplies and whatnot?"

"Yeah," Leighton lied, trying to sound enthused. But the truth was, he didn't want to do any of that because he wasn't excited to go to school, and a comforter or a notebook or a shower caddy wasn't going to change that.

"Fabulous!" Mom chirped. "We'll head out after lunch. Would you like some of my salad? It's delicious!" She took a big forkful of lettuce and shoved it in her mouth to emphasize just how tasty it was.

"No, thanks. I'll just have a banana. I want to shower and stuff before we leave."

"Suit yourself," Mom replied with a shrug.

Leighton went back up to his room to get ready. Last night, when he was informed of his punishment, he'd thought that being stuck at home all day was going to be bad, but this was so much worse. Just the thought of putting on a show for the next however many hours was exhausting. He let out a loud sigh and mulled over his options:

1.   Tell his mom that he didn't want to go shopping for school supplies because he didn't want to go to school.

2.   Pretend to be sick so he wouldn't have to go shopping for school supplies . . . and so he wouldn't have to tell his mom that he didn't want to go to school.

3.   Go shopping for school supplies and pretend to be excited so his mom wouldn't know that he didn't want to go to school.

Option number one was what Leighton should do. After all, honesty *was* the best policy. But dropping that kind of truth bomb on his mother just twelve hours after he was arrested for drunk driving was risky, at best. Option number two was the safest, but it was also the most cowardly. Did Leighton really want to take the easy way out? Option number three was the least attractive to Leighton, but it would appease his mother, which strategically was a smart move. By keeping her happy, he was ensuring that his punishment would not be extended past the twenty-four hours that she'd quoted the night prior. Mom could be petty, and if Leighton did something that she didn't like, she might retaliate just to spite him.

So, Leighton went with the final option. Sure, it might be excruciating, but it would set him up for the best chance to see July sooner rather than later, and the only thing he really wanted was to spend time with July. So, he'd go shopping with his mom, and he'd enthusiastically pick out items for college, and Mom would be pleased that he was doing everything that she wanted and expected him to do. And who knows, maybe it would end up being an enjoyable experience. Maybe, just maybe, it would make Leighton have a change of heart and he'd want to go to school after all. That would be ideal. Then he wouldn't have to worry about disappointing his parents or sacrificing his happiness. *If only things could be that easy.*

Mom was even more talkative than usual on the way to the store. She zealously shared stories about her time at Georgia State University and repeatedly emphasized how *transformative* her four years in college were. She gushed about Greek life, studying abroad, and internships. Leighton had to admit, it did sound nice, but Mom was also notorious for embellishing things, especially when she was trying to sell something. She was persuasive. "You'll see," she said again and again. "These are going to be the best years of your life."

Leighton nodded along, laughing here and there, pretending to be engaged in the conversation. The truth was, his mother's stories did pique his interest, and they made him feel the most optimistic about school that he had felt since, well, ever, really, but it still wasn't enough. It reminded him of when his buddies would talk about college. They were all so excited to go, and sometimes their excitement rubbed off on him, but it was only ever temporary. As soon as the conversation ended, Leighton would hear that voice in the back of his mind that was saying—no, *screaming*—that going away to school and studying politics and becoming the mayor wasn't his dream, it was his parents' dream.

Leighton thought about July and all the advice that she had given him these past few days. She had said many things that stuck with him, but there was one phrase in particular that kept playing on repeat since he heard it. It was from their first night together, when she said, *"My mom never told me what I should do. She always encouraged me to follow my heart and live a life that makes me happy."* Why couldn't Leighton's mother be like that? Why was it that with his mom, love and acceptance were conditional? Mom was happy with Leighton only when he was doing what she wanted him to do. As soon as he veered off course or even questioned the path that she so brazenly pushed him to follow, she became resentful and cruel. Leighton recalled how his mother had treated Kennedy after she decided to pursue her dreams. Mom had completely cut ties with his sister, speaking to her only when required for public functions. And even after Kennedy's bakery proved to be a huge success, Mom still wasn't proud—or even approving, for that matter. She continued to hold a grudge and act as if Kennedy's accomplishments were beneath the ones that she had wanted for her daughter.

Leighton felt that familiar lump forming in his throat. He tried to swallow it, like he always did, but it was to no avail. It never was. He wanted things to be different, but he knew that you can't expect change when you're staying stagnant. Change demands action, and it's usually the kind that requires you to step out of your comfort zone. Was he really ready to shift the trajectory of his life?

He looked out the car window, while he and his mother waited at a red light, and there, perched on the sideview mirror, was a beautiful butterfly, a monarch, to be exact. Leighton felt a flood of emotion as he remembered the words from Greta's letter: *Whatever you choose will be the right decision. Continue to be your most authentic self and always, always follow your heart.* He knew what he needed to do.

"I don't want to go to school," Leighton said with an abruptness that even he found startling.

The light turned green, but his mother didn't move. They sat there for a minute before the person behind them grew impatient and honked their horn. Mom started to drive, but she remained silent.

Leighton waited a few moments before he spoke up again. "Are you going to say anything in response?"

"There's nothing to say," Mom replied with a cool shrug. "You're not thinking clearly. Grief is messing with your head, just like it did last night." She took her right hand off the steering wheel and placed it on Leighton's shoulder. "It's normal to have questions, and doubts, and lapses in judgment, especially after losing a loved one. You've just hit a rough patch. We'll get through this." She gave his arm a comforting squeeze.

"That's not what's going on, Mom. This isn't some knee-jerk reaction to Greta's passing. I've been feeling this way for a while now. I even tried to tell you the other night, the night of Dad's party, I just didn't come right out and say it. Remember when we talked about setting boundaries and letting me make my own decisions? That all stems from this. From me not wanting to go to school. I've just been too afraid to flat out say it because I don't want to disappoint you. Or Dad. But I also don't want to sacrifice my own happiness by trying to make you guys happy. I was hoping that the idea of school would grow on me as it got closer, but it hasn't. If anything, I'm even more aware now than I was before that college and politics and the whole Prescott legacy isn't for me. That's just not the future that I see for myself." Leighton paused. "I'm sorry," he said quietly.

"It sounds like your nerves are getting the better of you, hun. I know that leaving home for the first time can be intimidating, but once you're on campus and you've set up your dorm room and made friends, you'll settle right in. By the time Thanksgiving rolls around, you probably won't even want to come back to Montclair!" Mom let out a self-assured laugh.

Leighton looked at his mother in disbelief. "Are you being serious right now, Mom? I'm trying to open up to you, and you're completely ignoring everything that I'm saying. It's like I'm speaking, but you're refusing to listen. Do you realize how frustrating that is?" Leighton paused, but his mother didn't respond. "So I'm going to say it one more time and I'm going to be very clear because I won't repeat myself again: I don't want to go to Emory, I don't want to study political science, and I don't want to be the mayor of Montclair."

Mom sighed heavily and shook her head. "I don't understand. This was always your dream. What changed?"

"No, Mom. It was always *your* dream," Leighton corrected her.

Mom sighed again. "What about your scholarship? You worked so hard for it . . . straight A's every semester, all those extracurricular activities, class president, valedictorian . . . Was it all for nothing?"

"Of course it wasn't for nothing. Those are still accomplishments that I'm incredibly proud of."

Mom clenched the steering wheel, and her hands were shaking.

"The scholarship can go to someone more deserving," Leighton continued. "It's not like I needed it anyway. Give it to someone who actually *wants* to be in school, someone who can't afford their tuition otherwise. That's who should have had it all along. It would be wrong for me to take that opportunity away from someone else."

Mom was quiet for a few minutes. "I don't know what to say. You're breaking my heart. You realize that, right?"

Leighton didn't respond. He knew what his mother was doing. She was trying to make him feel guilty in hopes that he'd change his mind, but he wasn't going to.

Mom pulled over to the side of the road and started to cry. Her weeping was big and exaggerated; it was more of a show than genuine emotion. Typical.

She continued to sob, waiting for Leighton to comfort her, to console her. She wanted him to take it all back. But Leighton remained silent. He kept his eyes fixed on his lap. They could stay like this for the rest of the day for all he cared. He wasn't going to give in.

"You're really just going to sit there and watch your mother cry?" Mom asked. "How dare you?" Her tone was angry now and her eyes were magically dry. "After everything that

I've done for you. This is how you repay me? By throwing it all away?"

Leighton took a deep breath. "I don't think this is how it's supposed to work, Mom," he fired back. "I shouldn't have to *repay* you for being a good parent. I'm grateful, of course, but I shouldn't have to do something that doesn't make me happy because it's what you want me to do.

"This is the same thing that you did to Kennedy, and now you're doing it to me. Your pride and stubbornness ruined your relationship with your daughter. Are you really willing to ruin your relationship with your son, too?"

Leighton let the question hang in the air. He knew that he didn't need to say anything else. He looked over at his mother. Her eyes were filled with tears, but this time, he could tell that they were real.

She surrendered after a few minutes. "Okay," she said, her voice hoarse.

Leighton couldn't believe it. *Did I actually get through to her?*

"And you're sure this is what you want?"

"Yes. One hundred percent positive."

"Okay." She wiped at her damp eyes. "Do you know what you want to do instead?"

"Kind of. I know that I want to do something with the bookstore. I just don't know exactly what that is, at least not yet."

"Well, you're going to have to figure that out soon," his mother pointed out.

"I know," Leighton replied. "I will, I promise."

The two were quiet for a moment before Mom interrupted the silence

"Would you be opposed to taking online classes?" she asked timidly. "I would hate for you to give up on continuing your education entirely. You could choose your major and your courses. You could even enroll part time so it doesn't interfere with the bookstore too much."

Leighton considered his mother's proposition. *It's actually not a bad idea*, he thought. He loved to read and write, so he would definitely be interested in taking some English classes. Maybe that could even be his new major. He'd also like to take a creative writing course, if they offered it. Leighton realized that he didn't actually hate the idea of going to school; he just hated the idea of going *away* to school and studying politics. If he could stay in Montclair and major in something that he was truly interested in, then the idea of college did sound appealing to him.

"No, I wouldn't be opposed to that," he replied. "Not at all. I actually think it's a great idea."

"Really?!" his mother exclaimed.

"Yeah. I don't know why I didn't think of it myself. I want to stay home so I can still work at the bookstore, but if I could do that *and* go to college, then I would be getting the best of both worlds. It's a perfect arrangement, really."

Mom squealed. "Oh, hun, I'm so glad to hear that!"

Leighton smiled. He was glad to see that he and his mother could find common ground, a place where they could both be happy. "Thanks, Mom."

"For what?"

"For being understanding. And cooperative. And accepting. I know this probably isn't easy for you, but I really appreciate you letting me make my own decisions."

"You don't have to thank me, Leighton. I'm your mother—I'm supposed to support you no matter what. And that's what I'm going to do from now on." Mom paused. "I'm not going to make the same mistake twice," she confessed, her voice shaky now. "What I did to Kennedy . . . Those are years that I can never get back. I don't want to have those same regrets with you."

His mother's words were laced with guilt, and Leighton couldn't help but feel sorry for her, even if the falling-out between her and Kennedy was her own fault. "I don't want that either," he replied earnestly. "Speaking of Kennedy, it was nice to see you two together last night. I know the circumstances weren't ideal, but I'm so glad that you guys are getting along again."

Mom's lips curled up into a heartfelt smile. "Me, too," she said before she and Leighton settled into a comfortable silence.

When they arrived at the store, Mom asked Leighton if he still wanted to go inside. After all, he wasn't going away to school anymore, so he really didn't need all the things that they had talked about earlier that day. Leighton suggested that they take a look around anyway; it'd be a good way to pass some time. He also pointed out that he could still use some notebooks for his online classes. Mom's face lit up when he said this, and Leighton was glad to see her happy, especially when it wasn't at his expense. *Compromise is a beautiful thing*, he thought with a satisfied grin.

The two perused the store for the better part of two

hours, taking their time as they browsed the aisles in each of the many departments. While they shopped, they shared lighthearted conversation, reminiscing on old memories and inside jokes. Leighton couldn't remember the last time he had enjoyed his mother's company this much. Without the pressure and expectations, their relationship really flourished. He just hoped it would stay this way.

When Leighton and his mother weren't talking, Leighton thought about July and all the possibilities between them now that he wasn't going away to school. He daydreamed about July staying in Montclair and working with him at the bookstore. He got lost in the idea of taking their relationship to the next step. He imagined himself calling her his girlfriend and July calling him her boyfriend. He pictured what it would be like to go on dates, to take road trips, to spend holidays together.

In the past week, Leighton had learned a lot about himself and who he wanted to be. His future was now his for the taking and he had a pretty good idea of how he wanted it to look. It seemed like he was on the path to achieving that vision, but there was still one missing piece: July. Although they had known each other for only a few days, Leighton was feeling more and more like July was someone that he couldn't live without. Now the question was, how was he going to convince her to stay?

On the way home, Mom and Leighton stopped at the farmers' market and picked up some homemade pasta, seasonal vegetables, freshly baked bread, and artisanal cheese.

"I have a special dinner planned tonight," Mom said with a sparkle in her eye. "We are going to celebrate because the whole family will be together."

At first, Leighton thought that his mother had just meant him, his father, and her—after all, he had been skipping out on supper for the past several days—but when Leighton saw his mom grab a bag of spinach and mozzarella ravioli, Kennedy's favorite, he knew that his sister would be joining them. This was a pretty big deal, considering the fact that Kennedy hadn't shared a meal with them in years, not since that infamous dinner when they had last had spinach and mozzarella ravioli.

When his mother approached him, clutching the cheese-filled squares like a prized possession, Leighton raised a brow and nodded toward the pasta, acknowledging its significance.

In return, Mom flashed him an exuberant grin, which confirmed what Leighton already knew.

He smiled and shook his head. He still couldn't believe that his mother and sister had finally made amends. *Who would have thought that something so positive could come from one of the worst decisions of my life?*

"When do you think I should tell Dad about my change of plans?" Leighton asked as he and his mother drove from the market back to their house.

"That's up to you, hun."

"You're not going to say anything to him?" he asked this hesitantly, treading lightly. Normally, his mother would be quick to tattle, but with her drastic change in attitude, what was once characteristic wasn't necessarily the case anymore. Leighton didn't want to offend her, especially when things were going so well.

"Of course not," she said. "This is your news to share. You talk to your father whenever you're ready. My lips are sealed until then." Mom pretended to zip her lips closed, lock them, and then throw away the key.

Leighton smiled. "Thanks, Mom. I'll probably tell him after dinner tonight. I don't want to wait too long. Better sooner rather than later, right?"

"Right," she agreed, giving his bicep a comforting squeeze.

Leighton leaned his head against the car window and turned his attention to the passing scenery. *I like this version of Mom*, he thought as he watched the sun-hazed blur of pastel buildings, neatly trimmed plants, and cobblestone sidewalks.

Mom's softer demeanor reminded Leighton of how she was when he was younger. As a child, Leighton suffered from frequent nightmares, and it wasn't uncommon for him to wake in the middle of the night, crying for his parents. Mom always came to his rescue. She'd climb in bed with Leighton and wrap him up in her arms. Then she'd sing him a lullaby until he peacefully drifted back to sleep. Leighton could still hear her song: "Sleep, pretty darling, do not cry and I will sing a lullaby. Golden slumbers fill your eyes, smiles awake you when you rise."

When they got home, Mom started preparing the food. Leighton offered to help, but his mother shooed him away.

"I've got it under control," she reassured him. "Go up to your room. Chill out before Kennedy gets here. I think she said she'd be coming over around six."

"Okay." Leighton was relieved to be off the hook. While he had undoubtedly been enjoying his mother's company, he was craving some alone time, especially before their family dinner that night. He had to center himself and get his thoughts together. A lot had happened in the past few days and Leighton hadn't fully processed it yet, especially the most recent events. The life that he had been living last week was drastically different than the one that he found himself in today, and in many ways, he felt like a new person. Everything that had occurred, both good and bad—a chance encounter, a tragic passing, a regrettable mistake, a long overdue conversation—had all helped him get to where he was right now, and for the first time in a long time, he felt like he was exactly where he needed to be.

Kennedy arrived at quarter past the hour. "Sorry," she called as she shuffled through the door in a flour-dusted T-shirt, "we had a customer come in five minutes before close and she couldn't decide between a traditional cake, cupcakes, or cake pops for her son's birthday party. She must've been from out of town because I've never seen her before. Maybe all that social media marketing is finally paying off." She entered the kitchen and placed a big white cardboard box on the island. "I've brought goodies, by the way."

"Oh, how nice of you, hun!" Mom said as she hurried over to Kennedy. She gave her a hug and a kiss on the cheek.

It was still weird for Leighton to see his mother and sister like this, after years of conflict and contempt. For so long, it seemed as if their relationship was in a state of disrepair, yet in one night they were able to turn the tables, to reconcile, to fix what was broken. Perhaps it was because it was long over-due or maybe it was because the timing was just right, either way, Leighton didn't want to question it. He was just glad to see his mother and sister getting along as if their falling-out had never even happened. *I guess it's been a transformative time for us all*, he thought.

"Hey, dude," Kennedy said as she sat down next to Leighton.

"Hey," he replied as he picked at the perfectly arranged charcuterie board that his mother had assembled.

"She really went all out, huh?" Kennedy nodded toward the impressive display.

"She got your favorite ravioli, too."

Kennedy's face lit up. "Spinach and mozzarella?"

"Yep."

"I can't believe she remembered," Kennedy admitted, her voice a bit shaky.

Leighton could swear that he saw tears well up in his sister's eyes, but she quickly wiped them away. Kennedy acted tough, but beneath her hard exterior, she was sensitive. And though she'd never admit it, Leighton knew that his sister had been deeply hurt by their mother's neglect these past few years and that she'd been yearning for her affection again.

"Dinner will be served in twenty minutes!" Mom chirped as she buzzed around the kitchen. "We're just waiting for your father."

She started humming while she bounced back and forth between stirring the pasta and the sauce. "Oh, this is going to be so lovely!" she exclaimed. "What a pleasure to have every-one back together again!"

A few moments later, Leighton heard the garage door open, which meant that his father was home.

"It smells great in here!" Dad said as he entered the kitchen.

"Hey, Dad!" Leighton and Kennedy said simultaneously.

"Hey, kids!" Dad replied with a big smile. He gave each of them a hug. Then he grabbed a handful of olives off the charcuterie board and popped them in his mouth.

Next, he gave Mom a hug from behind. "Hey, babe," he said as he kissed her on the cheek.

Mom giggled at the gesture before turning serious, or at least trying to, in an attempt to hide her enjoyment of her husband's flirting. "Go wash up, dinner is almost ready," she instructed.

"Yes, ma'am."

It was like a scene from a movie. Mom, the happy home-maker. Dad, the devoted husband. Leighton and Kennedy, the grown children, smiling as they watched their parents' public display of affection. They seemed like a picture-perfect family.

Leighton, with a grin still plastered on his face, shook his head in disbelief. *Who would have thought we'd be here after all the shit that has happened these past few days?*

When Dad returned from the washroom, the family sat down for dinner. Mom had prepared a remarkable spread: spinach and mozzarella ravioli in a herbaceous tomato sauce, garden salad with pine nuts and balsamic vinaigrette, and warm focaccia bread with seasoned olive oil. It looked amazing and tasted even better. As they ate, the family shared a lively conversation. Leighton looked on adoringly as his sister bragged about the bakery and Mom and Dad gushed over her success. Everything was perfect, and while Leighton was savoring the merry moment, he couldn't help but think of July. What was she doing? Was she alone in her motel room? Had she gone out? Was she catching up with her friends from back home? He also wondered when she'd last enjoyed a homecooked meal with loved ones. Had her last family dinner been with her mom before the accident? Leighton decided that if there were leftovers, and he hoped that there would be, he would bring them to July when he went to see her later that night.

Speaking of July, Leighton thought, *I never asked Kennedy if she delivered my letter.*

He scanned the table. His parents seemed to be enthralled in a deep conversation. If he wanted to be discreet about this, which he did, then now was the time to pounce.

"Hey," he said under his breath, just loud enough for his sister to hear.

Kennedy looked up from her pasta. "Hey," she replied, mimicking Leighton's hushed voice.

"Did you ever deliver my letter to July?"

"Of course," she said in a did-you-even-have-to-ask tone. "I slipped it under her door. Room 13. As promised."

"Okay, cool. Thanks, Ken."

"No prob." She scooped up a ravioli and spooned it into her mouth.

After the family finished eating, Leighton helped his mother and sister clean up the kitchen. While Mom and Kennedy washed the dishes that couldn't fit in the dishwasher, he packed the leftovers, making sure to put some food aside for July. He hoped that she'd appreciate the gesture. She'd said she was stocked up on snacks, but ramen noodles and candy bars certainly can't compare to a homecooked meal. When he was done, he wiped down the table and the counters before excusing himself. His mother and sister were deep in a conversation about Korean skincare and barely acknowledged his request, opting instead for a simple wave to let him know that it was okay for him to leave. He then went to the study to find his father. It was finally time for him to tell his dad that he would not be going away to school or pursuing a career in politics. Hopefully, Dad would be understanding. As Leighton neared the heavy mahogany door of his father's office, he expected to feel nervous, but surprisingly, he didn't. He actually felt excited. He *wanted* to tell his father about his new plans for the future. He wanted to make it known that he would be forgoing the beaten path and blazing his own trail instead.

Leighton approached the door and hit it with three confident strikes.

Knock, knock, knock.

"Come in!" Dad called.

"Hey, Dad," Leighton said as he entered the elegant suite.

"Hi, son." Dad was standing by a bar rack pouring himself a glass of scotch from an ornate crystal decanter.

Dad's office looked like it could belong to the president: a large stately desk, floor-to-ceiling bookshelves, grand furnishings, and a plethora of attractive decor, such as a vintage globe and a shiny brass telescope.

"What's up?" his father asked.

"I wanted to talk to you about something."

"Okay." Dad sat down at his desk and pointed toward the tufted armchair opposite him. "Have a seat."

Leighton did as he was told, though it did seem a bit too formal. He was hoping for a more laidback, candid conversation, but he didn't object. Sometimes in life, you just have to choose your battles, and this one wasn't worth fighting. Leighton settled into the stiff chair, cleared his throat, and started speaking. "I wanted to talk to you about my future."

Dad looked at Leighton with a steady gaze.

Leighton continued, "There's been a change of plans. I've decided that I don't want to go away to school. I don't want to study politics. And I don't want to be mayor."

Leighton paused, waiting for his father to react, but Dad stayed quiet. He tried to read his expression, but his father remained pokerfaced. He just sat there, cradling his drink ever so gently, just enough for the ice cubes to circle slowly around the glass.

So Leighton carried on. "I'm sure this must come as a surprise to you, but the truth is, I've actually never wanted to be a politician. I've been playing along with the idea for all these years because I didn't want to let you or Mom down. I hate to disappoint you guys. But I've come to the realization that I have to live my life for *me*, and not for other people. I have to prioritize *my* happiness. And I'd be doing myself a major disservice if I continued to pursue a dream that wasn't my own."

Dad took a big swig of his drink, so big that he practically finished it in one sip. He set the glass down on a thin gold coaster.

"Can I tell you a secret?" Dad asked, expression still deadpan.

Leighton scrunched his eyebrows in confusion. He didn't understand where his father was going with this. "Sure."

"I've had a hunch that you were feeling this way."

Leighton looked at his father in disbelief. "So, why didn't you say anything?"

Dad shrugged. "Because I knew you would eventually come talk to me, when you were ready to do so. And here you are."

"Are you . . . mad?" Leighton asked apprehensively.

"Mad? No, I'm not mad. Disappointed? A little."

Leighton dropped his head. "That's even worse."

"But not because you don't want to go away to school or become mayor. I'm disappointed that you felt like you couldn't talk to me about this sooner. I'm sorry if I put too much pressure on you, son. I know that I've been grooming you to follow in my footsteps since you were a young boy, but I never wanted to make you feel like this was your only option. Of course I'd want you to carry on the family legacy, but only if that's what you wanted to do."

Leighton looked at his father appreciatively. He was going to tell him that he didn't have to apologize, but he reconsidered. Instead, he forwent his typical people-pleaser response and continued to be as honest as possible.

"You and Mom did put a lot of pressure on me," he admitted. "I know it was just because you wanted to see me succeed, but it made me feel like any other life choice that I made would be viewed by you guys as a failure. I want to make you and Mom proud, I always have, but not at the expense of my own happiness."

"I *am* proud of you, son," Dad said earnestly. "So proud. And your mother is, too. I hope we don't ever make you feel like you have to question that again. Speaking of your mother, have you told her yet?"

"Yeah, she actually took it really well. Way better than I thought she would. She was upset and angry at first, which I expected, but after we talked some more, she accepted my decision. Hell, I would even go so far as to say that she supports it."

"See, she's not so bad." Dad winked. "You've just got to set boundaries."

"Yes. I've been working on that."

Dad smiled and stood, picking up his glass. At the bar rack, he poured himself another scotch on the rocks. "So now that you're not going away to school or becoming the next mayor of Montclair, what would you like to do with your future?"

"I'm still going to attend Emory, but I'm going to take online classes instead, that was actually Mom's idea, and I'm pretty excited about it. I'm going to switch my major, but I haven't decided exactly what I want to change it to yet. I do know that I want to take humanities courses . . . English composition, English literature, and a creative writing class, too."

"I think that sounds like a great idea. You've always loved to read and you're a very talented writer."

"Thanks, Dad, that means a lot to me."

Dad returned to his desk and took a sip of his drink.

"I also want to do something with the bookstore," Leighton continued. "In honor of Greta."

"Ah shit!" Dad exclaimed, hitting his forehead with his left palm. "That reminds me . . . Monica called this morning. Greta's wake is scheduled for tomorrow. I meant to tell your mother earlier today, but I got caught up with work." He shook his head in disappointment. "It's already short notice as is, and now I'm giving your mother even less time. She's going to kill me."

"Yikes." Leighton grimaced. "Yeah, I don't think she's going to be too happy about this." He scratched the back of his head. "You should probably go tell her now . . . before it gets any later."

Dad sighed. "Yes, yes. You're right." He got up from his desk. "I'll go do that now."

Leighton gave his father a tight-lipped smile and then followed him out of the office. He figured he might need some moral support. When they got to the kitchen, Mom and Kennedy were laughing over a bottle of wine. Leighton looked over at his father and he could tell that he was relieved to find his wife in a good mood. The two stood in the doorway awkwardly as they waited for the girls to pause their chitchat and acknowledge them. When they finally did, Dad explained their, well technically his, reason for interrupting. As expected, Mom wasn't thrilled, but she also wasn't as angry as she probably would have been as recently as just yesterday. Her attitude really had changed so much in the past twenty-four hours.

Leighton knew that his mother had never been a bad person

with bad intentions—she just got too caught up in the idea of being the perfect family. Mom put so much pressure on him and Kennedy because she, too, felt pressure to cultivate this image, and in her mind, that meant they needed to go to college and pursue careers that she deemed reputable and appropriate. When her children strayed from this path, Mom lashed out because she worried that it might tarnish the image that she worked so hard to maintain. It seemed, though, that the recent events were enough to make Mom reevaluate her priorities and realize that having a relationship with her kids was far more important than how others perceived her family, or rather, how she *thought* others *would* perceive her family.

After Dad shared the news of the wake, the Prescotts agreed that they would attend the service together, and Leighton, with the encouragement of his family, decided that he'd deliver the eulogy, which meant that he had about twelve hours to write it. After confirming that he was no longer grounded, Leighton rushed up to his room so that he could get started.

On his way there, he reminisced about the many happy memories that he and Greta shared. One of his favorites was when they took a day trip to Atlanta to go thrifting, acquiring inventory for the bookshop. Leighton was around ten years old at the time, and he was so excited that Greta had chosen him to accompany her. She normally went with Ivan, but her husband's health had started to decline that year and all the driving and walking would have been too much for him. Leighton remembered the pancake breakfast that they got on the way there and playing I Spy as they drove along the highway.

"Why did you ask me to come with you?" Leighton had asked as the city skyline came into view. He was starting to doubt himself. He had never done anything like this before and he didn't want to let Greta down.

"Why would you ask that, my dear?"

"I don't know," Leighton said apprehensively. "What if I'm not helpful enough?"

Greta had placed her hand on Leighton's back. "You're the most helpful young man that I know," she said, "and there's no one else that I'd rather have with me today."

Greta had always known how to make Leighton feel special, and now it was his turn to highlight just how special she had been, not just to him but to the entire town of Montclair.

Perched at his desk, Leighton opened his laptop and began to type. He worried that he might struggle to find the right things to say. He'd never written a eulogy before, but his fear proved to be unfounded as the words flowed out of him like a river meeting the ocean. Before he knew it, the once-blank page was filled with sweet sentiments, raw emotions, and fond memories.

Leighton read over his work, and then he read it again and again. With a tweak here and a tweak there, it was almost perfect. He went over it once more, applying a final round of edits. When he finished, he beamed with pride, knowing that he had written something that honored Greta in the way that she deserved; and on top of that, he had thought of a way to carry on Greta's legacy. While he was writing her eulogy, Leighton finally figured out what he was going to do with the bookstore.

In Loving Memory of Greta Larsson Federov

When I was a child, my favorite days were always those when my mother would take me to Twice Upon a Time. For many years, I thought that I cherished those days so much because I loved books, and while that was true, and it still is, there was something in that quaint shop that I loved far more than the secondhand paperbacks that lined the walls, and that was the soft-spoken, tenderhearted owner, Greta.

Like for many of you, Greta had a profound impact on me. She was a constant light in my life for as long as I can remember. In fact, some of my earliest, and my most treasured, memories were made with her, in that cozy bookstore. I can't count how many afternoons I spent at Twice Upon a Time, sitting on Greta's lap as she read me story after story, transporting me to new worlds that we'd get to explore together. When I grew too big to sit on Greta's lap and I was old enough to read on my own, I'd sit beside her, each of us immersed in different novels of our own choosing. We'd spend hours like that, shoulder to shoulder on the shop's old green sofa, simply enjoying each other's company.

Greta was the type of person who just felt like home: warm, comforting, inviting, safe. Her deep laugh and good nature brought joy to every room that she was in, and her kind eyes and affectionate smile made everyone who met her instantly feel like a close friend. Greta had a beautiful gift of making you feel like the most important person in the world. She radiated compassion, and I think that the number of people here today is a testament to how many of us were touched by her presence.

In addition to being a beloved member of our community, Greta was also a devoted wife. She and her husband, Ivan, could make even the biggest of skeptics believe that soulmates were real. When they first met, Ivan was a soldier in the Russian army who was just passing through Greta's small Swedish town. She was working at a bookstore that he visited during his stay, but despite their instant connection, Ivan had to leave and continue on his tour. Greta waited for Ivan for five years, never giving up hope that he'd come back for her, which he did, even after all that time. Greta and Ivan married upon his return and then came to America for a chance at a better life. They dreamed of opening their own bookshop and they made that dream come true, right here in Montclair.

Greta was gentle and sweet, but she was also resilient and tenacious. This was especially true after the tragic loss of Ivan, which was un-doubtedly one of the hardest challenges that she ever had to face, but she did so with both grace and courage. Greta could have closed the bookstore after his passing, but instead she kept it open, determined to honor him—and she continued to work in the shop until she physically couldn't anymore.

When I got the keys to Twice Upon a Time, I promised myself to love it as much as Greta did, and now that Greta is not here with us any-more, that vow is ever more important. That's why I'd like to make an announcement, which seems fitting to share with you now, while we are all together with Greta for one last time.

To commemorate Greta, and Ivan, too, Twice Upon a Time bookshop will now be Twice Upon a Time Memorial Library. Over the next few weeks, I will be renovating the space and making it a place where the commu-nity can come together. I know Greta would have loved that so much. You can look forward to your standard library amenities as well as daily activities such as writing workshops, art classes, and so much more. I hope you are as excited as I am to keep the memory of Greta alive in Montclair.

And with that said, I'd like to thank you all for coming to this service. I know that I can speak for all of us when I say that Greta left a lasting impression on our town and every person in it, and she will live on in each and every one of our hearts.

It was half past nine when Leighton closed his laptop, which was perfect timing considering he had told July that he'd meet her between ten and eleven. Before freshening up, he checked on his parents' whereabouts, hoping that they'd be getting ready for bed. Although Leighton wasn't grounded anymore, and he could technically come and go as he pleased, he still preferred to do so without answering any questions. Fortunately, neither his mother nor his father were anywhere to be found when he got downstairs. Plus, all the lights were either dimmed or turned off, which told him that they had already gone to their bedroom for the night. He went back upstairs to confirm his hunch, and when he heard the low hum of the television from outside their door, he knew that he was in the clear.

Leighton returned to his room where he changed his clothes, combed his hair, and sprayed himself with some fancy cologne that his mother had gotten him for his birthday that year. Then he went downstairs, grabbed the leftovers that he had packed from the refrigerator, and hurried out the door. It felt like he had been waiting an eternity to see July again, even though it had only been twenty-four hours.

July was already outside when Leighton pulled into the parking lot of the motel. When he came to a stop, she quickly started walking toward his truck, so Leighton hurried out to greet her, and to give her the leftovers that he had put aside for her earlier that evening.

"Are you out of your damn mind?!" she barked as she angrily hit his chest with her hands, shoving him backward. Leighton thought she might be upset with him, but he wasn't expecting her to be this mad.

"I'm sorry!" he exclaimed, with both surprise and regret. "It was a mistake. A very, very stupid mistake."

"You promised me that you wouldn't drive. You said that you would have your sister pick you up. You lied to me!" July cried. She pushed him again, and this time, it was with so much force that Leighton dropped the plastic container. He watched as the contents toppled out onto the pavement. He wanted to be mad at July for causing him to spill the food that he was so excited to give to her, but how could he be angry with her when there was so much pain in her voice? He couldn't, but he could feel guilty and remorseful and scared. *Is this it? Did I destroy my relationship with July?*

"I didn't mean to," he pleaded. "I called Kennedy when I got back to the bookstore, multiple times, but she didn't answer. I called Carson, too, and I even waited for a while, hoping that one of them would call me back, but they didn't, and it was so late by that time, and I just really wanted to go home."

"I don't want to hear your excuses," July seethed. "You *lied* to me, and you put yourself and others in danger. I didn't think you were the kind of person to do something like this, but you're obviously not who you've been pretending to be. I thought I knew you, but I guess I don't really know you at all."

Leighton grimaced. July's words cut deeper than a knife, and he was taken aback by her cruelty. He had messed up and he could never justify what he did, but for July to question his character seemed extreme. Leighton had spent the past few days being as honest with July as he could possibly be. He had opened up to her in ways that he had never done before with anyone else, and he'd done that because he wanted her to really get to know him. Hearing her doubt the authenticity of everything that he had shared with her broke his heart.

But instead of responding to July's hurtful remarks, Leighton reached out for her and then pulled her to him. He expected her to push him away, but she didn't, so he wrapped her in a tight hug. "I'm so sorry," he whispered in her ear as she nestled her head on his shoulder. "What I did was inexcusable, but I've learned from it. I'm not the same person that I was yesterday. I know that sounds dramatic, but so much has changed in the past twenty-four hours, and I really want to tell you about it."

July was silent, and Leighton worried that this might be it for them. He didn't want to lose her. He couldn't lose her.

"Can I please tell you about it?" he asked desperately.

"Okay," July agreed after several painful moments.

Leighton let out a sigh of relief. "Thank you." He relaxed his arms and released July from his embrace.

The hard expression that July had worn only a few minutes earlier was softer now. "You're welcome," she said.

Leighton gave her a small smile. "Do you want to go for a ride while we talk?"

July nodded.

"Okay, let's clean up this mess," Leighton said, gesturing to the food on the ground, "and then we can head out."

July winced. "Sorry about that, by the way. For what it's worth, it looks really delicious . . . even scattered across the parking lot." She gave him a sheepish grin.

Leighton let out a deep laugh, grateful that the mood was lighter. He picked up the plastic container, and with July's help, gathered the remnants of his family's dinner.

Then, they got into Leighton's truck and turned toward the highway.

Once they were on the open road, Leighton began telling July about everything that had transpired since he had last seen her: the DUI charge, Mom and Kennedy's reconciliation, the conversations that he had with his mother and father, his new plans for the future, Greta's wake, and the eulogy that he wrote for it. By the time he had covered everything, they had put nearly sixty miles on his old truck and had traversed a dozen towns and three counties.

"Wow," July said when Leighton finished his rundown. "You weren't kidding when you said that a lot had happened."

Leighton laughed. "No, I wasn't."

"I don't even know where to begin with my thoughts and reactions," July admitted. "I have so many feelings. I think what I want to say, first and foremost, is that I am so proud of you for finally speaking up to your parents about your future. That was huge and long overdue. You must feel so relieved!"

"I am," Leighton confessed. "It feels like a weight has been lifted off my shoulders. And for the first time in a long time, I am really excited for what's to come.

"You know," he continued, "I couldn't have done it without you."

July blushed. "You're just trying to butter me up now."

Leighton laughed. "I mean it. Before I met you, I let my parents dictate my life, but the conversations that you and I have had this week made me realize just how messed up that was. Then, Greta passed away and everything kind of came to a head. I realized that I have to live my life the way that I want to."

July applauded. "Yes, you do!" She beamed.

Leighton smiled and reached for July's left hand, which she happily gave to him. He laced his fingers through hers. "Hey, speaking of Greta . . . Would you want to come to her wake tomorrow? I know it's last minute, but I'd really like to have you there . . . as long as you feel comfortable, of course."

"I wouldn't miss it for the world."

Leighton's heart swelled, and he couldn't help but grin foolishly from ear to ear. It's no secret that actions speak louder than words, and July agreeing to go to Greta's wake told Leighton that she cared for him as much as he cared for her. And that was an amazing feeling.

On the ride back to Montclair, Leighton and July discussed Leighton's plans for Twice Upon a Time. July proved to be a valuable sounding board, not only providing helpful feedback but also coming up with some intriguing ideas of her own. The conversation was invigorating, and it lit a spark in Leighton's soul. He felt more determined than ever to make his dreams a reality. It was rare to find someone who inspired you the way that July inspired him. And once again, Leighton was left feeling unbelievably lucky and grateful to have someone like her in his life.

I think I might be in love with this girl, he mused.

When the pair arrived back at the motel, it was clear that neither one of them was ready to say goodbye, though they both knew that it was time to do so. It was past midnight, and the moon hung low in the sky. Leighton rolled down the windows and the two sat there as they listened to the static noise of the sleepy town.

"I should probably go inside now," July said quietly after about fifteen minutes or so.

"Do you have to?" Leighton asked with playful puppy eyes.

July laughed and nudged his arm. "Oh, stop it!"

Leighton gave her a flirtatious smirk. Then his face turned serious. "I hate this part."

"Me, too."

Leighton put his hand on July's cheek and pulled her into a kiss. It was a soft, sweet one, not the passionate, lustful kind, though he did enjoy those, too. But that wasn't right for tonight. Tonight called for the type of kiss that you give to someone who you can see forever in, and Leighton could definitely see forever in July.

When Leighton opened his eyes, he was met with July's sparkling gaze. The tiny flecks in her eyes were reflecting light like a kaleidoscope. She bit her lip and gave him a dreamy smile. Leighton sensed that she had something that she wanted to say, but she was holding back.

"What?"

She blushed and shook her head. "Nothing," she said.

Leighton raised a brow, but he didn't probe her. "Here, let me get the door for you," he said as he exited the vehicle.

When he opened her door, July slid out and gave him a quick kiss on the cheek. "I'll see you tomorrow," she whispered.

"I can't wait."

Leighton grinned the entire ride home, and when he got to his room and rested his head on his pillow, it was July he saw, vividly, as he drifted off to sleep.

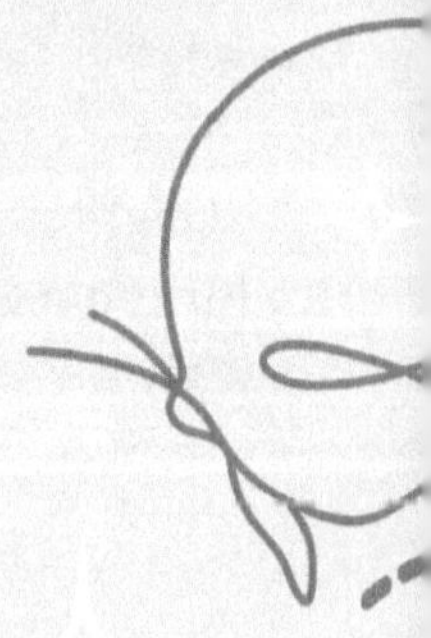

Day Seven

IT WAS GRAY AND GLOOMY when Leighton awoke the next morning. He decided not to open the bookstore since Greta's wake was later that afternoon. Plus, his emotions were all over the place, so he wanted to take some time to sort them out. On the one hand, he was still smitten over the night prior. Every time he thought about July, his heart swelled. On the other hand, there was a lingering sadness deep in his gut, like a storm cloud looming. Today was the day that he had to officially say goodbye to Greta, and he wasn't sure if he was ready to do that.

Leighton looked outside at the dreary weather. Rain was falling now, and he could hear menacing thunder not too far in the distance. He noticed a small blue jay singing a song from a branch on the oak tree right outside his window. Leighton smiled. He could relate to that blissful little bird; he, too, was a happy juxtaposition to the glum circumstances. Leighton continued to gaze outside for several more minutes, watching the leaden sky grow even darker. His feathered friend retreated to its nest, and Leighton figured that he ought to do the same, but he lingered, until an angry strike of lightning touched down from an ominous cloud.

"Shit," he said as he quickly backed away from the window. He looked at the clock; it was half past nine. Not yet ready for breakfast, Leighton practiced delivering Greta's eulogy. When he finished, he took a long look at himself in the mirror. He noticed that the person looking back at him seemed different from that of days past. This version of Leighton stood a little taller and a little straighter. He gave a skeptical look before settling into a smile, satisfied with what he saw.

In the kitchen, Leighton found his parents in their usual spots: Dad at the table reading the paper and Mom by the stove flipping pancakes.

Leighton laughed and shook his head. *Same scene, different day*, he thought. *They're such creatures of habit.*

"Hey, hun!" His mother greeted him. "Slept in this morning?"

"Hey, Mom," Leighton replied. "No, I've actually been up for a while now. I was just hanging out in my room, practicing Greta's eulogy and whatnot."

"Oh! Good, good! I'm so excited to hear it! Would you like some pancakes? The first batch is just about ready."

"No, thanks. I'm just going to have a bowl of cereal." Leighton pulled a box of Froot Loops from the pantry.

"Hey, son," Dad said when Leighton sat down beside him at the table. "How are you doing?"

"Pretty good. I mean, I'm still upset about Greta, obviously, but I'm also happy and excited for the future."

"Well, I'm glad to hear that. A lot has happened over the past few days."

"Yeah, it has," Leighton agreed as he poured a healthy serving of milk over the brightly colored rounds.

"So, what's on the agenda for today?" Dad continued, after a few minutes. "Other than Greta's wake, of course."

"I'm not sure," Leighton said with a shrug. He took a spoonful of cereal, ushered it into his mouth, and crunched loudly.

"It probably wouldn't be a bad idea to contact Emory and notify them that you'll be switching to an online program," Dad suggested. "You should also let them know that you will be forfeiting your scholarship. There may still be enough time for them to offer it to someone else."

"Good thinking," Leighton said. "I'll do that as soon as I finish eating."

"You could also start looking through their catalog of classes," Mom said from the other side of the room, her voice muffled due to her head being halfway in the refrigerator. "You don't want to miss out on the good ones!" She pulled out a variety of pancake toppings—two types of syrup, fresh fruit, whipped cream, and berry compote. She cradled the items and carried them over to the kitchen island.

"Definitely." Leighton took another bite of cereal. "I thought I was going to be bored for the next few hours . . . boy, was I wrong," he said with a laugh.

Leighton finished his breakfast and rinsed his dish out in the sink.

"Let me know if you need help with anything," his father called as he exited the kitchen.

"Will do!" Leighton shouted from the hallway. Normally he'd be dreading emails and paperwork, but today he was looking forward to it. It wouldn't be long until his decision was permanent.

When Leighton's parents first talked to him about college, he was only around eight years old, which in hindsight, seemed way too early to bring up higher education. It was Christmas morning and Leighton was getting ready to open his gifts.

"Open this one first!" His mother had instructed as she handed him a gold foil–wrapped box with a big red bow.

"Okay," Leighton said as he carefully tore the paper. Mom was meticulous with her gift wrapping and she got upset when he opened his presents too aggressively. "Cool, a new hoodie!" Leighton exclaimed as he held up a navy-blue garment with yellow block letters. He had asked for a new sweatshirt, but he wanted a *Star Wars* one. He didn't let his parents see his disappointment, though.

"Not just any hoodie," his father had pointed out. "It's from the college that I went to, and the one that your grandad and great grandad went to, also!"

"And it's the college that *you're* going to go to one day," his mother had cut in with an overzealous grin.

"Thanks, I love it!" Leighton lied. He didn't really know anything about college but he didn't like how his parents were making him feel about it. He couldn't identify his emotions at the time, but looking back now, he realized that it was in that moment that he started to feel the weight of his parents' expectations.

Leighton felt sorry for that little boy. Over the next several years, the pressure would only grow. Fortunately, that wasn't an issue anymore, because Leighton had finally spoken up and regained control of his life, and nothing felt better than that.

It was a little past one when Leighton finished everything that he had set out to do. It was official—he had switched from traditional to virtual learning and had forfeited his scholarship. And while he would still be attending his father, his grandfather, and his great-grandfather's alma mater, he was doing it *his* way. Instead of majoring in political science, Leighton decided to pursue an English and creative writing degree. He was so excited! He still needed to select his classes, but he did start browsing the catalog to see what was being offered during the fall semester. He jotted down the classes that he was most interested in, hoping that they wouldn't be full before he had time to enroll the following day.

Content with his progress, Leighton quickly showered and got ready. His family would be leaving for the funeral home at a quarter to two, and he didn't want to be the reason that they were late. This service was far too important not to arrive on time.

Montclair Mortuary was only a short drive from the Prescott estate. It was located on Main Street, not too far from the bookstore or Kennedy's bakery. When the family got there, Leighton was surprised to see that July was already waiting outside.

"Hey," he said.

"Hey," she replied sheepishly, tucking a piece of hair behind her ear.

"How are you?"

July opened her mouth to answer, but before she could say anything, she was interrupted by Kennedy, who scooped her up into a bear hug.

"July! It's so good to see you!"

"It's great to see you, too!" July said with a laugh.

Dad and Mom followed shortly after. Dad greeted July with a friendly pat on the back while Mom gave her a tight squeeze on the arm. Leighton was worried that his mother might be problematic again, but her kindness seemed sincere. He could tell that she wasn't just pretending to be on her best behavior. She actually seemed genuinely happy to see July. Leighton wasn't sure what had led to the change of heart, but he was grateful for it. There were few things in life that he hated more than conflict, especially between two people that he deeply cared about.

After their hellos, the group entered the funeral home. There were only a handful of visitors already inside, but as it grew closer to the top of the hour, more and more people began to trickle in. By two, the room was filled. If anyone had questioned the influence that Greta had had on that little community, they certainly didn't anymore. It looked as if the entire town was present that afternoon.

Leighton was seated in the front row alongside Monica. The two of them were the closest thing that Greta had to family after Ivan's passing. Greta was an only child, and she had lost both of her parents shortly after she left Sweden and moved to the United States. Ivan, on the other hand, was estranged from his family, so Greta never got the opportunity to get to know them, or even meet them. And as for children, the couple never had any of their own, though Greta did act as a maternal figure to many Montclair kids, especially Leighton.

When the service began, Leighton was given the option to be one of the first to pay his respects, second only to Monica. While he felt honored to be in such a position, he was also apprehensive. Because his grandmothers and Ivan had all passed away when he was so young, this was his first time *really* attending a wake, and it was an open casket, so he didn't know what to expect. He scanned the room for his parents or sister, but he couldn't seem to find them. He felt that familiar lump forming in his throat; anxiety was beginning to get the better of him. He looked around again, desperate for a reassuring face. Finally, he found one—July's. She was standing in the back left corner of the room, giving him a nod, as if to say *go on, it's okay*. The tension left his body. He smiled and mouthed *thank you* to her, knowing that she probably didn't even realize just how grateful he was for her in that moment. He had felt paralyzed by fear and uncertainty, but

July's support and encouragement nullified those feelings. She gave him the confidence that he needed to move forward, both figuratively and literally.

Leighton approached the casket after Monica finished paying her respects. He walked slowly toward the wooden box until he was standing over it. He looked down to see Greta in a pale blue dress with her hands crossed over her stomach. She looked so peaceful yet also so frail. He couldn't help but notice that the dress, which he had seen her in so many times—she had worn it to nearly every gathering that required more than casual attire, the last being his graduation ceremony—seemed much too big on her now. That had never been an issue before. He wondered if this was something that happened after you died, or if she had been slowly deteriorating for the past few months and he hadn't even realized. Leighton moved his attention to her face. Her skin was as pale as snow and her cheeks were sunk in like tiny craters. His eyes began to burn and the next thing he knew, he was sobbing. All the tears that wouldn't come that morning were flowing freely. He didn't even try to stop them; he just let them pour out. Leighton had known that this was going to be difficult, but seeing Greta like this broke his heart, especially because it would be the last time that he ever saw her, and he wasn't sure if this was the final image that he wanted to be left with. He wanted to remember her looking robust and jovial. He wanted to remember her when she was full of life.

Leighton wiped his eyes and took a deep breath. He had been standing there for quite some time now and other people were waiting to pay their respects. He wanted so badly to touch Greta's cheek, to feel warmth on her skin. But he knew that he couldn't do that, plus he wouldn't like what he felt anyway: cold, stiff, lifeless. He closed his eyes and clenched his jaw until the tears had dried. Then he bid Greta a final farewell, hoping, praying, that she was able to hear him. When he was done, he went outside. He knew what he was looking for, but he wasn't sure if he was going to find it. He sat down on the ground with his back up against the side of the building. He looked out on the town. There was no hustle and bustle, no one was coming and going. The signs on the doors of the pastel shops were all turned to Closed, their keepers at the funeral home, just like Leighton.

Leighton's gaze fell to the sidewalk. There was a small potted tree standing tall despite its diminutive size. It was then that Leighton saw what he needed to see—a monarch butterfly perched on one of the tree's branches, its wings wafting up and down in a rhythmic pattern.

"Greta," Leighton said aloud. He felt tears filling his eyes again, but this time they were happy tears. Grateful tears. "Thank you," he cried. "Thank you so much." And then the butterfly flew away, up into the summer sky until it was just a memory.

"Hey," Leighton heard from around the corner. He looked up to see July standing there.

"Are you okay?" she asked. "I've been looking all over for you."

"I'm sorry. I needed to get some fresh air. But yeah, I'm okay. I wasn't, but I am now."

July moved closer, a sympathetic look on her face. She sat down next to him. "You sure?"

"Yeah." He took her hand and placed it in his. "Thank you for coming today. I needed you here, more than you know."

"You're welcome, but I really didn't do anything."

"You did. Before I went up to Greta's casket, I wasn't sure if I was going to be able to do it. Then I saw you from across the room and you gave me the push that I needed."

July squeezed his hand. "That's what friends are for."

Leighton was caught off guard by her response. *Friends?* he thought. *Is that all she sees me as? A friend?*

He stayed silent for a few moments, unsure what to say next.

"Is . . . everything okay?" July asked after a minute or so.

"Yeah, I just . . ." Leighton swallowed. He hated confrontation. "I thought this was more."

July squeezed his hand again and then playfully bumped her shoulder into his. "I suppose you're right," she said. "We are definitely more than friends."

Leighton let out a sigh, relieved to hear that he was out of the friend zone.

"But that doesn't mean that I want to put a label on this," she continued. "On us."

"Okay, that's fair. I don't want to put a label on it either," Leighton agreed, even though he would love nothing more than to put a label on his and July's relationship.

The two sat there for a few more minutes before returning to the funeral home, still hand in hand as they walked inside.

"There you are!" Mom said as the two entered the building. She looked at Leighton's fingers intertwined with July's. She narrowed her eyes then checked herself, readjusting before bringing her gaze back up to Leighton's. "It's almost time for you to read your eulogy. Are you ready?"

"Yeah," Leighton replied. "I mean, I think so, at least. I've never done something like this before."

"You're going to be great," July said.

"Yeah, hun," Mom agreed, despite looking slightly irritated that July had beaten her to the punch and provided Leighton with the words of encouragement that she wanted to deliver. "You have nothing to worry about. You're a gifted writer and a talented public speaker. Plus, you and Greta were so close. There is no one better to do this than you."

"Thanks, guys," Leighton said with a timid, tight-lipped smile. "I just have some nerves. I'm sure they'll go away once I get started."

"We should probably return to our seats now," July suggested. "It looks like everyone is starting to settle down."

"Yes, we should." Mom turned around and walked back into the viewing room.

Leighton and July followed.

"You've got this!" July said. She let go of Leighton's hand and gave him a kiss on the cheek, then moved toward her spot in the back corner of the room.

"Thanks." Leighton brushed his shirt of any wrinkles, even though there weren't any, and walked to the front of the room, where his notes were already waiting on the lectern. He cleared his throat and positioned himself on the podium. *Here goes nothing*, he thought.

"When I was a child, my favorite days were always those when my mother would take me to Twice Upon a Time . . ."

The first words stumbled sloppily out of his mouth, as if they were drunk. His voice was shaky, and his nails dug into his palms. He looked to the back of the room to find July.

When he met her gaze, he felt the same rush of courage that he had felt earlier that day, before he visited Greta's casket. He continued with his speech, and now the words were coming out confidently, his voice firm. Twenty seconds in and he was passionately delivering the eulogy. He didn't even have to reference his notes anymore; it was as if he had memorized the whole thing without even realizing it.

When Leighton finished and looked out into the crowd, he was met with a sea of supportive faces. Some were smiling, some were wiping away tears, and some were giving him approving nods. It made his heart feel full. All he had wanted was to honor Greta and to move the guests in the same way that Greta had moved each and every one of them. Based on their reactions, he could guess that he had succeeded in this goal.

His mother, father, and sister were waiting for him when he returned to his seat. His mother kissed his forehead, his father patted his back, and his sister gave him a hug. Then they sang his praises.

"We're so proud of you!" Mom squealed.

"Nice speech, son," Dad said.

"Greta would've loved it!" Kennedy chirped.

"Thanks, guys." Leighton was grateful for his family's support, but the attention also made him feel a bit bashful. The speech was supposed to be about Greta, after all, not him.

The room, which had been quiet and orderly just a few moments ago, was now loud and busy. People were saying their goodbyes and packing up to leave. Leighton looked around for July, but he couldn't seem to find her.

"Hey," he heard from behind his right shoulder. He quickly turned around to find two big brown eyes staring back at him.

"There you are," he said.

"Sorry," July replied. "I walked around the back of the room to avoid all of the chaos."

"Gotcha. I guess I just got worried when I didn't see you near your seat."

"Haven't we gone over this already? I wouldn't bail on you, silly."

Leighton blushed and scratched the back of his head, feeling a bit self-conscious.

"Your speech was awesome, by the way. I'm really proud of you."

"Thanks."

"So, what now?"

"How about an early dinner?" Kennedy suggested, joining the conversation. Leighton wondered if she had been listening the entire time. "Mom and Dad want to go to Bella Italia, that new Italian restaurant that everyone is talking about."

Leighton looked at July. "Would you want to do that?"

"Sure, as long as I'm not intruding."

"Of course you're not intruding," Kennedy said. "We'd love to have you join us!"

"Okay," July agreed. "I *could* go for a big bowl of carbs right about now."

"You and me both, sister," Kennedy said with a laugh.

Dad approached Leighton and the girls. "Are you guys ready to head out?" The room was practically empty now, except for a few stragglers.

"Yeah," Kennedy replied.

"Alright, I'll go get the car, then. It started raining again, and I'm sure your mother isn't going to want to get wet. I'll be waiting out front in a few minutes," Dad said as he turned toward the exit.

"Okay!" Kennedy called after him. "I'll go get Mom," she said to Leighton and July before hurrying away.

"Are you sure about this?" Leighton asked July once it was just the two of them again.

"One hundred percent positive."

"Okay." Leighton gathered up the few belongings that he had brought with him and grabbed July's hand. "Off we go, then, my lady!"

It was half past four when the group arrived at the restaurant. It was some fancy establishment in the next town over. Apparently, the food was amazing; the people of Montclair had been buzzing about it since it opened a few weeks earlier. The Prescotts had yet to visit, but Mom had been incessantly asking Dad to go. She'd finally gotten her wish. There had been rumors swirling around about crazy-long wait times, but the place seemed to be practically dead when they got there. Then again, it wasn't yet dinnertime and it was a weekday.

Their party was seated immediately upon entering. They got a large circular booth near a window. A sharply dressed waiter came by to take their drink orders a few minutes after they got comfortable.

"We'll take two bottles of your best cabernet," Mom requested, before anyone else had the opportunity to speak, "for the table."

"Yes, ma'am," the waiter said with a nod of his head. "I'll get you all some water as well."

"Thank you," Mom replied.

"You didn't let me or July order our drinks," Leighton pointed out to his mother.

"You don't want to have wine with the rest of us?" Mom asked nonchalantly.

"I didn't realize that was an option," Leighton admitted.

"It is today," his mother responded. "We are celebrating, after all. We'll all have a glass to toast to the life of Greta."

"Okay," Leighton agreed. It felt good to be treated like an adult, especially by his mother.

He looked at July, who was seated next to him, to make sure that she was okay with this arrangement. She shrugged and gave him an it-sounds-good-to-me look.

The waiter returned with two bottles, both adorned in ornate gold labels. He displayed one to the table before pulling a corkscrew out of his apron and meticulously opening it. Then he filled each of their glasses with a perfect six-ounce pour, twisting the bottle in a swift upward motion at the end of each fill to ensure that none of the precious liquid was wasted.

After the waiter left, Mom raised her wineglass toward the center of the table. "To Greta!" she exclaimed.

"To Greta!" the group relayed back to her, lifting their glasses in unison.

They carefully tapped the five glasses together—*clink!*—and then each of them took a swig of the burgundy nectar.

Leighton wasn't really a wine drinker, so he didn't have much to compare this particular cabernet to, but even so, he was sure that it was the best wine that he had ever had, and possibly even the best wine that he would ever have.

He looked over at July, whose eyes were glowing in the dim restaurant light, and he could tell that she felt the same way.

Leighton placed his hand on her thigh, right above her knee. He gave her leg a subtle squeeze. July smiled and placed her hand on top of his, moving her thumb in circles on his skin. The hairs on the back of his neck stood up.

I really hope that I get to do more of this with her, Leighton thought as he took a big sip of wine and breathed in the delightful scene.

Over the next hour, the group talked, joked, wined, and dined. The conversation was lively, the laughs were full, the liquor was intoxicating, and the food was rich. Leighton understood why everyone spoke so highly of this restaurant, between the romantic atmosphere and the delectable cuisine, it really did offer its guests a one-of-a-kind experience. He hoped to have the opportunity to bring July here again. He imagined how nice it would be, just the two of them, tucked away in one of those smaller booths that were nestled in the corner.

"We should do this again sometime," he whispered to July, just loud enough for her to hear.

"I'd like that," she replied in a similarly hushed tone.

When the bottles were empty and their plates were cleared, Dad waved to the waiter to let him know that they were ready for the check. The waiter dutifully retrieved it and quickly came over to drop it off. Dad handed him his credit card without even looking at the total. July tried to give Dad a couple of twenty-dollar bills to cover her share, but he shooed her contributions away.

"Don't be silly, this was our treat."

"Thank you," July replied. "The meal was delicious and the company was even better."

"Thank you for joining us," Dad replied with a kind smile.

Leighton could tell that his dad was fond of July. He looked over at his mother, who looked equally enamored. This was exactly what he had wanted; all the people that he loved, together and getting along. Chatting, smiling, laughing, and just genuinely enjoying each other's company. The only person missing was Greta, but he knew that she was there, too; maybe not physically but in spirit. The warm glow of the candle, the happy hum of music, the intimacy in the atmosphere . . . it was Greta. She was everything good that was all around them.

"So, where are you two heading?" Dad asked Leighton and July once everyone was in the Prescotts' sedan.

Leighton looked over to July, who gave him a shrug. Her glazed eyes and flushed cheeks told him that one, she was feeling tipsy, and two, she would probably be happy doing just about anything.

"We're going to go to the bookstore for a bit," Leighton replied. He looked at July again, happy to find that she was giving him a nod of approval.

"Alright," Dad said. "I don't see that being a problem.

Before I drop you off, though, I would like to know how you plan to get home later?"

"I'll call one of you," Leighton replied. "Well, maybe not Kennedy. . . . She seems a little drunk." He nudged his sister's arm to let her know that he was just teasing her.

"Am not!" Kennedy chirped with a guilty, lopsided grin.

"Or I can take an Uber," Leighton continued, "if it gets too late and I don't want to make you guys come out. That's what I should have done the other night. The night of the, you know . . ."

"Yes, that is what you should have done," Dad replied before turning onto the highway and back toward Montclair, "but I'm glad to hear that you've learned your lesson."

On the drive into town, Leighton thought about the last time that he brought a girl out to dinner with his family, and just how different the experience had been from the one that he just had.

It was on his sixteenth birthday, two years earlier. Mom, Dad, and Leighton were going to Hibachi to celebrate, and his mother insisted that he invite Becca. Leighton would have preferred for Kennedy to join them instead, but she and Mom weren't on speaking terms.

At the time, Leighton hadn't yet realized that he wanted to break up with Becca, but he did know that her feelings for him were a lot stronger than his feelings for her. Becca had a tendency to be overly affectionate and desperate for Leighton's attention, but on this particular night, she was acting especially clingy. She practically hung on to his arm during the entire meal, snapping pictures of them every few minutes to share to her social media. It was awful.

When they finished eating, while Dad and Mom were paying the bill, Becca whispered in Leighton's ear, "Leighton Prescott, I'm in love with you." It was the first time that the *L*-word was ever mentioned, and he knew that she was probably expecting this to be a special milestone in their relationship. The problem was, Leighton didn't feel the same way. "Well," she continued, "aren't you going to say it back?"

Leighton had felt a lump in his throat. He didn't want to hurt her feelings. "I love you, too," he lied.

Becca squealed and clung to his arm even tighter. "This has been the best night ever!"

"Yeah," Leighton agreed, even though he felt the exact opposite.

Now, looking over at July sitting peacefully next to him, Leighton once again noted how being with her just felt easy, and their time at dinner only confirmed what he had already known. Leighton was in love with July, and he was going to tell her that night.

"So, what did you want to do here?" July asked when she and Leighton got to the bookshop. They were standing outside, but Leighton was making no effort to find the keys to open the door.

"I'm not really sure," Leighton admitted. "We don't even

have to hang out here if you don't want to. I just wasn't ready to go home. I wanted to spend more time with you."

"Aw, someone's getting soft on me again," July teased, playfully nudging Leighton's arm.

Leighton could feel his cheeks getting hot, but he tried to laugh it off. "Yeah, I guess I am," he confessed.

July gave him a sincere smile, and her face was more serious now. "All jokes aside," she said, "that's really sweet. I wasn't ready to leave you yet either. Plus, it's only what, six? Seven? We have the whole night ahead of us!"

"That's what I'm saying!" Leighton replied, shaking his head and throwing his hands up in the air in dramatic fashion.

July laughed at his charade and Leighton gave her a cheeky grin.

"So, my lady," he said, "what shall we do?"

July put her hand under her chin and tapped her cheek with her pointer finger. "Hmm," she said. "We still have all those options that you had mentioned the other day. The day we decided to go roller-skating. I don't remember what they were, though."

"Oh yeah," Leighton said, remembering the ideas that he had come up with. "There was a picnic by the lake . . ."

July shook her head. "It's too late for that and I'm way too full."

"Bowling . . ."

July scrunched her nose. "I'm not in the mood for bowling."

"Or the movies," he said as he gave her an inquisitive look. "Otherwise, we'll have to think of something else."

July tapped her finger against her cheek again. "What if we went back to my room and watched a movie? I saw that there were a few good titles available to rent."

"Okay, that sounds good to me," Leighton agreed. "What kind of movies are you into?"

"I'm not too picky. If I had to choose a favorite genre, it would probably be psychological thrillers, but I'll watch anything as long as it doesn't totally suck."

Leighton laughed. "Yeah, I'm pretty much the same way. My favorite genre is definitely horror, though. I love a gory slasher film."

July looked at him incredulously and then her lips curled up into a playful grin. "And here I thought you'd be a superhero-movie-kinda-guy," she teased.

"Why would you think that?!" Leighton asked, pretending to be offended. "Are you stereotyping me?!"

July laughed. "Because you're so mild-mannered, and polite, and"—she put her finger to her lip while she tried to find the right word—"righteous."

"I think you forget that I almost went to jail," Leighton replied with a mischievous smirk.

"Leighton!" July exclaimed, slapping his arm.

"What?!" he said, rubbing the spot where she hit him. "Too soon?"

"Yes! *Way* too soon."

"Okay, okay. I'm sorry. I thought girls liked bad boys."

"Not this girl," July said, pointing her finger to her chest.

"Well, in that case," Leighton said, flashing her a toothy smile. "I'll be your knight in shining armor, baby."

July's cheeks turned red. "Oh, stop it."

Leighton smiled again. He loved their flirtatious banter. "Ready to go?"

"Yeah." July nodded, her cheeks still pink from their playful exchange.

It was a calm, cool evening thanks to the rain from earlier that day, which not only lowered the typically high Southern summer temperatures but also the accompanying humidity, which was always thick in the air during this time of year. Leighton and July took their time walking back to the motel. They strolled slowly, hand in hand, soaking in the sights and sounds of Montclair: birds singing from a tree branch, children playing at the park, couples dining outside a restaurant, teens biking down the sidewalk, and squirrels running around the town square.

"I'm going to miss this," July said.

Leighton stopped walking. He was caught off guard by her statement. Although he hadn't yet asked July to stay in Montclair, he was hoping that she was considering it, but apparently she wasn't. Leighton hated the thought of July leaving. In fact, he had been doing his best to avoid thinking about it since meeting her. It also hadn't helped that since he'd solidified his new plans, he'd been daydreaming about their future together.

July turned to face Leighton. "Is everything okay?"

"Yeah, sorry," Leighton stammered. "I just . . . I don't like to think about you leaving."

July's expression softened and Leighton pulled her to him. He held her tight and rocked her back and forth, ever so gently.

"I don't like to think about it either," she whispered, putting her forehead against Leighton's chest.

"You don't have to leave," Leighton said quietly. "You could stay."

July pulled her head away and cupped Leighton's face in her hands. She looked at him for a few moments before responding. "I would like that," she finally said, "a lot, but I don't know. I feel like I have to go to Florida to see my dad. I mean, he's the only parent that I have left. Shouldn't I at least try to have a relationship with him?"

Leighton contemplated what to say. If he were being honest, he didn't think that July's father deserved to have a relationship with her, not after everything that she had told him about her dad. But Leighton also didn't want to say anything that could start a fight or be perceived as selfish.

"Yeah, that makes sense. But don't you think you could have both? You could still go and visit your dad in Florida, but you could live and work here in Montclair," he suggested.

July gave him a tight-lipped smile. "Okay, I'll think about it," she said before planting a quick kiss on his lips.

When she pulled away, Leighton tried to continue the conversation, but before he could, July was grabbing his hand and pulling him toward their destination.

Montclair Gas and Grocery was located right next to the motel where July was staying. It was a mom-and-pop business that had been around for just as long as Twice Upon a Time, maybe even longer. A few years earlier, one of the big gas station chains tried to buy it out, but the owners, Mike and Lynn Rogers, refused. Leighton was glad that they had not sold out. One of Montclair's quirks was its rich history and the people who helped build it.

It was quiet inside the convenience store. The cashier, who Leighton recognized as a girl named Amber, a sophomore from his high school, was chewing gum while reading a magazine. She didn't even look up when Leighton and July entered. The two made their way to the snack aisle to pick out some things to munch on while they watched their movie.

"What about drinks?" Leighton asked after they made their selections. He had an armful of chips, candy, and popcorn.

July gave him a mischievous grin. "I have something in mind," she said as she walked toward the refrigerators that lined the back of the store.

Leighton followed her as she passed by the waters, teas, sports drinks, and sodas. She moved intently to the back left corner, where the adult beverages were located. She placed a hand on her hip and leaned to the right as she examined the offerings.

"There we go," she said, and her lips turned up into a victorious smile. July opened the door and pulled out a six-pack of lager. "These should do the trick!" She turned to look at Leighton. "You in?" She motioned toward the beers.

Leighton hesitated before answering. He felt guilty drinking after what had happened the other night, but he wouldn't be driving later that evening, and his parents did let him have wine at dinner, so a few beers wouldn't be so bad. Right?

"Yeah, I'm in."

"Good," July said with a smirk, "because I was going to make you drink some whether you wanted to or not."

Leighton laughed and stuck his tongue out at July. *I like it when she's bossy*, he thought.

The cashier was still engrossed in her magazine when the pair approached the counter. Leighton rang a bell to get her attention. She looked up and blew a big pink bubble of gum. After it popped, she asked, "Is that all for today?"

Leighton nodded. When July put the beer on the counter, Amber gave Leighton an I-know-you're-not-old-enough-to-buy-that look, but she rang it up anyway.

July pulled out her fake ID and handed it to the cashier without being prompted. Amber brushed it away. "You're good," she said dismissively.

"Thanks," July replied with a kind and unrequited smile.

The cashier put the items in a plastic bag covered with the words 'thank you.'

"Eleven ninety-seven," she said as she pushed the package toward them.

Leighton pulled out his wallet and gave her twelve dollars. "You can keep the change," he offered.

"Gee, thanks," Amber said flatly.

Leighton picked up the bag and turned toward the door. When he caught a glimpse of July, he could tell that she was holding back laughter.

When they got outside, she couldn't hold it in any longer. "Well, she was a ray of sunshine," she said between giggles.

Leighton was laughing now, too. "Oh yeah, a real doll," he quipped.

When Leighton and July got to July's room, and July opened the door, Leighton was surprised to see a litter of garbage, clothes, shoes, and other belongings scattered haphazardly around the area. For someone who always looked so put together, July had a messy room. Leighton found the juxtaposition between her tidy appearance and her untidy living situation interesting.

July must've noticed Leighton's critical stare because her cheeks turned red. "Sorry for the mess," she stammered. "I would've cleaned up if I knew you were coming."

Leighton could see that July was embarrassed, and he felt terrible for making her feel that way. "No worries," he replied. "It's not even that bad. You should see my room," he said in an attempt to compensate for his uncharacteristically judgmental behavior.

July's stiff posture loosened. She gave Leighton an appreciative smile before leading him into her room. "Welcome to my humble abode," she said, motioning her right arm in such a way to display the setting.

"It's perfect," Leighton said as he placed the drinks and snacks on a small desk in the corner of the room.

"We can put the beer in the mini fridge." July grabbed the six-pack and brought it to a little kitchenette area, pulling out two bottles on her way. After she twisted off the tops, she handed one of the beers to Leighton. "Cheers," she said before clinking her bottle against his. They each took a big swig of lager before settling down on the bed.

Leighton leaned against the headboard, making sure to keep some distance between himself and July. He didn't want her to think he was trying to take this any further than watching a movie together, though he wouldn't be upset if it did turn into more. When the film started, they each sat on their respective sides of the bed, nursing their beers, with ample space between them. It wasn't until halfway through that July pulled herself close to Leighton, taking his arm and wrapping it around her shoulders. She nestled her head against his neck, sending a rush of electricity through Leighton's body. He was happy that she'd made the first move. It was one that he had been considering since the movie started. In fact, he had been so preoccupied thinking about how to get closer to July that he had hardly paid any attention to what they were watching. Had July been thinking the same thing? Had she been waiting for him to initiate something? Did she finally make a move on him because she grew tired of waiting for him to make a move on her?

Leighton shook his head and pushed the anxious thoughts out of his mind. He focused on being present in the moment and enjoying this time with July. He breathed in the scent of her hair, coconut and vanilla, and took in the feel of her skin, warm and studded with tiny goose bumps. He moved his fingers up and down her arm and took pleasure in the sensation of the hairs standing up. Touch was Leighton's love language, and while he enjoyed being touched, he enjoyed July's response to his touch even more. It made him feel wanted, and who doesn't want to feel that?

When the movie ended, July got up and grabbed a second round of beers for them. Instead of drinking hers slowly this time, though, she popped off the top and chugged the entire thing in a minute flat.

Leighton watched with wide eyes. "Impressive," he said as July put the empty bottle on the table.

"Your turn," she said with a mischievous smirk.

Leighton did as he was told. When he finished, July was back in the bed, and to both his surprise and his delight, she was crawling on top of him. Leighton grabbed her hips and pulled her body to his. When they were nose to nose, Leighton cradled her cheeks in his hands and looked into her deep brown eyes. Then he kissed her. Intensely. Passionately. Desperately. As if it was the last kiss that they were ever going to share. And July kissed him back, with just as much force.

After several minutes of crazy lips and wild hands, Leighton could hear that July was breathing heavily, almost as heavy as he was. The desire between them was mounting like a kettle about to boil. July reached for Leighton's shirt and frantically began unbuttoning it. Once loose, Leighton shimmied out while July ran her nails down his bare chest. The hairs on the back of his neck stood up. He took July's blouse and pulled it over her head, exposing a lacy black bra, perfectly smooth skin, and a small bumblebee tattoo on her rib cage.

"I like this," Leighton whispered as he traced his fingers over the tattoo.

"I like you," July breathed in his ear.

Leighton put his mouth to hers and gently sucked on her bottom lip. Then he cupped her breasts before moving his hands down her stomach. When he reached her waist, he hesitated. He wanted to ask her if she was okay with where things were going, but before he could, July was tugging on his pants. Leighton helped her remove them before sliding her out of the skirt that she had been wearing.

Skin to skin, Leighton couldn't fight his yearning for July for any longer. He wrapped his arms around her body and laid her down on the bed, switching positions so that he was on top of her. He brought his face close to hers and gave her a gentle kiss on the forehead and then down the bridge of her nose before landing on her lips. July dug her nails into his back and lifted her hips so that she was pressing against his groin.

"I want you," Leighton moaned.

"I'm already yours," July whispered.

"I've never done this before."

"Me neither, but I want my first time to be with you."

Leighton's heart skipped a beat and electricity, once again, surged through him. "Are you sure you want to do this?"

July put her hands on his cheeks and looked him directly in the eyes. "Positive." She pulled a condom out of the night-stand drawer.

Leighton gave July a long, passionate kiss and carefully removed her undergarments. Then he slid off his boxers, put on the condom, and angled his body toward hers.

As he pushed himself inside her, July let out a soft whimper.

Leighton moved slowly, gently, deliberately. He didn't want to hurt her. July squeezed his arms and pulled him closer. The two breathed each other in and out until they fell into a beautiful rhythm.

"July," Leighton said quietly. They were lying next to each other now. July's head was tucked into the pit of Leighton's arm. He ran his fingers through her hair.

"Yeah?"

"I think . . ." he paused. He was scared to put himself out there, but he also desperately wanted July to know how he was feeling. "I think I'm in love with you," he stammered. "No, I *know* I'm in love with you." He cleared his throat and steadied his shaky voice. "I'm in love with you, July."

July lifted herself up and propped her head on her left fist. She looked Leighton straight in the eyes. Her stare was intense, and Leighton couldn't read her expression.

She placed her right hand on his cheek. "Tell me tomorrow," she whispered.

Leighton gave her a puzzled look. "Huh?"

"We just"—she blushed—"you know. It could just be your hormones talking."

"It's not. I've never been so sure of something in my entire life . . . but I'll tell you again tomorrow, too."

July smiled and snuggled back into the crevice between Leighton's arm and his body. She traced circles on his chest. Leighton, with his arm wrapped around her, stroked her shoulder with his thumb.

As he drifted off to sleep, Leighton thought about the last conversation that he had with Ivan before Ivan passed away. It was a few days before Halloween and Greta was hosting her annual Trick-or-Read event where she invited the local kids to Twice Upon a Time for sweet treats and scary stories. Greta loved to dress up, so she not only encouraged the children to wear costumes, but she wore one herself. That year, she was a monarch butterfly. Leighton remembered sitting with Ivan in the corner of the shop as they watched Greta read to the little ones.

"That's my girl," Ivan had said affectionately. He had a big smile on his face. "You know, I've loved her since the day I met her."

Leighton smiled, too. "How'd you know that she was the one?"

Ivan put his arm around Leighton and said, "Because once I met her, I knew that I couldn't live without her."

One Day Later

LEIGHTON AWOKE GROGGY AND DISORIENTED.
He rubbed his eyes and looked at the digital clock beside
the bed. The bright red numbers were just a blur at first,
but once he cleared his vision, he could see that they read
10:15. Leighton didn't think much of it until he noticed
the sunlight creeping through the drapes. His stomach
dropped. It wasn't ten at night; it was ten in the morning,
which meant that he'd never made it home last night, and
when his parents realized that, he was going to be in big
trouble.

Shit, shit, shit, he thought, panic overcoming him. He
squeezed his eyes shut and took a deep breath. He didn't
want July to know that he was freaking out. They had
had such an amazing time last night and he didn't want
to spoil it. He could deal with his parents later. For now,

he was going to focus on July. After all, he had to tell her that he meant every word that he had said to her the evening prior.

Leighton rolled over, eager to wake July with gentle kisses and a reiteration of his feelings for her. He turned slowly, trying not to disturb her from her slumber, but when he finished his rotation, he was alarmed to find the spot where she was supposed to be empty. Confused, he sat up.

"July?" he called out, hoping for a response even though the room was small and there wasn't anywhere else she could be other than the bathroom, but the bathroom door was open and the lights were off.

Maybe she went out to get breakfast or something, he thought. Leighton rubbed his tired eyes again and looked around the room.

It was spotless.

Everything that had been scattered haphazardly on the furniture, the tables, and the floor just twelve hours ago was gone now. All that remained were the sunflowers that Leighton had given July the night of his father's party. If it weren't for them, the unmade bed, and Leighton's few belongings, he'd think that the room were vacant.

This can't be happening, Leighton thought. *There must be an explanation.* He grabbed his cell phone off the nightstand and with clumsy fingers, he called July. To his dismay, it went immediately to voicemail. He tried again and again, but it was no use. July's phone was clearly turned off.

Falling. No, plummeting. That's what it felt like. Plunging into a never-ending black hole.

Leighton stood up, but his legs were shaking. He wanted

to sit back down, but he knew he couldn't. He got dressed, gathered his belongings, and ran out the door with an urgency that he had never felt before.

When he got to the motel office, he practically crashed through the door.

"July Evans. Room 13," he said while gasping for air. "Have you seen her?"

The front desk clerk, Mrs. Carter, gave him a bewildered look.

"Jesus, boy! You startled me!" she said with a thick Southern drawl.

"I'm sorry, but I need to know if you've seen this girl," he pleaded.

Mrs. Carter's face turned sympathetic. "Yes, I saw her this morning. She checked out not too long ago . . . around nine, I'd say."

"Did she say where she was going?" Leighton asked desperately.

"No, but she did ask for the bus schedule," the clerk replied, pointing to a calendar hanging by the desk.

The room started to spin, and Leighton was fighting to stay grounded. "When does the next southbound bus depart?"

Mrs. Carter looked at the calendar. "Ten thirty."

"Thank you," Leighton said, already halfway out the door. It was 10:25, and the bus terminal was only a quarter of a mile away. If he ran, he could make it there before the bus left.

The sprint to the station was a blur. If it weren't for his heavy breathing and his fatigued legs, Leighton would've thought that he teleported there. He hurried up the stairs to the platform where a bus was waiting.

That must be it! he thought. The bus was already boarded and the doors were closed. It was obvious that it would be departing any second now. Leighton raced over, waving his arms in the air. "Wait!" he shouted. "Please don't leave yet!"

When he got to the bus, the driver, who must've seen him coming, opened the door, and Leighton scrambled up the steps.

"This is the southbound bus, right?" Leighton asked between deep breaths.

"No," the driver replied. "The southbound bus left a few minutes ago. We're headed west, to Texas."

The words hit him like a punch to the gut. He clenched his stomach to soften the blow but the damage had already been done. He stood there for a moment, cradling his invisible wound. Then he turned around and exited the bus.

"I guess you won't be joining us?" the driver called after him.

"No," Leighton replied glumly. "But thanks anyway."

The doors closed behind him and Leighton watched as the bus drove away. He walked over to a bench and took a seat. He looked down at the ground for several long minutes. The painful jab that had been terrorizing his midsection was now replaced by complete emptiness. He couldn't think. He couldn't move. He was totally numb. Then, out of nowhere, he felt the defeat and despair rushing through him like bile coming up his throat. He wanted to cry. He wanted to scream. But he didn't. Instead, he continued to sit there, in silent agony.

Why did she leave like this? he thought over and over again. *So abruptly . . . without even saying goodbye? How could she do that after everything that we shared this past week . . . after what we did last night? After what I said to her?* Leighton was desperately clawing for answers. *Was this her plan all along or was it a knee-jerk reaction to what I told her last night? Did I scare her off when I said that I was in love with her?* Leighton didn't want to be mad at July, but he couldn't find any good reason for leaving like she did. Even if she was freaked out by his confession, her actions still weren't warranted. If anything, that made them worse.

This is fucking pointless, Leighton thought, striking his thigh in frustration. *I'm never going to know the truth unless I hear it from her.*

Leighton stayed on that bench for another two hours, watching the people come and go, hoping that one of them might be July. He saw scenes of lovers kissing goodbye and hello; tearful departures and happy reunions. He would do anything for the latter. *Maybe she'll change her mind*, he thought, but deep down he knew that she was gone for good, and waiting at the bus station was only perpetuating the heartache.

Buzz, buzz, buzz.

It was his phone vibrating in his pocket. *July!*

Leighton pulled his phone out so quickly that he nearly lost grip of it and sent it flying across the platform. When he looked at the screen, his heart sank into his stomach. It wasn't July; it was his mom.

"Hello," he said cheerlessly as he put the phone to his ear.

"Leighton!" his mother barked. "Where in the hell are you? I thought you had been sleeping this whole time. I figured you were tired from Greta's wake yesterday, but when I realized that it was almost one in the afternoon, I got worried, so I went into your room and lo and behold, you're not even here!"

"Sorry, Mom," Leighton replied flatly. "I left early to go to the bus station."

"The bus station?" his mother repeated.

"Yeah . . . July left this morning," he choked through the lump in his throat.

"Oh," his mother said, clearly surprised by this new information. "I didn't know she was planning to leave today."

"Me neither. Anyway, it doesn't matter. Can you come pick me up? If you're busy, it's okay, I can walk."

"No, no," his mother said quickly. "Of course I can come pick you up. Where are you? Are you still at the bus station?"

Leighton hesitated. "Yeah . . . I'm still here." He waited for his mother to say something snarky, but to his surprise, she didn't.

Mom arrived at the station less than ten minutes after Leighton hung up the phone. Leighton watched as her white sedan entered the parking lot. When she pulled up to the platform, she gave the horn a friendly honk to let Leighton know that she was there.

Leighton gathered his belongings and stood up from the bench that he had been slumped on for the past two hours. As he neared the steps that brought him down to the parking lot, his heart sank once again. Staying at the bus station gave him a sense of hope, even if it was false hope. It made him feel like there was still a piece of July for him to hold on to. Leaving the station forced him to say goodbye, to close the chapter, and he wasn't sure if he was ready to do that. But his mother was waiting, and July wasn't coming back, so he forced his legs to descend the stairs, and he got into the car without looking back.

"Do you want to talk about it?" Mom asked.

"Not really," Leighton replied with his head against the window. He looked out at the world. Everything seemed so dull and lackluster. Even Montclair's pastel buildings, which always appeared bright and cheerful, were missing their characteristic vibrance.

If being in love is seeing the world through rose-colored glasses, being heartbroken is seeing the world in a single shade of gray, Leighton thought.

When they returned home, Mom attempted to talk to Leighton again, but Leighton declined. What was there to say anyway? July was gone, and there was nothing he could do about it. Everything he felt, all that they had shared, what was the point?

Frustrated, Leighton went upstairs. He wanted to escape the heartache, but it was swallowing him whole. How was he supposed to stop the memories from replaying again and again in his mind? Her eyes, her smile, the way that she laughed—it all felt so tangible yet completely out of reach. He could still hear her awful singing, still smell the scent of her hair. What hurt the most, though, was thinking about the parts of July that he only just got to discover, like the little bumblebee tattoo on her rib cage that he liked so much, and all the things that he still hadn't discovered but would never get the chance to.

"Fuck!" Leighton shouted before collapsing on his bed. He put his face in his hands and sobbed, and then when he couldn't cry any longer, he got up and pulled himself together.

Leighton decided that he was going to go about his day as usual. If July could so easily forget about him, then he could do the same to her. He'd shower, get dressed, grab a fruit, and head to the bookstore. Just like any other day.

It's just like any other day, he thought while he shampooed his hair.

It's just like any other day, he said as he pulled on his jeans.

It's just like any other day, he chanted between bites of banana.

But it wasn't just like any other day, because when he got to Twice Upon a Time, there was a letter hanging on the door.

And it had his name on it.

Leighton's heart started to race.

It must be from her.

Leighton removed the note and opened it slowly. Then, he began to read.

> Dear Leighton,
> It's just about two in the morning and you're currently asleep in my bed. We had the most incredible night tonight. It was a night that I'll never forget.

By the time you find this letter, I will be well on my way to Florida, and you'll probably be wondering why I left so suddenly. The truth is, though, that it wasn't sudden at all. I've been meaning to leave for a few days now, but you've made it so hard to go.

This past month has been the darkest time of my life, yet you've managed to bring back a light that I was so certain had burned out. I can't thank you enough for that.

I'm sure that you are probably upset with me. After all, leaving like I did was pretty shitty. But if I didn't go now, and in the way that I did, I don't think that I ever would have left.

See, when my mother was my age, she fell in love before she had a chance to learn who she was, and although she never admitted it, I know that she had regrets. After she died, I promised myself that I would do things differently. That's why I had to go.

You're an amazing person, Leighton. And you have an insanely bright future ahead of you. Hopefully I'll get to be a part of it someday.

Love,
July

When Leighton finished reading July's note, his eyes were burning from the tears that he was fighting back. The letter had given him the answers that he was looking for, but it also sparked a flurry of conflicting emotions: anger and forgiveness, confusion and clarity, heartbreak and love. He stood by the door for several minutes, trying to navigate his feelings. He breathed in *one, two, three, four*, and he breathed out *one, two, three, four*. When he finally felt grounded, Leighton folded up the note and put it in his pocket. Then he unlocked the bookshop and went inside. He walked to the back of the building and pulled a small box from the storage closet. Inside the box was a single sheet of paper—the letter from Greta. Leighton had put it in there so that he would never lose it. It was far too important to him. He smiled when he saw the floral stationery and the familiar handwriting. Leighton read Greta's letter again, even though he had already practically memorized it. When he got to the end, he held it close to his chest before carefully placing it back in the small box. He took July's letter out of his pocket and laid it in the box with Greta's. Then he closed the box and put it back in the closet.

Leighton returned to the front of the store and sat at the desk. As he looked around, he couldn't help but reminisce on the memories that he and July had made over the past few days. It was as if she had left a mark on every inch of that cozy shop. He could still see her reading on the worn green sofa, he could still hear her singing while drunk on tequila, and he could still taste her kissing him with her sweet, warm lips. The thought of never getting to experience any of those things again made his body ache in a way that he had never felt before. Leighton wished that he had better prepared himself for the occasion. After all, he had known that this day would eventually come. But would it have even mattered? If he were more prepared, would it have actually made it sting any less? Or does losing love hurt like hell whether you're ready for it or not? Despite this being his first heartbreak, Leighton had a good hunch that it was the latter.

I have to get myself out of this funk, he thought as he stood up from the desk. *Yes, I miss July. And yes, I feel like my heart has been ripped out of my chest. But I can't let this break me. I have so much to look forward to. And the only way to move past this is to focus on all the good things that I have in my life.*

Leighton walked around the shop, taking note of every characteristic, blemish, and quirk: the tiny chips that peppered the mahogany bookshelves, the uneven texture of the cream-colored walls, the way the light danced haphazardly through the weathered glass window. It was hard to feel sad when he had so much to be grateful for, like Twice Upon a Time, which was his favorite place in the entire world, and now he could call it his own. Leighton traced his fingers along the tattered spines of the secondhand books while he imagined how he was going to transform the store into Greta's memorial library. He decided that he wanted to remove the aisles of bookshelves that currently took up the majority of the space and line the walls with the shelves instead, which would allow for a large gathering area in the middle of the room where he could set up tables, chairs, and couches for reading and activities. It would also help make the space appear bigger than it actually was. Maybe one day Leighton could even expand. He'd love to set up some computers and a place to watch movies, too. The possibilities were endless, and for the first time in a long time, he was genuinely excited for the future. For so many years, he felt dread every time he thought about what would come after high school, but now that he had spoken up to his parents and changed his trajectory, his future could be whatever he wanted it to be.

Leighton took out a pen and paper and jotted down all his ideas for the bookshop. When he finished, he read over his plans and grinned from ear to ear. He felt liberated and invigorated. But most importantly, he didn't feel hopeless anymore. Sure, there was still a hole in his chest (metaphorically speaking, of course), but the dismal depression that had been suffocating him all morning had relented. He could see the light at the end of the tunnel despite the heartache still being so raw. Thinking about his future and everything that he wanted to accomplish helped him better understand why July had left. It even helped him accept why she left like she did. They both had their entire lives ahead of them. He would never want to keep July from fulfilling her dreams and aspirations, and he knew that she wouldn't want to hold him back either. Of course, he wished things could be different; he wished that he could have it all, but that wasn't an option right now. It made him think about Ivan and Greta. It seemed like they wanted to be together when they first met, but Ivan had to complete his duty as a Russian soldier. He had no choice but to continue his journey. July had to continue hers, too.

Today is the first day of a new chapter, Leighton thought as he took another trip around the store. He walked to the second to last aisle and quickly skimmed the titles. When he found the book that he was looking for, he pulled it off the shelf and carried it over to the old velour sofa that he loved so much.

Leighton looked down at the paperback in his hands. It was beaten and battered, kind of like his heart. Despite its poor condition, though, it still held so much value; it still had so much more to offer. And Leighton did, too.

He ran his fingers over the cover. "*The Outsiders*," he said aloud. "It's been far too long since I've read you."

Leighton opened the book and turned to the first page. There was something comforting about a new beginning.

Five Years Later

"TODAY'S THE BIG DAY!" KENNEDY squealed. She was making scrambled eggs when Leighton entered the kitchen. They were in the guesthouse. Leighton had been living there since Kennedy moved back into her swanky new apartment a few years ago. "I let myself in, by the way," she continued, "as you can obviously see. Are you hungry?"

Leighton was about to respond when his phone started to ring.

Ring. Ring. Ring.

It was Miranda, his literary agent. He had been expecting her call.

"Hey, Miranda," he said as he answered the phone.

"Leighton!" she exclaimed. "It's finally here!"

Leighton laughed and brushed his fingers through his hair. "I know! I can't believe it." He shook his head in disbelief.

He really couldn't. When he started writing his novel five years ago, he never would've guessed that it would actually get published. And now today, his book, *One Week of July*, was being released. To celebrate, he was having a launch party at Montclair's local library, Twice Upon a Time.

"How are you feeling?" Miranda probed. "Nervous? Excited?"

"I guess a little bit of both."

"Perfectly normal! But you have nothing to worry about. Everyone's going to love it."

"Thanks, Miranda," Leighton replied, getting ready to hang up the phone. Miranda was always busy, and their phone calls never lasted longer than a minute or two.

"Well, I've got to run," she said, to no surprise to Leighton. "You're going to do great today. I can't wait to hear all about it. I'll give you a call tomorrow so you can fill me in on all the juicy details."

"Okay, sounds good," Leighton replied, but Miranda had already hung up. He laughed. *Typical Miranda.*

When Leighton and Kennedy arrived at Twice Upon a Time, a line of people was already waiting outside. There were some familiar faces—Monica, Carson, Becca, Buster, even Sheriff Montgomery—but a lot of unfamiliar faces, too. Leighton had expected many of Montclair's residents to attend the party; it was a supportive little town. He hadn't been expecting all these strangers though. He wondered how they had even heard of his book or the event. Then again, he did sign a deal with one of the biggest publishing houses in the country, and their marketing team was top-notch, so maybe it wasn't that surprising after all. Regardless of how word had spread, Leighton was thrilled by the turnout. This book was a true labor of love, and to see people excited to read it gave him a sense of pride that he had never felt before.

Leighton and Kennedy pulled into the parking lot behind the library and entered the building through the back doors. Thankfully, they had spent the night prior setting up, so there wasn't much for them to do now.

"I cannot believe how many people are here!" Kennedy chirped as she arranged plates of fruits, breads, and pastries. "I was not expecting this!"

"Me neither," Leighton admitted. "I just hope they like the story. If it could have an impact on even one person, I would be happy."

Kennedy gave him an encouraging smile. "I have no doubt that it will."

"Thanks, Ken," Leighton said. He had his books placed in neat piles next to a table where he'd be doing his signings. He picked one up and looked at the cover. It still felt surreal to actually hold his book. After a minute or two, he placed it back on the table and squeezed his hands together. "Alright, let's do this!"

Leighton walked to the front of the shop and took a deep breath. He had imagined this moment in his head so many times, and now it was finally here. He put his hand out and opened the door. "Hey, everybody!" he called. "Welcome to the *One Week of July* release party and book signing. I'm so glad you're here! Come on in!"

The crowd cheered and eagerly followed him inside.

The next few hours were filled with friends, food, and fun. Leighton sold all but one copy of his book, and he penned his signature so many times, he was practically on autopilot by the end of the line. It was the best day of his life.

After everyone left, Leighton cleaned up and prepped the library for the next day. He had an arts and crafts project planned for the local kids, and he was really looking forward to it. He was rummaging through a box of supplies when he heard the soft jingle of the door's bell.

Ding, ding.

"Hey!" he called with his back facing the entrance. "The party's over. We're actually closed for the evening."

"Oh no," the visitor said in a disappointed tone. "I drove all the way from Florida just to be here."

A huge smile spread across Leighton's face. "I thought you had to work today," he said as he scooped July up in his arms and placed tiny kisses all over her face.

July giggled. "I did, but I found someone to cover my shift at the last minute. Did you really think that I was going to miss your big day?"

"Maybe."

"We've been dating for five years," July said as she playfully slapped his arm. "You should know me better than that!"

Leighton blushed. Even after all this time, he still got butterflies whenever he was with July, and he still couldn't believe that he got to call her his girlfriend. When July had left Montclair on that fateful morning, Leighton was certain that he'd never see her again, but a few days later, she called him. She explained that while she planned to stay in Florida with her dad, she didn't want to give up on them. July suggested that they try a long-distance relationship, and of course, Leighton agreed. Five years later, they were happier than ever, and July would be moving to Montclair in a little over a month. Leighton couldn't wait.

"I have something for you," Leighton said. He picked up the last copy of *One Week of July* and handed it to her. "The author even signed it." He grinned.

July took the book and ran her fingers over the cover. "I think you've finally dethroned that copy of *The Outsiders* that you gave me when we first met. *This*"—she hugged the novel—"is definitely my favorite book that I own."

Acknowledgments

I'VE DREAMED OF WRITING A novel for as long as I can remember, but actually doing it required discipline, determination, and the help of some really great people. Fortunately, I had all three.

To my editor, Nicole: thank you for being my mentor throughout this entire process. From editing to formatting to proofreading, you've done it all, and I can't stress enough just how valuable your guidance and expertise have been.

To my line editor, Elyse: thank you for massaging my words and elevating my prose. Your feedback and recommendations greatly improved the readability of my novel.

To my copy editor, Anne-Marie: thank you for whipping my manuscript into shape. My book wouldn't have been publication ready without you and your eagle eye.

To my cover designer, Lucy: thank you for bringing my

artistic vision to life. I couldn't imagine a more perfect cover for my book.

And of course, to my family . . .

Dad: thank you for being my first beta reader and for investing so much into this passion project of mine. *One Week of July* would still be a document on my computer if it weren't for you.

Mom: thank you for being my fiercest supporter. You've always told me that I could do anything, and by instilling that tenacity in me, you've helped to make this dream a reality.

Steven: thank you for being the soundboard to all of my ideas and ramblings. Your encouragement made the times of stress more manageable and the times of celebration more special.

Melissa Mastro was born and raised in New York but now calls North Carolina home. A lifelong lover of words, she has a Bachelor of Arts degree in English from Stony Brook University, where she graduated with honors. When she's not writing, Melissa enjoys reading, red wine, and Pilates. *One Week of July* is her debut novel.